SHATTERED ILLUSIONS

a novel by
Karen D. Bradley

Ambrosia Sands Books
Dolton, Illinois

This is a work of fiction. All characters and events in this book are purely fictitious, a creation of the author's imagination and any resemblance to actual persons, living or dead, is coincidental.

Shattered Illusions
Published by:

Ambrosia Sands Books
PO Box 827
Dolton, IL 60419
www.ambrosiasands.com

Second Edition
Trade Paperback ISBN: 978-0-9833560-8-0
Digital ISBN: 978-0-9833560-9-7
LCCN: 2017950092

First published by AuthorHouse May 4, 2007
ISBN: 978-1-4259-9783-0 (sc)

Cover Art by: J.L. Woodson www.woodsoncreativestudio.com
Interior Design by: Lissa Woodson www.naleighnakai.com

Manufactured and Printed in the United States of America

SHATTERED ILLUSIONS

ACKNOWLEDGEMENTS:

This journey was unexpected. Writing books was not on my check list of things I wanted to do in life. It was born out of need to survive. When this book was rejected by publishers, I sat it aside and moved on to writing the next one without really looking back. The only reason this book isn't collecting dust on my bookshelf is because of my sister. So, thank you Jenetta M. Bradley for that as well as for reading my stories over and over again without complaint.

To Ebony Walker, thanks for being willing to chime in when an honest opinion is needed.

Thanks to Michelle S. Chester for making this novel better than when it was first released.

To J. L. Woodson, I appreciate you for being flexible and easy to work with. Thank you for the time and energy you put into revamping the book cover.

A special thanks to Lissa Woodson (Naleighna Kai), for your time and efforts in helping me with the interior design. I truly appreciate you yanking me out of my comfort zone. The experience reminded me that what you believe will either feed your fears or fuel your dreams, and who you surround yourself with will do the same.

To my friends, family and core group of readers, I would have been one and done if it wasn't for your kind words and support. You have been an amazing group to experience the panel and book discussions with. Those discussions are some of my most cherished memories.

Most of what I have accomplished has been due to the encouragement and nudging of those around me providing fuel for a journey on a path I wasn't sure was mines to take. Life is full of unexpected twists. While I can't predict what's next for me, what has transpired so far has been a blessing.

Thank you to everyone who purchases a book, know your support is appreciated.

DEDICATION:

For those who build protective walls,
Know that those bricks are meant to create launching pads for
your dreams. Don't let what you've been through negatively define
you but let it refine you and lift you higher.

SHATTERED ILLUSIONS

PROLOGUE

The darkened sky and impending storm were not going to dampen Terry D. H. Johnson's spirit. Confirmation she was having her first child had her overjoyed. It was the best early birthday gift. There was no doubt no one could top that in two weeks.

Thunder rang through the air only a few minutes after the lightning brightened the sky. She was determined to beat the storm. She had to tell someone the news. Her husband was on a business trip and could not be reached. Her sister and best friend, Gena, was the next best thing. She was glad Gena was back in town. Otherwise, she would have had to track down John, who was like a big brother to her. Her excitement about this baby could not be contained. The baby wasn't coming at the perfect time with her opening her own clothing company in less than a month, but the best-laid plans change. She was happy to adjust her plans for this kid. It was funny to her that in her husband's little gentle persuasion speech, he said that she should take this opportunity to pursue her dreams before they started a family.

Terry quickly studied the dark clouds overhead. She wasn't so sure that she would be able to make it to Gena's before the full storm hit. She slowed as she turned onto Gena's block making sure she didn't miss the entrance to her driveway, which happened to be surrounded by thick bushes. In the front, the only breaks in the thick bush fence were the exit and entrance for the circular drive. She silently cursed as she missed it. She rolled through a Stop sign as she went to circle the block. Her eyes darted to the rear-view mirror at the sound of sirens. Fortunately for her, they were in the distance. The last thing she needed or wanted was a ticket. Terry sighed her relief at seeing only parked cars on the street. One of those parked cars looked awfully familiar; it was too dark and too hard to see the plates. *But it couldn't be him.* She shrugged off that thought. Terry relaxed in knowing she wasn't about to be pulled over.

Gena had a way with kids but she didn't want any full time. She always told Terry, "I love kids but also love sending them home to their parents." Terry's laughter filled the car. That made for a perfect babysitter. Truth be told, she knew if Gena got pregnant, there was no way she was having an abortion.

Terry tried to focus her mind as she neared the house again. Out of habit, she flicked on her turning signal as she neared the driveway even though it wasn't necessary. It was raining so hard that she almost had to make a complete stop to keep from turning into the bushes. She crept around the circle driveway. It was storming so hard now, Terry could barely see what was in front of her. The wipers swished back and forth at top speed as the rain pounded on the windshield. Each raindrop sounded like hail against the glass. Terry leaned closer to the steering wheel to see better.

The windshield wipers might as well have been off, for all the good they were doing. The thunder made a resounding noise as the lightning lit up the sky. Terry flicked on her bright lights; Gena would have a fit if she scratched her beloved Mustang, let alone hit it. She put her car in park behind Gena's car, grateful Gena had pulled up enough to let her park in front of the door. Terry had forgotten her umbrella, and if the rain so much as looked at her hair, she'd have an afro. She took her hand and ran it through her long, reddish-brown hair that hung down her back in no particular style.

It was a good thing she thought to phone ahead. Gena told her to use her keys to let herself in. Terry was relieved she didn't have to ring the doorbell. It could have taken forever depending on what part of the house Gena was in. In this weather, if she had to wait to be let in, she'd be soaked to the bone. Terry opened the car door and pulled her trench coat off her shoulders and over her head. She did a quick trot to the front door while reaching into her coat pocket for the key. There were two different sets of keys in Terry's pocket. The question was which set had Gena's door key on it. Once she was at the door, she fumbled through the keys on the first ring only to find the key on the second one. She was getting soaked. Her trench had fallen back onto her shoulders before she unlocked the door.

Terry entered, immediately pushing the door closed and making sure it was locked. On nights like these, there were a lot of crazies that wanted to come in out of the rain. She wasn't trying to help them out by leaving the door unlocked. She took off her coat and threw it haphazardly on the antique brass coat rack near the door. As Terry walked down the hall, she stopped and looked in the antique mirror. If she didn't know what a drowned rat looked like before, she had a good idea now. She was tempted to yell for Gena, but she had a feeling that she wouldn't be heard over the storm. Gena was probably waiting in the living room for her anyway.

She loved Gena's house or Gena Holmes Estates as she often referred to it. It was a little too extravagant for her, but it was immaculate. Terry was afraid to touch anything for fear that it might break. There wasn't an item in the house that was cheap. Each item was either antique or expensive, right down to the food in the kitchen cabinets. There was some very expensive food in Gena's kitchen that had been there so long that they qualified as antiques.

Terry's favorite room in the house was the living room. Two beautiful cherry wood doors with exquisite hand carved designs opened into the living room. When entering the room, before the stairs leading to the lower level, there was a section that was higher than the rest of the room, it was relatively small compared to the size of the room. On either side of the center stairs, directly in front of the door, were two cherry wood banisters. These banisters slanted upward from the bottom level to the top, curved in opposite directions and went the length of the upper level and then curved into a downward slope as it neared the other sets of stairs to the lower level.

There was a magnificent crystal lamp sitting on a smoked black glass table to the right of the door, the same side as the beautiful old-fashion black lounging chair and cherry wood bookcase, opposite the bar. Both the bar and lounging chair could be reached from the bottom level without going back to the center stairs. The sunken level of the living room was decorated with exquisite, expensive, deep burgundy Italian furniture, so rich in color that it looked black. The unique bay window was the reason she loved this room. It looked out over the relaxing water in the Olympic size pool which was to die for.

A distinctive pattern had been etched into the glass and different colored lights were directed at various points on the window. This cast an exotic, sensual, and alluring image on the surface of the water that was mesmerizing. Gena and Terry loved the beautiful picture it made as they lounged poolside during the warm summer nights. The only problem was that Gena had trouble figuring out how to set up the lights so they could look at the pool while sitting at the bay window. For a time, the lights had been scattered all over the floor, the seat, and the window. Finally, Gena had the lights installed at various points in two panels on the side of the wall near the bay window.

Once the lights were off the floor and in the wall, a person could sit at the window and stare at the exotic picture in the pool. Gena only had to flip the switch on the wall to the right or left of the living room doors to control the bay window lights. Terry couldn't remember which side it was since Gena always kept them on even during the day; it was just easier that way. The bay window's lights lit the room up enough that a person entering could see the stairs. With the bay lights on, people had no problem finding the main light switch that was oddly placed on the wall panel in the sunken part of the living room. Whoever thought of that must have really wanted someone to fall down the stairs.

"Gena, are you in here?" Terry opened the doors and walked in, automatically closing them. "I have the best news ... Argh, what the ..." Terry cried out as she tripped over something. If she had been paying attention, she would have noticed that the only light in the room was coming from the corridor.

That's odd for the lights to be off, Terry thought. *Why weren't the lights on in the living room, not even the special ones?*

Terry searched for the lamp in its usual place to the right of the door, but it wasn't there. Blindly, she explored the wall in hopes of finding the switch that turned on the bay window's lights. It became apparent that it wasn't on that side as her legs hit the lounger. Terry sunk her hands into the cushion to prevent herself from falling face first into the chair. She pushed off the cushion and groped until the cool wall tickled the palms of her hands. In an angry fit, Terry turned around, kicked the wall, then leaned on it. She felt like an idiot for taking out her frustration on a wall.

Terry laughed as the thunder drowned her out. She thought about how this was a great setting for a horror film. Gena would get a kick out of this. She laughed harder when she thought of what Gena would say. "My poor dear older si ..."

Her laughter stopped instantly as lightning illuminated the room. It was a mess. It looked as if someone had an all-out "pick-up-anything-you-can-throw" fight.

"Oh God! Where's Gena?" Terry turned back around to face the wall and frantically searched for the door, her heart raced and her adrenaline shot up. Something crunched under her feet as she stayed close to the wall. Once she neared the door, her foot hit the object that she'd tripped over and she stepped over it. She groped for the door handle, glancing down quickly to see what she'd stepped over as the light poured into the room. Terry's eyes skimmed over the glass table and the shattered crystal lamp. She hit the hallway running. Maybe it was a good thing the kids back in school used to chase her around. She'd learned to run when necessary, fat or not. She ran, searching every room on the first floor.

"Gena! Oh God! Where are you?" She continued calling out though she knew even if Gena was right next to her she'd have trouble hearing her over the storm.

Terry decided that it might be in Gena's best interest if she called the police before she started searching the upstairs. Just as Terry reached the kitchen and headed towards the phone, she thought she heard a noise coming from upstairs. She couldn't really tell because of the thunder. The storm had quieted down compared to earlier but it was still pretty loud. All thoughts of calling the police vanished. She went to check out the noise. Terry ran up the stairs taking them two at a time. She was breathing heavily by the time she made it to the top. She thought to herself that she really had to work on losing some weight.

"Gena! Gena, where are you?" First instinct led her to the master bedroom. Maybe Gena had been so tired from work she had gone straight to bed and because of this she hadn't noticed that someone had broken into her house. Hopefully, they got what they came for and left long before Gena made it home. Terry knew this was just wishful thinking.

Gena's bedroom door stood open. Terry ran in, then stopped mid-step. What Terry found was not her wish come true but her worst nightmare. Gena was on the king-sized bed with her dress ripped apart.

The masked assailant stood, releasing Gena's wrists, which he held over her head with one of his hands. He grabbed the knife off the nightstand holding it to Gena's neck, then reached down, zipping up his pants.

Terry had not realized she was screaming until his head snapped towards her. They stood frozen, staring at each other. He started to point the knife in her direction. The sight of Gena sitting up and pulling her knee towards her sent a new level of rage coursing through Terry's veins. Running at top speed, Terry launched her body at him. She heard the clatter of the knife hit the floor and his grunt as his body hit the bed. Gena barely made a sound as they struggled on the bed below her feet. Terry could feel him trying to push her body off him, but she refused to let go. The momentum sent both of them off the foot of the bed. Their body's hit the floor with a thump. He tried to push Terry off him again, but she was not having it. She put her knee in his groin area and placed every ounce of her 223 pounds into it. He started yelping like a puppy. As he was cringing in pain, she stood up and proceeded to kick him in the stomach as he rolled to his knees.

Terry placed her foot in his back to knock him back to the floor. She started to stomp on his back, but before she knew what was happening, he grabbed her other leg and yanked her to the floor. He stood up and grabbed her by the arm, trying to make her stand. She swiped his arm away from her. He stepped back and stumbled over a decorative basket. Terry got to her feet and began punching him. The first punch landed on his jaw and the next on his chin. He placed his hands up to deflect another blow to the face. She took her right leg and swiped his legs from under him. He hit the floor and she put her foot and most of her weight into his neck. He held fast to her foot to prevent her weight from crushing his neck but he couldn't budge her. Terry then saw that the knife wasn't lying too far from them. If he got the upper hand, he'd also have the knife. She realized this was the first time ever that she didn't mind being overweight as she pushed more weight into his hand.

"Gena, grab the knife, dammit! Gena, snap out of it!" Terry was unsure of what to do next. Gena was no help. She was just sitting on the bed trembling, crying, and rocking back and forth. When it came to business and her money, Gena was a tiger, but personal crisis and things like this, she was anything but. Anger built in Terry; her teeth sank into her bottom lip as she forced more weight onto his hand. She heard Gena call her name and quickly looked over. Gena had stopped rocking and was no longer hugging herself.

Terry knew she had made a mistake. She gave the assailant opportunity to get the upper hand by alleviating enough of her weight where he could push her off. Terry stumbled back. The assailant was instantly on her. As they fought, Terry grabbed a statue off the dresser and smashed it across his head. He grabbed her head and banged it against the dresser. Terry was stunned briefly, but it gave him adequate time to retrieve the knife. Terry tried to get up, but molasses moved faster than she did. The assailant reached her in a matter of seconds. He snatched her up and pushed her against the wall. He placed the blade against her neck.

He growled, distorting his voice. "You weren't supposed to be here." He moved the point of the knife under her chin. "I should kill you just for that. It will make me at least a million dollars richer." His breath was heavy on her face.

Gena came from behind and pulled his arm down away from Terry's chin. She had no problem moving his arm since he hadn't expected it. He flung Gena to the floor, easily. Terry pushed passed him and ran. Gena was getting up when Terry ran by, grabbed her hand, and headed for the stairs. Terry pulled Gena slightly to get her to move her butt. They were not far from the top stair when Gena tripped. Terry turned and caught Gena before she hit the ground, steadying her. The assailant, right on their heels, lunged at them. The force of his body connecting with theirs sent them tumbling down the stairs.

Terry woke up in a daze. *Where am I?* She remembered. *Gena's. Oh no.* She tried to sit up too swiftly and got light-headed and had to lie back down. She sat up again, slowly this time. Her head throbbing. She was slightly dizzy. It didn't feel like anything was broken.

Once she looked around, she found the assailant knocked out next to her with Gena face down over part of his chest. Terry felt faint as she stood but she walked over to Gena anyway. She knelt next to Gena then leaned over. Terry shook her ever so slightly and whispered in her ear.

"Gena! Wake up! We need to get out of here before he wakes up. Oh lord, Gena, get up."

Terry was scared to move her. She rested her hand on the floor next to Gena as she checked the pulse in her neck. She exhaled, relieved she was still alive. Terry tried to use the hand on the floor to push up to stand. Her hand slipped a bit. Glancing down, she saw liquid was on the floor, a small pool of blood. "Oh, no! God, no."

Her heart beat wildly against her chest as she ran to the kitchen. She picked up the phone and dialed 9-1-1. The dispatcher answered the phone and Terry started speaking rapidly.

"Miss, we need you to slow down and repeat what you said." The voice was calm and steady.

Terry took a deep breath and clearly stated. "My sister has been stabbed. I need an ambulance at 212 Bell Oak. Oh!" Terry cried out in pain then hit the floor, landing on her knees. With the phone muffled against her, her head fell forward onto her lap as she wrapped one arm around her stomach trying to stop the pain.

"Miss! What's wrong? What's happening?" The dispatcher's voice rose slightly to indicate her concern but not enough to sound alarmed.

The pain was so severe, Terry was struggled to speak. She ignored the dispatcher's questions. She held her head to the side so that her voice wouldn't sound stifled. "I also need the police. The assailant is still in the ..."

Terry looked up and saw the assailant standing above her with his finger on the hook, cutting her off.

CHAPTER ONE

The words were like shards of glass through her soul. One phone call on a morning that started off so normal resurrected the past that had destroyed Danya Holmes' life. Her name kept echoing in her ear. She could hear his voice, but she couldn't respond. Did he really say that her murdering bastard of an ex-husband would be released from prison? Her hands tightened around the phone, as the panic coursed through her veins. She glanced over at her gorgeous 6'1" roommate, Sharrita Drew, who stood leaning on the window panel. Danya smiled at her as if everything was okay when it couldn't have been farther from the truth. Slowly she inched further into the kitchen while she worked to calm the thoughts racing through her mind.

"Officer Bally, you've made a mistake. He can't be getting out." Danya attempted to keep her tone normal. She noticed Rita had moved to the couch and sat on the end closest to her.

"He's getting out on a technicality," Officer Bally replied.

"Technicality! What kind of bullsh ... Mmm ..." Danya took a deep breath. "A technicality, huh? So when will he actually get out?" She tried her best to keep the tone of her voice calm and low.

There was a slight pause before he spoke. "He'll probably be out by the end of the week if—"

"That soon! This is freaking unbelievable. How could you idiots let him off on a technicality? Tell me that! How in thee hell did you all manage to blow it?" Danya yelled, only pausing to catch her breath.

Officer Bally tried to explain, "I—"

"I've heard quite enough, bye." Danya hung up the phone not waiting for a reply. Taking a deep breath, she turned towards Rita. As if nothing happened, she continued their conversation where she had left off.

"As I was saying, I don't think a different style of clothing is going to alter your problem," she stated, referring to the oversized, shapeless, ankle length black dress Rita wore. "You have to decide what you are willing to do to 'earn' your promotion."

Danya barely glanced Rita's way as she strolled over to the window. She turned towards Rita, then leaned on the window ledge. Rita sat on the couch with her mouth wide open. She stood and walked over to Danya with a look of utter disbelief on her face.

"Hold on, sister girl," Rita said as she threw her hands up. "I'm confused. How did you go from 'how in thee hell' to calmly stating 'as I was saying'? What was that call about, exactly? Don't even think about saying it's about the past so ignore it, because that phone call was certainly in the present."

"Truly, it's nothing," Danya replied nonchalantly.

"That's a lie, and the truth is nowhere to be found." Rita stepped back and looked at her. "No, you didn't just try to play me for boo boo the fool!" Rita shook her head as she stood there saying no with a waving hand that moved back and forth. "I'm not having it! Now just in case you didn't understand the question, let me break it down for you. Who got out on a technicality? And, what does this person have to do with you?"

Walking away from Rita, Danya grabbed her coffee cup off the table heading into the kitchen. She rinsed the cup and threw it into the dishwasher then opened the refrigerator and grabbed her lunch.

Rita sauntered over to Danya, put her hands on her hips, and tapped her foot waiting for an answer.

Danya frowned as Rita blocked her way. "It's part of history, my history. You know how I feel about talking about that. I hate doing it, so I don't do it. Besides, I think your problem is more imminent than mine. I have to get to work." Danya brushed past Rita, grabbed her coat and purse, then headed for the door. When she selected Rita as a roommate, the agreement was her past was off limits as a topic of conversation. Now her past wasn't as far behind her as it should have been.

"If I'm in danger, don't you think I should know?" Rita called after her.

Rita didn't receive a response. Danya paused at the door. Rita was right but Danya couldn't handle addressing the issue right now. She could not believe this was happening. Just when she was finally getting her life together, he had to come back into it. Damn him, she thought as she opened the door. The door began closing. Danya stopped it, leaving enough room so Rita could see her face.

"Sharrita, we'll discuss it later, okay? And do me a favor?"

Rita stepped closer to the door. "What?"

"Take off that awful outfit!" Danya stated with a fake smile plastered on her face.

Rita shook her head and laughed. Danya closed the door the rest of the way, but closing that door had opened the door to the emotions that she'd been trying so hard to ignore. Her life was coming together so nicely. Now, she didn't know what it would be. Fighting the tears, she walked towards the elevator telling herself that crying wasn't going to change anything. Not a damn thing. There was no way she would get through work and dinner with Rick if she kept this up. Not to mention Rita. There was no getting around talking to her. No matter how late she got in, Rita would be up waiting. By the time the elevator opened and closed, Danya had cried, wiped her tears, and gone into deep breathing mode. When she finally stepped out of the elevator, her breathing had returned to normal.

All the things Danya typically paid attention to on the way to work went totally unnoticed today. Usually, she'd find something nice about the scenery to look at. Most of the time it turned out to be Lake

Michigan. Danya loved looking out over Lake Michigan; it seemed so blue compared to the lake behind her house when she lived in the suburbs. She remembered the lake was the reason she'd bought the house, but that was another lifetime. One that seemingly was coming back to haunt her, literally. As she parked her car on the seventh level of the garage, Danya realized that if anybody asked her which route she took to get to work, she wouldn't be able to answer. All she remembered was getting into her car and now parking it. She climbed out, walked towards the elevators, and went into work.

"There are several messages here for you," Mary said as she approached Danya's desk. "One from a Daniel Gritssom. He wants you to get back to him immediately about the fabrics you ordered."

Danya shook her head. She'd done it again. She'd lost the space of time between her walking to the elevators until when her receptionist spoke. Danya glanced down at what she was doing. She'd been pulling a file out of her cabinet, what she'd originally planned to do with it she had no idea, but she grabbed it anyway.

Mary flipped through several more messages, reading only the important ones, setting the rest on the desk. "I don't think you're going to like this message much. It's from the FBI. A Mr. Casey Waller wants you to call him. He said it is urgent and private. There's also two here from Trish. She wanted to remind you that John has an early morning breakfast meeting and won't be in until 10:45. She also wanted me to tell you she'd be in around 9:15 or so. Do you want me at Trish's desk or the receptionist desk until 9:15?"

Danya glanced at her watch. It was about 7:45. Trish would be in less than two hours. "It would probably be best if you stayed at the front desk. I don't have any appointments until 9:00, so if anybody walks in earlier than that in hopes of being squeezed in, tell them to check back after 11:30. One more thing, tell Trish I need to speak with her as soon as she gets in."

Why is the FBI calling me? Danya wondered. Whatever the reason it would have to wait. She needed to pull herself together before making that call. This was going to be a rough day considering how many times in the last five minutes she had to tell herself that she had to concentrate on work if she planned to be of any use today. She came into work forty-five minutes early with the intention of working on some files and getting all her paperwork in order before her first meeting. Danya had been actually hoping to free up some time to work on designs but her hopes were not to become a reality. Her memories wouldn't let her focus enough to create any good designs. Past events continued to play over and over in her mind like a song on repeat. Danya made it through her meeting, but her mind was back in another time when her secretary walked in.

"What's on your mind?" Trish stood in front of her desk smiling.

"Trish, there are a few things I need you to do. First, I need you to cancel all my appointments after twelve and rearrange them to fit into John's schedule. Second, I need you to work on these files." Danya picked up three thick files and handed them to her blue eyed, blonde, petite, and perky secretary. "Reduce some of the paperwork in these files. I've already been through them to make sure they could be condensed. I haven't had the time to do so."

"What you mean to say is, you have something on your mind and you can't concentrate." Trish took the files then cheerfully commented, "So you're passing the work off to me and John. Am I correct?"

Danya leaned back in her chair and smiled. "You know me too well."

"Not well enough for you to discuss it with me, huh?" Trish inquired as she shifted the folders in her arms.

Danya moved items on her desk as she contemplated on how she would respond. "No, but don't consider it an insult. I need a person like you around that knows me well, but not too well."

"Why?" Trish asked confused.

"I might feel guilty for pushing my work off on you. And instead of feeling guilty all the time, I'd just fire you," Danya replied matter-of-factly as she logged into her computer.

"In that case, we're fine the way we are. The fact is I know my upbeat attitude is why you hired me." Trish pulled her notebook from under the files and flipped through it. "You needed someone to perk you up. Besides you won't fire me because you think I'm a perfect flunky white girl."

"What does color have to do with?" Danya looked up from the computer at Trish.

Trish shrugged and chuckled, then explained, "Nothing, I don't mind being the token white."

Danya laughed. Trish was right, Danya had hired her because she needed an employee that could stay chipper all day, get the work done, and keep the office spirits up without working her nerves. It was hard to have an attitude when Trish was around. Mary was like that too, the only difference was when she was having a bad day, the other employees could tell despite the smile on her face. Trish, on the other hand, always seemed to be having a good day. It was the office's joke that it must be "a white thing." Trish would laugh and keep on going. There were some of every race in the company but Trish thought of herself as the token white because she was the only Caucasian in the main office.

When Trish brought Danya some coffee, not even fifteen minutes later, Danya asked, "Hey, has John made it in yet?"

Trish set the coffee on the desk and gave her a puzzled look. "Either, you have something very important to discuss with him, or Mary didn't remind you that he wouldn't be in until 10:45. It's not even ten yet."

"You're right." Danya glanced at the time. "Mary did tell me."

Trish pushed the coffee cup closer to her. "Is it that bad?"

"What?" Danya looked away from her blank screen.

"Let me put it this way. I'm glad you only have one more meeting this morning. I'd hate to lose my job and you to lose a company that you worked so hard to start. If your 9:00 meeting went anything like this conversation we're having, then I have a feeling we might have lost a potential client. Maybe you should think about taking the rest of the day off, boss. Once John comes in, he should be able to handle any problems." Trish leaned on the back of the chair as she stared at her.

Danya could hear the genuine concern in her voice. "Thanks. I can handle things but I'll think about it, okay?"

Walking to the door, Trish stopped and said, "I hope I didn't over step my boundaries." She smiled as she exited the office.

Damn that girl. She's right again. Danya recalled barely making it through her meeting. She seriously doubted that she'd hooked the potential client. The flashes back to a time in her life she'd rather forget kept distracting her. Maybe if she stopped avoiding the problem and started dealing with it, she wouldn't feel the need to think about it so much. Going home to drown in the memories of the past wasn't a good solution. Talking to Rita would be the first step or at least a step in the right direction.

Danya called Rita and asked her to meet her at home in half an hour. In truth, part of her hoped that her schedule wouldn't allow for it. The other part of her was committed to making it happen. Rita said she'd tell her boss she had an outside business meeting and she'd be there. Danya informed Trish that she'd be leaving the office for a while, but she didn't want any more of her meetings canceled. Any meeting Danya missed Trish could handle. Trish knew enough to get through the meetings.

When Danya stepped into the door of the apartment, Rita was sitting on the couch waiting for her. She took a deep breath, then walked over and sat on the big leather chair that matched the couch. The chair was directly in front of where Rita sat.

"I know you want the whole story. It happened six years ago. I haven't come to terms with it. Since we both have to get back to work, I'll give you the edited version."

"That's all I can ask for." Rita leaned forward.

Danya knew by Rita's voice when she called that she was surprised, she probably expected her to avoid her. "Here's the story. I was excited about having my first baby; the same day I found out I went over to Gena's place to tell her she was going to be an aunt."

She paused, then stood, walked over to the window, and looked out. Danya refused to let Rita see the tears that were threatening to fall. With her back to her friend, she cleared her throat and told her story as the tears made a trail down her face. "That night was the last time I saw her alive. Gena died later that night in the hospital from a fatal stab wound. You know how you've always wondered why John was the only person that calls me by my first name."

In the reflection of the window, she could see Rita nod her head. "I associate that name with that night. When I moved here I introduced myself as Terry Danya and asked people to call me Danya or I'd simply say that my name was Danya. Since John has always known me as Terry, I didn't expect him to make the switch."

"What was the call this morning about?" Rita questioned.

"This morning I was informed that Marcus, her killer, is getting out. He promised to make sure that I ended up just like Gena." Danya wrung her hands and played with the bracelet on her wrist as she spoke.

"Why would he threaten you?" Rita frowned as if she was trying to make sense of it.

Danya shrugged then unconsciously shook her head. "Instead of standing by his side, I wanted him prosecuted to the fullest extent. Anyway, the cops believed he murdered her because he had gambling debts." He had to be out of his mind to think she would stand by his side after what he had done. She never would understand how his mind works.

"That doesn't sound like much of a motive." Rita's cell beeped. Danya glanced back at her.

"I don't really believe that was his motive. If it was, it was only part of the reason. What I never understood is where Gena came into the picture." Danya felt drained by this conversation as she spoke aloud the questions that had been on her mind for years. "How does him having gambling debts have anything to do with Gena?"

Rita gathered her stuff as she asked, "Did Gena know about his gambling debts?"

"Even if Gena found out about it, why would he need to shut her up? And if he was trying to get the money from her to pay off these people he owed, why ... Look, all I really know is money has always been said to be a powerful motivator. What I cannot figure out is why it caused that man to do what he did." She was grateful Rita phone beeped again.

"I have to get back to work. Just one more question before I leave. What happened to the baby? Did you give it up for adoption?" Rita grabbed her purse, tucking it under her arm.

"That's two questions, but the answer is no. I was never given the choice or the opportunity to have the child let alone give it up for adoption. Gena wasn't the only person I lost that night." Rita's phone beeped again. "You better get out of here. We'll talk about it later."

The instant Rita exited the apartment, tears rushed down Danya's face like a dam bursting. Her body crumbled to the floor as memories flooded her mind. For as long as she could remember, it had been her and her sister against the world. The one constant in her life through the death of her parents, her grandmother, and her uncle. When Gena was murdered, a part of her died. The guilt for bringing Marcus into their lives had kept her awake many nights. Only recently that she had begun to reflect on the good memories without them constantly being over shadowed by that one night. Now Marcus may be out on the streets again to wreak havoc on her life. She couldn't stop thinking about it. Stop, Danya thought as she took a moment to pull herself together. *You can't rewrite history but you damn well can make sure it doesn't repeat itself.*

CHAPTER TWO

Danya made it back to work before 12:15, determined to be more productive. She had only one more meeting since her afternoon meetings were rescheduled. She thanked Trish and headed for her office. Closing the door, she took a seat and began thinking about her talk with her roommate.

It actually felt good telling Rita. It was something that needed to be done, but her mind was stuck in a time warp. She started to play the "what if" game with herself. She should have been paying attention when she arrived. If she had been paying attention she would have noticed that the pool that could be seen at a certain angle on the circular driveway didn't have any lights shining into it. If she had noticed, she would have known that something was wrong and called the police from her car. What would she have told the police if she had observed that small fact?

Maybe if she'd only phoned the damn police immediately when she entered the house some of those events would not have occurred. Maybe if she hadn't been pulling Gena by the arm to the stairs. If she had just carried Gena's body to the car instead of calling 9-1-1. Maybe if they made it to the hospital in time. *If only we had made it to the hospital in time then my sister would still be alive,* she pondered, putting her head on the desk. If she could only stop thinking about that night after she turned Gena over at the bottom of the stairs.

The soft knocking didn't snap her out of her daze. Trish opened the door and leaned against its frame. "I hate to interrupt. I know you didn't answer my knocks, but I thought you would want to know that John called. He wanted to let you know that he won't be in until three. He's sorry he didn't call in earlier but he's at the factory checking on things. I told him that you had something urgent to discuss with him. He said he'd try to get back within the hour."

"Thanks." Danya snuck a quick look at her empty sketchbook page. *So much for being productive*, she thought as she closed the book. "Do I have time to grab a bite to eat before my meeting?"

Trish nodded as she replied, "Yeah."

"Well, I think I'll get something. My breakfast, which actually was my lunch, didn't hold me over. If, by some miracle of God, John gets here before I do, tell him to call me on my cell phone." She stood. "It's gotten quite busy, you think you can hold down the fort until I return or John gets in?"

"Yeah, I can handle it. It can't be any worse than this morning." Trish straightened up and flipped her hair over her shoulder.

"Trish." Danya tapped her sketchbook on the desk.

Trish paused and turned back towards her. "You need something else?"

"No. Thank you." Danya slipped her sketchbook into her purse. "I really appreciate having you around."

"No problem. I already told you that you need me." Trish smirked as she added, "Tell Rick I said hi."

Danya couldn't stop laughing as Trish walked out of the office. She knew that was Trish's subtle way of reminding her that she had better check in with Rick about their dinner date. They had been dating for about a year. He called yesterday to remind her he had something special planned for tonight. He even placed a call to Trish to make sure Danya didn't work late. Danya was about to call him when she decided it could wait until after she got back. Trish was definitely due for a raise. Danya had grabbed her purse and coat and was heading out the door when she thought better of her original decision. She'd forgotten about the dinner date once. She better not give herself the opportunity to do it again. She picked up the receiver and dialed Rick's number at work. Thinking about the call that had put her day in a tail spin quickly returned to the forefront of her thoughts.

"Hello, Cameron and Cameron. Laurie speaking. How may I help you?" The voice had more energy than the law allowed.

"Yes, Laurie. Could you put me through to Rick?" Danya asked in a dry, irritated, and snippy manner unlike herself.

"Whom may I say is calling?" Laurie questioned.

"Danya," she replied in a gruff tone.

"Hey, Danya, I didn't recognize your voice. Sorry about that. It's just you sound so different. How's your day going?" Her voice remained professional but Danya could hear a hint of attitude in it.

Laurie probably did recognize the voice but was unaccustomed to Danya being anything other than pleasant when she called. She knew Laurie had a habit of either not transferring the call, leaving people on hold, or simply hanging up. By Laurie's tone, she'd been in danger of that happening to her until she said her name.

"Let's just say, I've had better." Danya was getting extremely irritable for no reason. All she wanted the child to do was connect her to Rick's office. It felt as if she couldn't control her attitude. She knew she was upset with the Marcus situation and not Laurie.

"Well, let me transfer you to Rick's office. Maybe he can cheer you up. Hold on, please," she stated in her best kiss up voice.

The phone began to ring again, then a deep, sexy voice answered. "This is Rick Cameron of Cameron and Cameron. How may I help you?"

"I don't know, you tell me," she said in a low, soft, sexy voice.

"Hey, I was just thinking about you," Rick stated in a more relaxed voice. "Why didn't you call me directly?"

"Because half the time you're not in your office. If I call the receptionist she'll usually find you or at least attempt to." Danya's voice changed to a syrupy sweet 'I really don't want to have to tell you this' tones. "Listen, Rick, sweetie, the reason I'm calling is because I don't know if I'll be able to make dinner tonight."

Rick chuckled. "That's fine because I wasn't asking you to cook."

"You know what I mean!" Danya mentally debated her decision to cancel.

"Look, there is no way I'm letting you out of tonight. I told you I had something special planned," Rick explained. "If I have to pick you up at work, you're going."

Damn, she thought, *there I go again letting Marcus ruin my evening with Rick.* Danya had finally found a good man. She'd better not let him go. Marcus wasn't even out of jail yet. He may not even come looking for her when he gets out; at least she prayed he wouldn't. There was no reason to let him interfere with the special night Rick had planned.

"Danya! Are you still there?" Rick repeated himself twice before it registered.

"Yeah, yeah, I'm here. Um, Rick, I was just thinking we could still go out. Just call me when you're on your way. I'll be leaving work about 6:30. If I'm not home when you call, call me at work or on the cell. Okay?" Her voice was somewhat distant.

"That's fine. Is something wrong?" Rick asked with an increased level of concern in his voice.

"No. No, nothing's wrong," Danya stammered. "If you were asking why I wanted to cancel dinner, I was canceling because something popped up I needed to handle."

"If you really need to handle some important business," he hesitated and said, "we can have dinner some other time."

Danya found herself shaking her head as if he could see it, then replied, "No! I think I can take care of it before our date."

"You're sure?" Rick questioned.

She tried to sound more like her usual self as she answered, "Positive."

A tiny bit of excitement returned to his voice as he stated, "See you later. Love you, bye."

"Love you, too." Danya hung up the phone. She did love him, until this moment she just didn't know how much.

Grabbing a bite to eat never happened. She ran a few personal errands before coming back for her meeting. After her last meeting, she found herself thinking about her past, present, and future.

The way Danya handled her meeting earlier that morning, Trish had a right to be scared of losing her job. First, Danya continued to lose track of the conversation. Then, she sounded as if she wasn't even prepared for the meeting. She couldn't afford to lose her company. It meant too much to her. Mystic Fashion was the only other thing besides John that represented her past, present, and future, something solid she could depend on. There was no way she was going to let Marcus ruin it by occupying her thoughts. This business and John were the reasons she survived the worst time in her life.

It was three years ago with the help of John Davis that she started Mystic Fashions. She and John moved from the suburbs to downtown Chicago and rented a factory, bought a store and office space. Luckily, John had taken care of all the paperwork needed to get the business up and running. About six months later, she worked her butt off to chase away the ghosts of yesteryear. John was right alongside her, keeping her on track and picking up any slack. Without John and Mystic Fashions, there wouldn't have been a future for her. She was grateful that John had given her Gena's business concept. She instinctively touched her wrist with the distinct bracelet with symbols that represented her life elegantly weaved throughout it, from her company logo to the yin yang symbol to her zodiac sign. John had it custom made to represent her past and celebrate her new beginning. It meant a lot to Danya when he had given it to her on her first day in the office. When she looked at it, she was reminded that she was not only doing this for herself but doing it for Gena, too.

At present, Mystic was a combination of her and Gena's dream. She had wanted a store offering handmade clothing with options to have it tailored to fit for the everyday woman. Gena wanted to do high-end designs for the wealthy and elite. Her business did both. It made her feel like she was honoring Gena's life. Danya kept Gena's dream alive with every design she created. There was no way she could let this distraction become a habit. She'd be damned if she would let Marcus ruin it. Danya needed someone to talk to that knew her before and after Marcus had destroyed her life.

She worked well up until 2:30; by that time her concentration was shot. Her mind started going back in time. As she looked around the office, she realized she only had a few pictures up—one of Rick and her and an employee Christmas party picture with her, Rick, Rita, Trish, John, and few other employees.

Where in the hell was John? she pondered, anxious to talk to him. She had to discuss her feelings with somebody that understood what she was going through.

John walked into the office as if her thoughts had conjured him up. He closed the door and took a seat. Danya glanced up at her friend. She was glad that she had this 6'3" lean, well-built man to depend on for over twenty years, especially the last six. John's style had always been clean cut; usually, he dressed in slacks and a sharp dress shirt but he was the kind of man that even looked sophisticated in jeans. Most women thought John was handsome and sexy. Since he was like a brother to her, he only looked okay to Danya, but he was a gem. She wondered why she hadn't fallen in love with someone like him instead of someone like Marcus.

"Terry, I thought you needed to talk to me," John said, stopping Danya's contemplation.

Danya didn't waste any time as she got straight to the point. "Marcus will be getting out due to some glitch in the system."

"When did you find out?" His face expressed the concern he felt.

"This morning." She pushed back her chair.

He glanced at her with his mouth open then shook his head as if in shock. "What loophole did they find to get him out?"

"I'm not sure. Officer Bally tried to tell me but I was too upset to listen. That was not the question I wanted answered. What I want to know is when he gets out, is he coming after me?" Her erratic hand movements reflected her frustration at the situation.

"Maybe it's time you took a vacation. I can handle things here for a while." John gave her the worried look.

"I can't. That would be the worst thing for me. Where would I go? I'd be all alone. Just me and my nightmares, no thank you. How would I explain that to Rick? Just tell him, 'Oh honey, I have a business trip. I don't know where I'm going or when I'll be back. I'll call you.' You know that won't wash with Rick, not to mention Rita, who overheard my end of the conversation with the police this morning." Danya stood and paced the small office not giving John a chance to speak. "I don't even know if he's going to bother me once he's a free man. It could have been an idle threat. He may be so thrilled to be free that he doesn't even give me a second thought."

"Don't kid yourself. It just may end up getting you killed." John's eyes tried to follow Danya's pacing body.

"That's true but I can't go into hiding forever." Danya ran her fingers through her hair, so distressed over the entire situation. The hair that had been previously rested on her forehead was now brushed to the back with several strands that refused to be pushed back sticking out here and there.

"That's a valid point. Are you going to tell Sharrita? She does have a right to know. She'll be at home waiting to speak to you. Knowing you like I do, if you wait, you'll find every excuse in the book not to tell her." John crossed his arms.

Danya stopped pacing and said, "Wrong, you are so wrong. I guess you and Rita don't know me that well after all. You both underestimate me based on—"

"Based on the fact that if it has to do with anything that happened before the last three years you won't talk about it," John interjected.

"Don't underestimate my ability to do things that I don't want to do but need too. I've already told Rita about some of it." She could tell John was surprised by the way his eyes grew bigger as his arms dropped to his sides. "I had to. This morning, I tried to avoid the topic but she made a legitimate point that I couldn't ignore."

John leaned on Danya's desk. "Which was?"

"If there's a possibility that she's in danger then she has a right to know. Since Marcus is getting out, I needed to tell her. Not that I really wanted to." Danya sat on the edge of the desk. John looked relieved she had finally stopped pacing. They discussed the situation intensely for a long time.

"I forgot to ask. How did your meeting go this morning?" Danya asked.

John frowned and gave her an update. They discussed business for a while until they realized how long they'd been talking. John and Danya slowly wrapped up their conversation.

"I still can't believe that Marcus will be back on the street by the end of the week, possibly sooner," John stated as he stood.

Her forehead creased as she frowned. "How did you know?"

"Didn't you tell me?" John looked at Danya, confused. "How else would I know?"

This Marcus thing was really getting to me, she thought because she could have sworn that she hadn't mentioned it. "I guess I did. I guess I did."

Danya laid her head in her hands. She couldn't believe that this was happening. Lifting her head, she asked John if he could handle things if she left out earlier than usual. She had a few more things that were imperative for her to take care of before going home.

"Sure, I can handle things, no problem." John headed to the door then paused. "If I need you, I'll just give you a call on your cell phone. You are carrying it today, aren't you?"

"Yeah, something like that." She grabbed her purse, ignoring the look John gave her for the comment she'd made.

"Something like that?" John asked, questioning her meaning since she chose to ignore the look he'd given her.

Danya had her cell phone but it wouldn't make much of a difference whether or not she was carrying it if the battery died on her. Danya hoped to have time to get a new one by the end of the week if she remembered. She knew from this morning that she could be easily diverted from her original train of thought. The fact that Marcus was getting out of jail upset her equilibrium. It terrified her to know she'd soon come face to face with the person who had, all in one night, ripped her life to shreds leaving a devastated soul with disintegrated dreams and a debilitated foundation on which to rebuild her life. Danya wasn't about to grant Marcus another opportunity to destroy her life when he came after her. While she tried to be somewhat nonchalant with John, the truth was, there was no doubt in Danya's mind Marcus was coming after her. When he did, she would be prepared.

CHAPTER THREE

Danya left right after her conversation with John. Entering the café, she ordered a coffee then made her way to the seats in the back. After plugging in her dying phone, she scrolled through looking for associates that she had crossed paths with in the past. She opened her briefcase and pulled out her sketchbook. She flipped past her clothing design ideas to a blank paper to make a list of individuals she wanted to reach out to. She contacted the two most important ones first. She would only need the rest of the list if they could not help her out. Once she contacted them, she ordered a new phone then headed home to get out of her monkey suit and into something more comfortable. It dawned on her how ridiculous it was for her to design clothes, but not design for herself.

Rita looked up from her tablet when Danya walked into the apartment a little before seven. Danya sat on the couch, kicked off her pumps, then took off her suit jacket. She glanced over at her friend who looked as if she had something to say. Rita stared at her like she'd grown a third eye, but didn't say anything.

Danya tried to ignore her by watching the movie on the screen but she finally asked, "What is it, Rita?"

"I was uh, well I ..." Rita shrugged her shoulders as she paused then said, "I was wondering if we could talk more about what we discussed earlier."

Danya cringed a bit before asking, "What in particular do you want to discuss?"

"I was curious as to why you didn't believe the motive the police gave." Rita angled her body towards her.

"Because certain pieces of the puzzle don't fit and still don't. If he wanted to kill Gena to prevent her from talking, why did he have to rape her?" Danya fought to keep the attitude out of her voice. She had finally stop thinking about it. Now she wondered if it was a good thing after all telling her roommate.

Rita sighed. "Maybe, he was just sick."

"I know that, but there is something missing. I can feel it in my bones, but I can't place my finger on it. It could be something that they didn't tell me, something I forgot, or something that was too painful for me to remember, I don't know." She shrugged and leaned back onto the couch. "What I do know is there is a key ingredient missing and without it, the motive that Officer Bally supplied doesn't hold water with me."

Rita and Danya talked until the doorbell rang. Danya lifted her arm to look at her watch. It was eight o'clock already. Rick was here and she hadn't even changed clothes. Now she didn't have time to. *I thought I told him to call me,* she pondered as she slipped her pumps back on. Adjusting her skirt and blouse, her plan to look nice was out the window. What she had on would just have to do. Instead of letting Rick in, she went out to him noticing her cell was dead as she slid it into her purse.

As they got in the car, Danya asked, "So, what are our plans for the evening?"

"You'll have to wait and see," he replied with a wickedly sexy smile.

During the drive, Rick made small talk which made Danya even more curious. Her mind slipped back to Marcus. How would this affect her relationship with Rick? It worried her that it may not survive the revelations of truths she had yet to tell him. As she reflected on her current situation, she was surprised as they pulled in front of his condo. Rick got out the car then went around to open the passenger door. She looked at him strangely. His condo wasn't the location she expected this special night to occur.

Danya entered his condo, all thoughts of Marcus exited her mind. Rick's place was dimly lit with Luther Vandross softly playing in the background. The apartment reminded her of walking into her grandma's kitchen with the aroma of all the fresh cooked foods drifting out to tempt the taste buds. That smell made her hungry every time.

"Mmm, I do love a man that can cook." Danya smiled at Rick as he closed the door. "So, what are we having for dinner?"

"Some of your favorites—salad, seafood lasagna with lots of shrimp, and for dessert, peach cobbler and me, of course. We're also having your favorite, white wine." Rick took Danya by the hand and led her into the dining room then pulled out her chair. "What is your aversion to red wine anyway?"

"I'd rather have the cobbler with ice cream, but you will do. It sounds delicious. Lead the way to the dining room." She glanced up at Rick as he poured her a glass of wine. "And there's nothing wrong with red wine, I just don't like it. Besides, white goes better with the seafood lasagna."

Rick gave her the 'whatever' look as he set the wine back. The memory of the incidents that caused her aversion to red wine flashed in her mind. She took a sip of her white wine and tried to shake it off.

Danya examined the table. There were two white candles with a beautiful rose centerpiece. "Oh! Rick, this is beautiful."

Rick placed the salad in front of her, then retrieved the rest of the meal from the kitchen. He served her a slice of lasagna with garlic bread then took his seat. She smiled as she used the fork she was eating the salad with to taste the lasagna. It was delicious. Danya was enjoying the evening and the conversation despite her mind often slipping in a few unwanted thoughts.

Rick stood and took the empty plates. When he returned with the dessert, he made a comment that threw Danya for a loop.

"I've known you for about a year now. You've told me how your parents died when you were eleven. That you lived with your Uncle Chris instead of living with your grandmother. I also know that your grandma died when you were sixteen and your uncle died when you were twenty. Yet there is still a span of years I know nothing about. Why is that?" He took a bite of the peach cobbler.

Danya kept shoveling cobbler into her mouth, no longer paying much attention to the taste. Rick's question had made her nervous. He'd never asked so bluntly about her past before. She didn't know if she wanted to ruin her evening by discussing it or if she wanted to wait to tell him later. The plan was to enjoy this evening and discuss the news she received tomorrow. Danya decided to stall for more time.

"The food was delicious," she blurted out. "Better than the seafood lasagna we had at that restaurant last week."

"After the way you complained about how the restaurant couldn't cook. 'Where's the seasoning? A little pepper in my life would be nice! They didn't put enough shrimps in here to feed an ant. The garlic bread tastes as if it was bought at a store where it's been sitting for centuries and it's hard as a rock. I think I may have chipped a tooth on it.'"

Danya laughed as Rick imitated her voice and facial expression from that night. Rick paused, laughing himself then continued talking. "Hey, I had to make sure everything was on point." He grinned. "Dinner turned out pretty well if I do say so myself. Now that I told you that, you can stop avoiding the subject. We'll enjoy our dessert."

Danya was relieved but couldn't enjoy the dessert as much as she had before his question. She began to eat the cobbler slowly like her middle name was molasses. Even eating slowly, she was finished before she knew it.

She avoided what she knew was coming with a single question. "Why cook instead of going out?"

"Because you're a private person, so I thought this should be done in private," he replied.

Danya cut her eyes at him. "This?"

Rick paused as if he was contemplated whether to say something. "You made a brother work hard for a date. I had to fall on the friendship sword to convince you to give me a chance."

It was true but after what had happened to her, who could blame her? She tilted her head and studied his face. "What does that have to do with this evening?"

"I never believed that I could love one woman so much, but I do." Rick slid out the chair onto one knee and pulled out the engagement ring. "Will you marry me?"

Danya was stunned for a moment. It never crossed her mind when he said that he had something special planned it was this. She wanted to say yes, but she didn't know how he'd feel once he learned about the missing years he'd just inquired about. Danya knew she had paused too long when the ring box closed and Rick stood.

"You don't have to answer right now." He slid the ring box into his pocket and started clearing off the table.

She decided that she had better talk to Rick instead of trying to think of ways to avoid the problem.

"Rick." She stood reaching for his arms as he picked up her bowl. "Let me explain ..."

"There is nothing to explain. Let's enjoy the rest of the evening, okay?" Rick turned away and carried her bowl into the kitchen.

"No, it's not okay. I have something to say and I want you to listen." She could hear in his voice that her slow response really hurt him. His male pride would never admit it.

"Go, ahead." Rick came back to the table and picked up the rest of the dishes then went back into the kitchen and placed them in the sink. "Let's go into the living room."

Following him into the other room, Danya sat on the end of the couch. Rick walked over to the stereo, turned it off, then went back in the dining room.

"Rick, come sit down!"

Rick walked back to where Danya was. He sat down on the couch and turned where he could be face to face with Danya. "You've gotten a little bossy, haven't you?"

"It's not that I don't want to marry you. I need to tell you a few things first, things that may change your mind about us getting married." She ran her hands through her hair. Danya didn't want to discuss this, but she had no other choice, not really. Rick needed to know this if they were to get married.

"Like what?" he asked as if there wasn't anything she could say that would change his mind.

"Several years ago I witnessed the murder of my sister, Gena, the one person who knew me better than anyone." She wasn't looking at Rick. Her focus was on the wall beyond him.

"Oh, baby. I didn't know." He reached for her hand.

She glanced at him, squeezed his hand, then stood. "Not too many people do."

"I know it must have been awful to witness something like that but …" he paused. "What does that have to do with us?" Rick asked. "Wait … Sister!"

When they met, Danya told him all her family was dead. Since she didn't have any living relatives, she knew he assumed she didn't have any siblings. Danya didn't have any pictures of her family. Her eyes scanned the family pictures that his mom had insisted grace his wall. She turned towards him and stated, "Yes. She was raped and murdered by my husband, Marcus Anthony Johnson."

"Hold on. Are you trying to tell me that you're married?" He stood quickly, advancing towards her.

"No." She rested her hand on his shoulder. "I'm telling you that these are two facts I hid from you."

His head dipped as if he was relieved. "I'm sorry about your sister, baby."

"Sometimes I feel like I knew her better than I know myself." She walked away from returning to the couch. "I'm extremely uncomfortable discussing this particular topic with anyone."

"I'm glad you felt comfortable enough to tell me now." Rick took a seat next to her on the couch.

The anger at Marcus built in her chest. He was screwing up her life and he hadn't even been released yet. She blinked back the tears as her mind considered the possibility that she could lose Rick. "I thought you needed to know that I used to be married."

"As long as you're not married now then that's all I need to know." He pulled her towards him. "What you've just told me doesn't change a thing. I still want to marry you and I love you. Why did you think telling me this would change that?" He held her chin, looking deeply into her eyes.

Her eyes shift down. "I thought you'd feel that you couldn't trust me since I wasn't completely honest with you."

Rick released her chin, reaching into his pocket.

"It's beautiful!" Danya exclaimed as he opened the box and she got a closer look at the ring.

Rick got on one knee beside Danya. "Will you marry me?" He took the engagement ring from the box and placed it on Danya's finger.

"Yes!" She hugged him tightly and started crying. This was her second chance with love. The first had been a disaster because she married a murderer. The second time, she hoped she'd live long enough to appreciate it. Danya hugged Rick tighter not wanting to let him go.

She felt if she released him, he'd disappear as if he were only a figment of her imagination.

"Baby, uh, honey, you're choking me." He grabbed her arms from around his neck. Rick took a deep breath as Danya leaned back. She grinned like he was joking. She realized he was serious. Her grip on his neck was cutting off his air supply.

"There's one more thing," she stated as if it pained her to say it. "He's getting out of prison soon."

"Is there any chance he might come after you?" Rick's tone became serious.

Danya attempt to sound nonchalant as she replied, "Yes, a slight one."

"Do you want to stay with me awhile? It's not a—"

"No! I'd better tell you the whole story, at least most of what I remember." Danya went into most of the story, ending at the last time she saw Marcus. "The last thing Marcus said to me was that I betrayed him. He made it clear to me he'd make me pay dearly for wanting my own husband to be severely punished, and I believe him. For three and a half years, I thought he was playing with a full deck. That night I found out that he was playing cards with a full deck but he had lost some of his marbles."

"What?" Rick gave her a confused look.

"He was crazy but smart. He had to be crazy to think that I wouldn't try to see to it that he got punished for murdering the only family I had left. To think, if I hadn't decided to tell Gena about the baby, he would have gotten away with his plan and I would have been none the wiser." Danya took the napkin Rick handed her and wiped her tears away.

"You know what really hurt was when the wool was finally removed from my eyes, I had lost everything. I lost my baby, my best friend and sister, and they were the last of my family. For a while, I even thought I was losing my mind." Danya leaned into his arms.

Rick's hands slowly went up and down her arm. "Why?"

"After I lost the baby, I was in the hospital for a year. Marcus almost slipped the system but things worked out and he went to prison." Danya paused.

"The first six months I spent in the hospital, I barely talked, ate, or did much of anything." The one thing she remembered when she was lucid was wanting a divorce from Marcus. Her body straightens up as she peered up at Rick and realized she had stopped talking. "Most of the time I laid in the fetal position replaying that night over and over again. I was always sick, but doctors couldn't find anything physically wrong with me. They assumed my physical sickness was caused by my emotional state. A lot of the time, I was confused. I just felt awful. There were times when I was feeling fine and then all of a sudden I'd be sick.

"The only person left that I could trust was John. He was the best. He took care of everything while I was in the hospital. He even hired a private nurse to keep an eye on me. He believed that the hospital didn't have enough staff to watch me constantly or to give me the care I needed. The hospital agreed, which I am now grateful for."

"You have been through a lot." Rick grabbed her hand.

"If John hadn't come to the hospital every day to visit me, I probably would still be there. He talked about things like how he was getting divorce papers drawn up for me. Or, how he was getting the paperwork for my business together. He would sit and talk to me from the beginning of visiting hour to the end." Danya lifted Rick's arm and slipped underneath him.

He pulled her closer and kisses her on the forehead. "I'm glad John was there for you."

"One night before John left, he gave me what I believe was the kick in the behind that I needed to get going. He simply stated that while I was laying there ignoring life, and everyone in it, I was letting Gena's murderer walk away without even a smack on the hand. He walked to the door then turned to me and said, 'Don't decide to start talking and wanting your life back then find out it's too late.' The next evening when he walked in I gave him a piece of my mind."

"Mmm. I can imagine that." Rick smirked.

"I told him if he came to get on my case, he'd have to cut his visit short. That day was the first time in months that I was not sick. For the next couple of months, I went to therapy. They wanted to make sure I had mentally pulled it together. When they felt I indeed had made a recovery, I was released from the hospital about a month or two later in spite of the fact I still wouldn't talk much about that night." Danya sat up and put her leg on the couch. She studied Rick's face for a moment trying to gauge his reaction to the news before saying more.

"Baby, you look tired. You don't need to keep talking about it." Rick took his finger and wiped a lingering tear from her face. "Why don't you rest a bit? I'll turn the music back on and you lay on the couch while I wash dishes. After I finish, I'll take you home, if that's what you want."

Danya was relieved to see the love in his eyes. She felt silly for not saying something sooner as she replied, "That's fine."

* * *

Rick turned the stereo on and went into the kitchen. Looking back, he wondered if he did the right thing not allowing her to finish her story. The way her eyes became more distant and void as she told the story worried him. He hadn't known when he asked her that question she'd actually have a story to tell. Danya had been married for well over three years if you count the time before her divorce was final. If it had not been for that night, she would have a child about five. Rick hated Marcus for what he'd done to Danya, but he was also grateful. If Marcus hadn't, they'd be married with children and Rick would have never met her. Rick couldn't even imagine not having her as a part of his life.

When Rick returned to the living room, Danya was laid out on the couch snoring lightly. She looked so peaceful that he couldn't bear to wake her up. He decided if she woke up when he carried her to bed then he'd take her home. If she didn't wake up then he'd take her home in the morning. In the end, he did neither. He covered her with a blanket. He decided it wouldn't hurt if they took the day off tomorrow. Before leaving the room, Rick bent over and kissed Danya on the forehead.

"Marcus will not lay a hand on you, not if I can help it," Rick promised.

CHAPTER FOUR

The next day Rick woke up with a start. Danya came bursting into the master bedroom with her hands on her hips and her neck rolling. If he'd wondered about her having a cramp in her neck, he had to wonder no more. Rick squinted at her then fully closed his eyes and turned back over. Danya began shaking him vigorously. He jumped into a sitting position and wiped the sleep out of his eyes.

"Richard Cameron, wake your booty up! What happened to taking me home? Did you even call Rita to let her know I was staying the night?" Her arms swung through the air frantically.

"The answer to your first question is I didn't want to wake you. And yes, I had enough sense to think to call your roommate. If this is the way you are in the morning, I don't know if I want to marry a grouch." Rick pulled Danya into his arms and began kissing her.

She smiled as he ended the kissed. "That was nice but I think you could do better."

"How?" He nuzzled his face in her neck.

Danya playfully pushed him back. "By brushing your teeth; your breath is kicking!"

"I don't think it should matter since I know you don't think your breath smells like fresh cut roses." Rick laughed and kissed her again. "Besides, when you're in love things like that don't matter."

"Whoever said that was full of crap. Are you telling me if I smelled like I haven't even looked at a bathtub in months, you'd still love me?" She wrapped her arms around his neck.

His hands roamed her upper back. "Yep, I just wouldn't touch you with a ten-foot pole."

"You're lying. If I smelled like ten-year-old funk, your love would be a thing of the past." Danya pulled the covers back and straddled him. She placed her hands under his T-shirt and seductively moved them upwards. The shirt was rising with her hands so she pulled it off. "Richard, you've been a very bad boy. It's time for me to teach you a lesson." She began slowly making a trail from his belly to his lips with her full lips. Then she placed her fingers in the elastic band of his boxers and moved her fingers around the elastic waistband, pulling them down slightly.

"If it's the kind of lesson I think it is, maybe I should be on top," Rick joked.

"Whatever for? Besides, this is my lesson." She began unbuttoning her blouse. "First lesson. I am thee only woman you'll ever need to satisfy you. If I'm not, you better become a very good teacher or call it quits." His hands slowly walked up her thighs. Her skirt began rising as his hands went further up. Danya knocked his hands away.

"Must I remind you? I am the teacher this go round. When I'm finished, then you can take over." Danya moved off him and stood. She slowly finished unbuttoning her blouse and let it hang open, revealing a cream bra resting against her dark brown skin. Rick quickly removed his boxers as he watched Danya undress. She unzipped her skirt then pushed it down her hips, rocking them provocatively from side to side before letting the skirt hit the floor. She then took her hands and slid her blouse seductively off her shoulders.

Rick reached into his night stand drawer when he noticed she was no longer wearing clothing. He was prepared by the time she'd straddled him again. She began titillating him with her tongue, working from the base of his neck down, as her hands massaged his muscles. Danya's lesson was absolutely getting a rise out of Rick. He was lightly moaning at Danya's sensual love play. Their passion had built by the time her lower body began moving. His eyes glowed with passion. Rick didn't mind helping out with this assignment. His hands were on her waist until his fingers began tracing the scar on her mid-section. Her body moved in ways that made the penetration deeper and deeper. He moaned in pleasure as they went on a ride through ecstasy. He pulled Danya to him and began kissing her, pleased with his lesson. Then he rolled her on her back.

"My turn," he said, his voice heavy with passion.

Rick went to work setting her body on fire. With his body against hers, he caressed her gently. He took his time, whispering erotic things in her ear. He entered her with a powerful thrust. He kept the intense rhythm going until Danya was trembling. Rick moved deeper within her, each movement more potent than the last until Danya was reaching for anything to hold on to. Their love making became so intense that the bed could no longer hold up. The final thrust happened as the bed hit the floor sending erotic ripples through their bodies. The bed frame couldn't handle their spirited love making. After their bodies stopped quivering, they were too drained to talk. Rick rolled next to Danya and held her in his arms.

Once some of their energy returned, Rick started nibbling on her ear. "I would have been bad sooner if I'd known this was the lesson I was going to be taught."

"Umm, don't make it a habit." She moaned as his lips worked their way down her body.

Rick looks up at her. "How about we spend the rest of the day practicing for our wedding night?"

"That sounds like a good idea. At least we don't have to worry about breaking the bed. I told you when you bought this bed that it wasn't made to last. But, no! You had to have this expensive, fancy looking piece of junk when you could have had that beautiful antique bed that was built to last for centuries."

"It doesn't matter. You get to choose my replacement bed since you'll be the one paying for the next one. I guess you can start looking tomorrow; it was your lesson that broke it."

"Lesson number two, males are always responsible for fixing or replacing anything that breaks before, during, or after the lesson." Danya laughed and cuddle against his chest.

Rick was surprised. Never had she been the aggressor when it came to sex. She'd developed an insecurity about her weight in her early years but to him she was thick and shapely. Rick actually had to convince her that he didn't mind her being overweight. Danya's fingers began to roam over Rick's muscular chest and his flat abdomen.

* * *

Danya watched Rick as he slept. The only thing that mattered in that moment was she had found a man that really loved her. She hoped that she was not making a mistake like last time. For the first time in six years, Marcus was not Danya's main focus in the morning. In fact, he was only a passing thought. Up until this point, Marcus had been like her alarm clock, the first thought she woke up to. She felt as if she were really starting to deal with everything that had happened to her, or at least coexist with it.

Rick began kissing her, making any other thoughts of Marcus exit her mind. Danya and Rick spent the rest of the day getting to know each other better—much better.

The next morning Danya drove to work smiling and singing. As she walked past Trish's desk, her assistant asked, "Are you okay?"

Danya laughed and replied, "I'm fine. The only reason I took yesterday off was I needed the rest."

She gave her a look of disbelieve and said, "Hmmm ..."

"You've been hanging around black people too long." Danya laughed as Trish gave her the sister girl look.

"You know that I was not referring to you being sick. I'm talking about the glow you got about you. Mmmhmm, so what's new?" Trish lifted her eyebrow at Danya and leaned closer.

"I'm trying a new make-up, girl," Danya joked.

"Mmmhmm." Trish leaned back and studied her boss's face.

"I'm serious." Danya looked down and tried not to laugh as she lied.

"Very funny. I'm serious. In all the time I've known you, I've never seen you look so happy." Trish studied her face.

Danya finally told her that it was because she had never seen her engaged before. Trish's reaction was much calmer than Rita's had been that morning. Rita had jumped up, hugged her, and began screaming in her ear about how she couldn't believe her roommate was getting married and congratulated her. She went on about the engagement ring and how beautiful it was. Trish told her how happy she was for her and to make sure she got an invitation to the wedding. The only reason that Trish didn't say more was the phone began ringing off the hook. Danya could say she was quite relieved that Trish wasn't given the opportunity to tell the entire office. One thing that Danya wanted to make sure of was John heard about her engagement from her and no one else. While Trish was on the phone, Danya went into her office. John was sitting at her desk. Danya threw her coat on the coat rack and set her purse on the desk.

"John. Great, you're here. I have something to tell you. Rick asked me to marry him and I said yes."

"That is wonderful news, but did you tell him—"

"Yes, I did," she stated with a slight attitude before he could finish his sentence.

"Now that's really wonderful," John replied without an ounce of enthusiasm.

Her smile instantly hit the floor when she looked into his eyes. She could tell he was happy for her but something was bothering him. From the look in his eyes, she guessed it was not good news. John seemed to be debating telling her.

"What is it? Don't say it's nothing just because I am in a good mood."

"Marcus was released yesterday. I found out after work. I tried to call you at Rick's, but I couldn't get anyone."

"I guess I have to ask." She paused. "What are the chances he'll come after me?" Danya sat on the edge of the desk facing John.

"It doesn't matter." He leaned forward and slowly stated, "You need to protect yourself regardless."

She crossed her arms then asked, "What do you suggest?"

"Self-defense classes and ..." John hesitated then said, "And ..."

Danya knew she wouldn't like whatever came next by the way he paused. "And, what?"

"Emotional therapy," he stated in almost a whisper.

She stood, walking over to the office door. "What? Did I hear you correctly?" Danya shouted as she slammed the door closed. She walked over to John with her neck rolling, one hand on her hip and the other cutting through the air. "What, do you think I'm crazy?"

"Calm down!" John held his hands up.

Danya continued ranting. "Or is it that you want to check my degree of sanity now that Marcus is back in the picture?"

John attempted to interrupt. "Terry, I—"

"I can't believe you." She shook her head. "You of all people should know that I'm not crazy!"

"I'm not suggesting that you're crazy. But it's time for you to deal with what you've been through. Gena and you were like two peas in a pod."

Danya agreed with a head nod. "What does me being close to my sister have to do with it?"

"This is the first time in six years that we've talked about it without you changing the subject. The way you walked in this morning tells me that talking about it has done you some good. Look, I don't want Marcus's weapon against you to be what happened, and if it is and it will be, he'll win. Why? You can't handle it. Because you haven't dealt with it."

"Okay. As mixed up as that sounds, it does make sense." Danya resumed her upbeat mood. "Now get out of my chair! And why are you in my office anyway?" She refused to give up her happiness for anyone today, especially Marcus.

John laughed, stood up, and headed for the door. "It's nice having the old Terry back. I didn't care for this Danya character much, she was kind of boring. If you're serious about what we talked about, I've already made an appointment for you at twelve with the best therapist in town. Tonight, if you and Rick don't have any plans, we could go to a self-defense class. Just let me know."

"Thanks, John. I'll talk to you later." Danya dismissed him, not missing the fact he'd ignored her question. "You know what?"

"What?" he asked as he turned back towards her.

"Danya is the old Terry and she has never been and will never be boring. Otherwise, I wouldn't have such an exciting friend. Unless you're saying you're a boring man."

John chuckled. "Terry Danya, I'm more exciting and complex than even you know."

"Well, well, well. The man has spoken. You're very conceited, you know that? Oh, I need the name and address of the therapist if I plan to go. I don't have ESP."

John gave her the information and left. After she had a moment to think, she was quite surprised that she was so content in spite of learning that Marcus was out.

Later that day, Danya found herself in Dr. Adams's office. The doctor was an older white woman who had a soft and calming voice. After introducing herself, she told Danya to take a seat on the couch and relax. Dr. Adams's office was in her home, which made Danya more comfortable. She had pictures of what she assumed were her family on the wall. It didn't look like she imagined a psychiatrist's office would look like. It was much cozier.

"You may start whenever you want and talk about whatever you want. This session is just to get you relaxed and more comfortable with me. We'll work our way up to the deeper feelings when we think you can handle it. How's that?"

"That's fair," Danya said, wondering if it was a mistake to come.

"I have one question to ask, though. Would you like me to call you Terry or Danya? The appointment was made for Terry but you introduced yourself as Danya." The doctor grabbed her notebook off the desk.

"Danya," she answered, glancing down, hoping that she wouldn't probe deeper. She begins to nervously play with her bracelet. She noticed the doctor scribbling in her notebook. Her mind went back to the reason she went by that name. She closed her eyes and tears began rolling down her face. Dammit, she didn't want to go there today.

"Well, we will not be getting into anything deep today. We'll only talk about your life in general," Dr. Adams explained as Danya wiped her tears away.

Danya was relieved. Although she'd thought she was ready to discuss her feeling about it, she wasn't. Danya could easily talk about trivial things as long as they weren't related to that night. By the time the session was over she had addressed more important feelings like how she felt about marrying Rick and how good it felt to be totally honest with him. Danya left Dr. Adams's office thinking John had been right. Talking about things may do her some good.

Danya got into the office a little after 1:30 p.m. Despite not talking about the past, the session with the therapist triggered her unpleasant memories.

"Boss lady, I hate to interrupt, but we have a meeting with a distributor in five minutes." John leaned into her office. "Are you up for a little self-defense tonight?"

"Yes." Danya smiled at John. "You know, John, without you, I don't know where I'd be."

"Lucky for you, you're not without me. See you in three minutes. I have some data to collect before the meeting." John took a glance back at Danya. "It's great to have you back."

The meeting went smoothly. It was after the meeting ended that everything went haywire. The problem arose right before they were going to leave for the day. Trish received a call stating the fabric company messed up Mystic's order again. They couldn't find their original copy of the order. John and Danya had to find their copies and get them to the company, otherwise their production would get behind. Their supplier contract would be up soon. Danya needed to start looking for a new supplier. She hated to be stuck any longer with a business that was continually messing up. What she didn't need was Mystic Fashions getting a bad reputation because the people that supplied her fabric couldn't get her orders right. Her customers didn't want to hear that. They wanted the items they ordered on time.

Trish looked through Danya's files for the hard copy. "You go to the self-defense class, I can handle this."

Danya glanced up from the computer that she'd been searching for the digital copy to see John entering her office doorway. She turned back to Trish and replied, "I can go next time."

"I looked through my emails. I don't think I was cc'd on this one," John stated as he approached her desk. "But you can go. Trish and I can handle this."

Danya couldn't understand why she couldn't find it. She recently had scrolled across it in her email. Now it's not there or saved on her desktop. "No, I'm fine."

"I'm your trusted friend, right?" John stared at her.

Danya gave him a funny look. "Yeah and you're saying this because ..."

"I'm saying this because I think, from one friend to another, you need to go." John looked at Danya sincerely as if not to hurt her feelings.

"One of these days I'm going to find out how trustworthy you are." Danya kissed him on the cheek and grabbed her things. Danya didn't think John wanted to go to the self-defense class. He was only going to ensure she went. This situation had handed him the perfect excuse to wiggle out of it. "If you and Trish have something going, make sure it's not going on on my desk, okay?"

Both John and Trish's head snapped towards her giving her a dirty glare. Danya smirked then smiled at them before leaving the office. Something was up with those two. They had been working a lot of late nights together, more than the norm. Maybe that's why John rarely brought the women he dated to company functions; he wanted to leave his options open with Trish. Danya suddenly remembered, she hadn't call Agent Waller back. She couldn't imagine what it was that he could want to talk to her about but she would give her lawyer a call first then call him back.

CHAPTER FIVE

The past was tugging on her soul like it was trying to drag her down to kiss the gates of hell. Danya took a terrible trip down memory lane as she sipped coffee in the living room with the News watching her. The only time she didn't think of Marcus and the past was when she was in Rick's arms. There were moments she wished she could turn back the hands of time. If she could, she would have listened to Gena and Uncle Chris when they warned her about Marcus.

Rita sashayed into the room and cleared her throat, interrupting Danya's thoughts. When Danya looked at her, she saw Rita with a bottle of champagne in her hands. *Isn't it a bit early to be having a drink?* she thought as she smiled up at her roommate.

"My dear, after you get in tonight we are celebrating!" Rita announced, swaying her hips like she was already drunk.

Danya clearly saw that Rita was delighted about something. Rita had on a new silk outfit, her slacks were white, her blouse and heels were the same color as her hazel eyes. How she managed to pull that off was amazing to Danya. Rita had even taken her hair out of her usual French roll she wore to work. Her hair looked just like a silk scarf flowing over her shoulders.

"What are we celebrating?" Danya questioned.

Rita's grin grew larger. "Could it be my promotion that I got without any strings attached?"

"Congratulations, girl." Danya stood and went over to hug her. She wondered if that meant more sales trips for Rita or less. As she ended the embrace, she gave her a questioning stare. "I am thrilled for you, but how did you manage to cut those strings?"

"I threatened him nicely." Rita threw her head back and laughed.

Danya cut her eyes at her. "What did you do?"

"I told him three things could happen to him if I don't get the job because I wouldn't have sex with him." She shrugs her shoulders nonchalantly then headed towards the kitchen. "Either I would file a sexual harassment suit against him."

Danya grabbed her coffee cup off the table and followed Rita to the kitchen. "What he say to that?"

"It wouldn't get far. I told him even if no charges were brought against him, the company would be watching his actions carefully. Or, I'd just tell his wife, and his wife is not a woman to be crossed. Trust me." Rita gave Danya a 'you know what I mean' look as she put the champagne in the refrigerator to chill.

"What was the third option?" Danya questioned as she rinsed out her cup.

"It's the third option that I love. I grabbed his arm, twisted it behind his back, and whispered in his ear, or I'll break your arm." Rita paused, looking like she'd just finished a delectable chocolate. "I know, Danya, that isn't what self-defense class is for, but, to see that smug look get wiped off his face."

Danya knew Rita's boss started with small comments about them dining together. When Rita became interested in the new position, it escalated to suggesting on the sly that sleeping with him would help her career. While one part of her was glad she did it, the other part wished she'd went through human resources to help prevent it from happening to someone else.

She shook her head. "Rita ..."

"Mmm, it was worth it. After I let go of his arm, he tried to play bad boy saying he chose none of the above." Rita chuckled as she filled her coffee cup. "He said he'd just inform his superiors that I threatened him then I told him the same exact thing he told me."

"What was that?" Danya was trying hard not to laugh at the picture of Rita having a confrontation with this man.

"That this was between me and him. Who's going to believe that a sweet girl like me would go to those extremes?" Rita started laughing as they walked into the living room.

"Look, I have well over an hour before I'm due to go to work. If you have some time too, maybe we can talk. We haven't had time to have our usual girl talk in the last few weeks. When we do get a chance, we're working out or something and you know how hard it is to talk and work out." Danya plopped onto the chair swinging her legs over the side as Rita sat on the couch across from her.

"I have about forty-five minutes since I got an early start this morning. Excitement will do that to you, you know? What you want to talk about?" Rita asked as she sat her cup down.

Danya slid her legs off the arm of the chair, planted her feet on the ground, then leaned forward and said, "I want to hear about how you met this Cory character you've been talking about lately."

"I actually met him after work. I was getting my usual steak sandwich with hot peppers when he decided to make his move. He introduced himself as Cory Jones but I wasn't paying him no never mind, I was trying to get my eat on. Anyway, he asked me out and I turned him down, but he insisted that I take his number. I took his number, smiled, walked away, and threw it in the first trash receptacle I saw."

"Was he that repulsive?" Danya asked, frowning.

Rita smiled. "Not at all."

"Then what was it?" She gave Rita a perplexed look.

"It's just that he gave me an uneasy feeling. I even thought for a minute he was stalking me."

Danya watched Rita's animated recall of the incidents that had her thinking he was following her. Rita's cheeks brighten as she revealed that he worked in the building and shared similar schedules. Danya tried to contain the laughter, but a snicker slipped out. "So, he wasn't following you?"

"Nope." Rita covered her face with her hands.

That conversation explained why Rita became so interested in going to self-defense class with her and then all of a suddenly she lost her enthusiasm. Now she knew. "How does he look?"

Rita's face lit up as she told Danya Cory was the nicest male she'd been out with in a while. Rita, after feeling like an idiot for believing he was following her, gave him her number. He called. They talked and hit it off pretty well. The next night they went out on a date on the Spirit of Chicago. They sat on the deck after dinner and talked. The cool wind from the lake blew through her hair as he kept her laughing about his wild years. Rita had been dating this guy for a little less than two months. She didn't consider them as having a serious relationship as they both were seeing other people but he was a top runner. Danya was surprised when Rita stated that if he wanted a serious relationship, she was all for it. Danya knew it was serious if Rita was willing to stop dating other men.

"Are you going to tell me how he looks before or after our forty-five-minute talk session is over?" Danya knew time was winding down. "Or are you going to sit there with that damn dreamy idiot look on your face?"

"Let's just say he's that universal fine with a well-built body to match." Rita pressed her lips together and tilted her head at Danya. "And missy, it wasn't too long ago you had this same idiotic grin on your face."

"Anyway," Danya waved off her comment, "when do I get to meet this mystery man?"

"Hopefully soon."

Rita and Danya continued their conversation. Before Danya knew it, it was time for Rita to head to work. "You better get out of here before they decide to revoke your promotion."

"Yeah, I'd better get going. I'll see you tonight." Rita took her cup into the kitchen.

Danya watched as Rita gathered her stuff. "Oh Rita, what time does our celebration begin?"

"What time is your class over?" Rita beamed, lifting her shoulder as if it didn't matter.

Danya replied, "About eight, I should be home around eight-thirty."

"Eighty-thirty it is. See you then." Rita waved as she exited.

Once Rita left, Danya took a seat on the couch and turned on the television. She had fifteen minutes left before she had to get dressed. The next thing she knew, the phone's constant ringing was waking her up. Danya hadn't planned to fall asleep. Groggily she answered the phone. It was John reminding her they had several important meetings that she should not miss unless she wanted to be stuck with the same suppliers. Danya told him she was going to be late, but she should be in before their first meeting.

Danya ran to her room, kicked off her bunny slippers, grabbed a towel, and headed for the shower. Damn, she hated taking jump in-jump out type showers but she hated keeping the same suppliers she had even more. She brushed her teeth, washed her face, showered, and threw on her clothes she'd just gotten out of the cleaners the previous night.

Man, she wished she hadn't fallen asleep, rushing wasn't something she enjoyed doing especially on a bad hair day. Danya fought with her hair for more time than it took her to get showered and dressed just to get it to look halfway decent.

* * *

The day flew by. Agent Waller had left another message for Danya. With all her best intentions, she hadn't managed to call him. She called her lawyer and was instructed to find out what he wanted but to not divulge any information. Danya closed and locked her office door and returned to her desk. She called the general number and asked to be routed to Agent Waller. She wanted to make sure he was who he said he was.

Danya unlocked her desk drawer and pulled out her sketchbook as she introduced herself then said, "Agent Waller, I hear you wanted to talk to me."

"Ms. Holmes, I'm glad you finally returned my call." She could hear paper shuffling in the background.

"Call me Danya," she replied as she flipped through the sketchbook and put a sticker on the page that she needed then closed the book.

Agent Waller cleared his throat then stated, "I was hoping that we could schedule a meeting."

Danya was all about preparing for Marcus's appearance and making sure she didn't lose her fiancé in the process. "My schedule doesn't have an opening until six months from now."

"I believe someone close to you can't be trusted and is using your business for illegal purposes."

"That is not possible." Danya couldn't imagine any of her employees doing something illegal. Then she had to remind herself that she never suspected Marcus was capable of murder.

"I can't stress the importance of squeezing me into your schedule," he stated in a stern voice that almost sounded like a veiled threat.

Danya glanced down as someone knocked on her door. "Give me a minute," she yelled at the person on the other side of the door. "Agent Waller, I appreciate you reaching out to me, but I have a meeting to get to. I will look into it and get back to you."

"Ms. Holmes, don't. I just need you—"

Danya hung up the phone reflecting on her conversation with Agent Waller. This was the last thing she needed. She bounced from her chair and unlocked and opened the door.

John stared at her momentarily before speaking. "We're locking doors now."

"Yes, when I need to make an adjustment to the wardrobe." Danya returned to her desk. "What's up?"

"I was hoping you could give me an update on this off-site meeting Trish mentioned you have today." John grabbed a seat.

"A quick one. I need to leave out shortly." Danya changed her passwords on her computer as they spoke. "Remember that company that pitched us the idea of combining forces for the classic man event."

"Yes. You said his designs weren't classic." John leaned forward.

"He has built quite a following. I thought I'd hear his latest pitch." Danya grabbed her sketchbook, put it in her briefcase, and stood. "I'll give you an update when I get back."

John rose to his feet and gave her a weird look as if he sensed she was lying. "See you when you get back."

Danya couldn't worry about it. "Oh, I'm not coming back to the office. I'm going to self-defense class," she announced as she headed out the door. The last thing she needed was to be late for a meeting she requested. She felt bad about not being honest with John, but it wasn't a complete lie. She was meeting someone that had previously pitched her an idea to work together. It was not for an event, but to design upscale protective clothing. Now she was trying to see if he could make something for her.

* * *

Danya entered a none descript building in the warehouse district. She hit the buttons and announced she was there to see Jax. The door buzzed and she entered. The outside didn't hint at the beauty that greeted her within. The dark hard wood floors ran down a hallway with modern paintings leading to an artsy but elegant reception desk. As she made it to the receptionist, Jax came out of what once looked like a smoked glass wall display that turned clear.

"Ms. Holmes, great to see you. Follow me into the conference room." Jax turned back towards the room he'd exited.

She pulled out the sketchbook and opened it to a design of a simple quilted jacket. He looked at the design then looked at her. "Don't you want more of a suit?"

"Wouldn't a suit design take longer?" Danya had thought about it but she didn't know the development process. The one thing she knew, she wanted this item back as soon as possible.

He nodded. "Yes but …"

"I need this made and tested quickly," Danya explained.

"I'll do it on one condition." He tapped the sketchbook. "You design a suit that I can work my magic on."

"Consider it a deal." Danya ripped out the page with the design of the jacket on it.

From here on out, I'll have to guard my personal sketchbook, she thought as she wrapped up the meeting with Jax. Out of habit, she wrote design notes on the rough drafts of the sketch. The last thing she wanted was John or anyone to know what she was doing. She was getting lectures from Rita about being too focused on Marcus. Rick was frustrated with her for dragging her feet on their wedding plans. John was usually her go to guy. The fact that he felt he needed to send her to a head doctor had her feeling some kind of way, even though she knew he meant well.

Danya walked out the conference room and shook Jax's hand before he walked away. She slid out her sketchbook as she walked over to the receptionist desk to make another appointment. As she waited, she heard one of the two ladies at the receptionist desk say she wanted a sleeper gun. Danya had recently started going to the gun range to learn to shoot, but she had no idea what kind of gun it was or if it was a nickname for one. She overheard the receptionist say she would order it. The supplier was supposed to contact her to arrange payment. Once that was done it would come with the lady's selected outfit. Danya waited until they left to ask the receptionist what they were talking about. She showed her the catalog and Danya ordered before rushing out to make it to her class.

When John suggested self-defense class to her, she thought it was absurd. Now she was glad she did it. The one time she had debated stopping was when Rita had stopped. John had reminded her that she was much lighter than when she first tangled with Marcus. It had been her extra weight that allowed her to take Marcus on like she had. If she hadn't been heavier, Marcus would have taken her out immediately.

John mentioned that in prison Marcus was probably given two choices, either learn how to handle men twice his size with three times his strength or bend over and get stuck. Knowing Marcus, the second choice wasn't an option if he could help it. Danya decided that John was right and began taking the classes faithfully. It was a good thing she didn't let those first few take her under. The schedule was draining her energy. She came home tired and worn out. The fact that she always checked her messages to see if Marcus called and left a threatening message, kept her going back which lead to her increasing her skillset.

Glancing at the time, Danya wondered if Rita would show up for the last of the 8-week sessions. Once it started she knew for sure. She wasn't surprised. Rita had been spending a lot of evenings with Cory. The class had her full attention. As it came to an end, the instructor reminded them to take a refresher course every so often to keep the moves fresh in their muscle memory. Everyone dispersed and grabbed their things. The instructor, Ross, walked over to Danya as she grabbed her water.

"You're a rare breed," Ross said as he waved at other students heading into the studio.

Danya took a sip of water. "Why do you say that?"

"You're a quick study. There is a difference between learning self-defense and it becoming a natural response when attacked. Normally once a person feels they got it, they stop coming like your roommate did."

"I can see that." Marcus's face crossed her mind and she added, "But I'm highly motivated to learn."

Ross glanced at her with concern in his eyes. "Fear, adrenaline, shock, or whatever, it sometimes causes people to react differently than they thought they would."

She didn't know how to take that comment. It felt like a warning not to do something crazy. "This class has been a great stress reliever. I hate the course is ending."

"I also teach beginning karate. If you're interested stop by my office before you leave and I'll give you the schedule," Ross stated before walking away.

Danya headed to the locker. "Crap!" she muttered as she realized she'd left something in her office.

Ross stopped short of his office, turned around, and asked, "What?"

"Nothing." She waved him off. "I just realized I left some documents that I needed to look over at the office."

He cut his eyes at her. "Does the building have security?"

"Didn't you just say I was a quick study?"

"One of the best self-defense moves is to avoid placing yourself in situations where you need to defend yourself." He repeated what he had said many times in class.

She reassured him that she would be fine and that there was security in the building. It was the truth. The thing she failed to mention was they were normally not at the building this late. She waved bye as she entered the locker room. Quickly grabbing her things, she bolted out the gym.

Danya rushed into her office and grabbed the sheet of paper she'd left. She gazed at the wall briefly as she imagined someone coming across it. She couldn't believe she left her Marcus to do list in the office. It would have been a disastrous conversation trying to justify why she was now working with Jax and no one in the company knew. There was one item of that list that she knew would be a three-hour conversation. Danya jumped at the sound of a knock at her door. The sheets of paper in her hand slid to the floor.

John stepped in the office. "I didn't mean to scare you."

"What are you doing here so late?" Danya bent over, picked up the list, then walked over to her purse and stuffed it in it.

He crossed his arms. "I could ask you the same thing."

Danya shrugged. "There were a few items that I needed."

"Tonight? What's going on?" John questioned.

"Nothing," she replied as John studied her face, not blinking under the scrutiny.

John broke the stare as he leaned on her desk. "My investigator friend called to say that you were trying to hire him to find and track Marcus."

Danya's head snapped towards him. "Clearly I didn't pick the right man for the job."

John replied, "He is selective about his clientele and he wanted—"

"You to vouch for me." Danya walked towards her desk.

"Yeah …" His voice trailed off.

She crossed her arms and frowned. "Why shouldn't I track Marcus down?"

"And do what? There's a very thin line between protecting yourself and becoming a vigilante." John's eyes trailed her as she began to pace.

"Keeping tabs that all." Her movement stopped as she lifted her eyebrows and stared at him. "Did you vouch for me?"

John stepped into her path and crossed his arms. "Yes but ..."

"But?" she questioned with a challenging look.

He gave her a stern glare. "How does Rick feel about you chasing Marcus instead of planning a wedding?"

The muscles in her face tighten as she gave him the evil eye. Danya shook her head before going around him and placed her purse on her shoulder. "I'm sure he'd rather have me around to marry than for me to sit around and allow Marcus to do me like he did Gena."

He walked towards her file cabinets then he glanced at her. "Don't—"

"I don't want to argue with you. I just came in to grab a few things." Danya scowled at him as her fingers strangled the purse in her hand. She hadn't missed how his eyes had scanned the area she was standing when he arrived. "Rita's waiting for me back at home."

John leaned on the file cabinet looking at her. "You need to stop and think."

"I am," she replied as she headed for her office door.

John followed her. "You're so worried about Marcus that you came out late at night by yourself to the office alone, for what?"

Danya stopped in the doorway and turned around. She was not going to answer that question especially in the middle of this conversation. "Okay, I give you that but I'm—"

"Didn't you tell me your instructor told you the best self-defense move is to avoid putting yourself in the situations where you needed to defend yourself?" John questioned.

Danya refused to give him the satisfaction of knowing that Ross had repeated those very words to her tonight. "Okay. I give you that. Coming out alone to the office may not have been the best move."

"At least let me walk you to your car." John moved towards the door.

Danya didn't turn him down. Once she was in the car, she called Rita to tell her she was running late. Rita insisted that they would still celebrate. Danya made it home after 9:30 p.m. and wasn't exactly in the mood to celebrate, but what the heck. There was no sense bringing Rita down, too.

CHAPTER SIX

Marcus entered the luxurious condo with a small envelope in hand. He dropped it on the table as headed to the bedroom. He thought things would be different when he returned. But he was glad to be back living the life he enjoyed. He hated being away. He couldn't believe that he and his partners were going their separate ways. They had been in business together since college. He understood why, but there had to be a better way than breaking up the team.

Sometimes he wondered if this plan was about getting him out. His thoughts went back to the night that changed things. He probably shouldn't have been drinking before going to Gena's. While he was quite good at stealing money, it was normally via computers and routing numbers. Not holding knives to people's throats to get them to open a safe. He had no clue seeing the version of his wife that he wanted to have would have such an effect on him. His partners came up with the plan to marry one of the Holmes' sisters. The death of their parent had already left them rich but it was the inheritance of their multi-millionaire uncle that made them extremely wealthy. Gena was the sister he wanted, but Terry was the easiest target. Gena was good for spotting a gold digger from a mile away. If Terry would have only been as fit as her sister, he would have been happy to stay married to her and her millions until death did them part.

The water beating over his head begins to remind him of running out into the rain after Gena was stabbed. His heart began racing. He quickly washed up and turned off the water. It had been a while since he had a moment like that. He wondered if it was the fact that his ex-wife's money was their backup plan if things hit a snag and they had to get out fast. It felt like the backup plan had his partners questioning his ability to handle things. As he dried off, he heard his cell phone ringing. He wrapped the towel around his waist, walked out the bathroom, and grabbed the phone off the night stand. Partner One appeared on the screen.

"Yeah," Marcus answered as he walked to the closet pulling out his most expensive tailored suits.

His partner asked, "Are you ready to hit the ground running?"

"I got this." He put on a Bluetooth earpiece so he could dress.

"Stay away from your ex," he commanded.

Marcus slipped into his suit. "I have no intentions of seeing her unless we decide it's required."

"Be alert. Your ex is not following her usual routine," he instructed.

Marcus checked himself in the mirror. "As long as I see her first, I will avoid her."

"Good." His voice lowered as if someone had walked in the room. "We have enough on our plate."

"I should have an update for you tonight when we meet at Gena's." They said their goodbyes and disconnected the call.

He laughed, wondering how his former wife would feel if she knew they were using her deceased sister's place to hold their meetings.

She hadn't been back to the house in years. They knew she wouldn't accidentally catch them together. He couldn't lie, part of him wanted them to use the backup plan just to burst his ex's bubble about the damage she'd done. Not that she didn't have an impact on his life, it's just not the way she thought she had. He imagined her face when she found out the truth and smiled.

The drive to meet an old associate left Marcus a decent amount of time to reflect. His partner's mistrust of him had him wondering if he needed leverage. The question was, would his best friend, Peter, side with the other partners or him? Peter didn't even get into it for the money. He came from money. He was in it for the thrill of it. He recalled how much trouble Peter got him into. Every time, his father would get them off without so much as a blemish on their records. When they started out up until six years ago, he would have never imagined Peter not having his back. Now he wasn't so sure. He decided it was better to be safe than sorry. Peter was addicted to the high of living a double life. The money was a bonus.

If Peter had inherited his family's money at that point their business hit a snag, maybe that night wouldn't have happened and their friendship wouldn't have changed. They had moved passed it but now that he was back in play with the potential to reconnect with his ex, the friendship was back to feeling off. The associate he was meeting, he decided would have to help him with two problems. Finding out who's leaking information to the authorities and gathering material on the one partner he thought was gunning for him. The one thing he knew was that man had skeletons in his closet. He needed to find the right one to use for an emergency trump card.

* * *

Danya's heels rapidly clicked on the floor as she headed to the door. She saw an extremely tall white man wearing a black suit entering the building. He approached her but she blew pass him. Her hand was on the door when she heard, "Ms. Holmes. Can I have a word with you?"

She turned back. "Have another appointment but you can schedule time with my assistant."

Danya pushed through the door. Moments later he was by her side. "It's about your ex-husband."

She stopped in her tracks.

He extended his hand towards Danya. "I'm Agent Waller."

"Call me Danya." She shakes his hand.

"That's a beautiful bracelet." He nodded towards her wrist.

She adjusted the custom-made charm bracelet John had given her. "It was a gift to celebrate opening my business. But it's not my bracelet that brought you here. I have somewhere to be so you have until I make it to my car to say what you need to say."

Agent Waller began talking. When they reach her car, he pulled out his phone and showed her some pictures. Danya stared at him for a long moment, shocked and confused. She shook her head. He nodded his head. Danya opened the car door. Agent Waller grabbed her arm before she could get in. She gave him a blank stare. His eyes seemed to say be careful. He handed her a business card then released her arm. Danya got in the car and started it. She rolled down the window and promised to make time to speak to him then drove off.

As she drove to the address Jax gave her, she silently berated herself for not making time to meet with Waller. Her mind couldn't imagine what would have had Marcus in the same space as Trish and Mary. She parked and entered the building following Jax's assistant instructions. She entered the room and waited. Jax was dressed in a designer blue suit and was on the other end of the room talking with someone. He did a slow swagger towards Danya, handed her a gun, then nodded. She wondered if he knew she'd been going to the range or he just assumed she knew how to shoot because of her order. She put on the protective ear and eye gear, then aimed the gun and fired several shots at the target.

She stopped and sat the gun down. The target started to move towards her.

A man came and took the black quilted jacket down. There were bullet dents in the jacket. The only bullet holes are in the zipper and the seam where the sleeve meets the jacket. She examined the bullet proof material. She pointed the holes out to Jax. They took off their protective gear then sat them on the counter. Jax nodded his head as the attendant handed him a tablet then took the jacket away.

He pulled up the jacket design and made notes. "I'll take care of the upgrades."

"I appreciate it," Danya replied, silently berating herself for going to this extreme.

"You need to get going. You don't want to be late for the meeting." Jax looked at her then the door. "He's a hard man to catch up with. You might not get a second chance."

Danya checked the time then said a quick goodbye and headed to her personal items. She sped walk, retrieved the items, and rushed out the door. She made one stop and made it to the park in record time.

She tried to act normal as she moved towards the designated spot. Her heart raced as she neared the secluded bench. At that point, she herself questioned her sanity. As she lowered her body onto the bench, her thoughts started to wreak havoc on her. What if Marcus had followed her? There was barely anyone in the area. Could she take Marcus? It's not like Ross didn't say people react differently when adrenaline kicked in.

A man dressed in the described outfit approached the bench. He nodded at her. Danya dug a small envelope out of her purse. She hesitated and made sure no one was around before she put her purse on the bench next to her then placed the envelope behind it. The man sat down next to her reading a newspaper. He placed the paper between them and pulled out his cell phone. She picked up her purse and listened to his call which she assumed was his girlfriend asking him to bring something home. He stood and grabbed the paper then tilted his head at Danya and waved his phone at her. She nodded. He strolled down the path back in the direction of the parking lot. Danya couldn't believe she'd done that. She sat there speculating on how many laws she may have broken. Finally she stood, wandered around the more populated part of the park. Her cell phone rang. She assumed it was Rick calling about their pizza night. Reaching into her pocket for her phone, she noticed it was an unknown number. She answered.

"You order has been processed." He then proceeded to give her quick instructions and warnings about her purchase.

Danya slid into her car as the call wrapped up. She managed to get a thank you in before the call was disconnected. She went on autopilot to get home. Rick pulled up as she got out the car. She grinned as he made his way towards her. It was no question that she would do whatever it took to preserve the life she had. Rick leaned down and kissed her.

"I expected you to already be upstairs with the pizza ordered." He wrapped one arm around her as they headed in.

Danya turned her lips up at him. "You expected no such thing."

He laughed. "You are absolutely right which is why I ordered the pizza while I was on my way over here. Then I prayed that I wouldn't have to accept the delivery from the car."

"Whatever." She unlocked the apartment door. "I'm not that bad."

"I want this to be a good night so I'm going to plead the fifth on this." Rick chuckled as he locked the door behind him.

They got comfortable and settled on the couch. She leaned over to grab her briefcase so they can review wedding books. There was no excuse tonight not review wedding stuff. She pulled out her sketch book first placing it on the table then the wedding books. They flipped through a few before finding themselves cuddling on the couch watching television. Rick leaned forward and grabbed her sketchbook off the table. She reached to grab it out his hands but wasn't quick enough. He turned his back to her and flipped through the pages. She tried to reach around him.

Rick peeked back at her. "I'm not seeing wedding dress designs in here."

"Who said I was designing it myself?" Danya continued to try to grab it.

"We are getting married, aren't we?" Rick inquired as he moved his drink back and sat the sketchbook on the table. He turned to her. "Because …"

"Yes, I plan to become Mrs. Cameron. It's been months. Marcus hasn't made an appearance. Life is good." She grabbed one of the wedding books from the table waving it in front of him.

Rick's forehead filled with creases as she shrugged then sat the wedding book down. A knock on the door drew their attention. Rick picked up the cash off the table and headed for the door. "I'm going to do everything in my power to keep life good for us. I still think we should move in together."

Danya sighed. "I don't think us moving in together right now needs to be one of those things."

Rick handed the delivery guy the cash as he grabbed the pizza. He closed the door and returned to the couch. He sat the pizza on the table. "Have you even asked Rita to be your maid of honor yet?"

"She's got a new friend keeping her busy," Danya explained as she opened the pizza.

Rick smirked. "Rita always has friends."

"This one is isolating himself from the pack." Danya went into the kitchen.

Rick picked up a slice of pizza as Danya returned with paper plates, napkins, and beer. "Is this the guy that works in her building, Cory or the ..."

Danya's nod stopped Rick mid-sentence. "Maybe we should invite them out to dinner."

Rick chuckled. "You haven't met him yet, have you?"

"No." Danya put a slice of pizza on her plate.

He opened his beer. "Rita isn't moving fast enough on the introductions, I take it."

"Whatever." Danya bumped his shoulder with hers. "It's been months. I can't help but be curious about the mystery man that has caught her attention."

Rick shook his head "Well can you bump up asking her to be a part of the wedding above being a nosey rosey about who she's dating?"

Danya playfully hit Rick. He pulled her into a kiss. She broke the embrace then tilted her head towards him. "I was thinking of asking John to walk me down the aisle. He's family."

"That is a great idea. He's like family," Rick replied.

"No. He's family. He doesn't know that I know, but he's my cousin. I found a letter from my uncle to his mother." Danya picked up her slice of pizza and took a bite.

"What letter?" Rick asked.

Danya started thinking about how John's mother used to babysit her and Gena. They spent so much time with her, they called her Aunt Kesha. The only time Aunt Kesha didn't baby-sit them was when their Uncle Chris was in town for a few days for his 'once or twice a year if then' visits. As John got older, he always found time to check on them in spite of what he was doing, especially after their parents died and they moved in with their Uncle Chris. Uncle Chris didn't too much care for John, but John couldn't care less. It wasn't until she and Gena were helping Aunt Kesha clean out her attic and found the letter from Uncle Chris to Aunt Kesha that they understood why.

She stopped reflecting on the past and answered Rick. "A breakup letter from Uncle Chris. That's how we found out Aunt Kesha was my Uncle Chris's former fiancée."

"Wait." Rick looked at her then looked away and returned with a confused stare. "Fiancée?"

"According to the letter, Uncle Chris didn't believe the baby was his and ended their engagement. He accused her of cheating and being a gold digger. I don't know how he managed to get her to promise not the tell anyone." Danya shrugged and took another bite of pizza.

"Man." Rick grabbed his beer. "Does John know you're related?"

"I think he does now, but I'm not sure. In all these years, we've never talked about it." She grimaced as she said, "If you knew my uncle and the way John felt about him, you'd understand why I never bring it up. Gena and I had talked about giving him a part of our fortune." John hadn't known it at the time but he was a beneficiary on both their wills. They didn't think he should have to wait to one of them died to receive a part of his dad's fortune.

"What happened?" Rick sipped his beer.

Frowning, she cut her eyes over at Rick. "Marcus happened. Gena was overseas when we made the decision. We decided to start the paperwork when Gena got back."

Rick grabbed her hand. "Babe, I know Marcus did major damage to your life, but I don't understand how he prevented you and your sister—"

"He killed her shortly after getting back to the states." Danya cut him off and stood grabbing her glass and headed into the kitchen.

CHAPTER SEVEN

Danya stood near her window looking over Lake Michigan wearing only an oversized sleeping shirt and her bunny slippers. Part of her felt stupid for worrying about Marcus. It had been the middle of May when she started taking self-defense classes. Now she was taking karate and it was almost the end of August. Not once had Marcus made an appearance. After the last three months, part of her was relieved she had not seen or heard from him and the other part was terrified.

Something good had come from all that worrying. Danya realized how out of shape she was and joined the health club and began working out on her lunch break. If those classes weren't whipping her behind, she probably wouldn't have started working out on a regular basis. Once she started getting in better shape, she began enjoying the karate more. It was a plus that in the process of getting in shape she'd lost 25 pounds. This time around she had a little extra ammunition that was not weight.

She also accepted that John had been the driving force in her life. That had begun to change. Danya knew that if that night hadn't happened John would have never had so much influence in her life. She loved John for all he had done for her, but it was time Terry Danya took control over her own life again. She had been a woman with a strong mind before that night. She knew people's advice was just that—advice. In the end, it would always have to be her decision. Over the last several years, that hadn't been true. Danya hadn't started her company, gotten a divorce, or even gotten herself out of the hospital. It had been John. He was right there getting her business started, getting her divorced, and getting her out of the hospital. When Marcus got out, she ran to John, taking his advice. He had never led her astray. It was time to start taking his opinion into consideration but making her own decisions.

Once her decisions had become based on what she thought was best, John's influence in her life decreased dramatically. She'd always value his advice. Danya felt good about taking her life back into her own hands. It was nice being that strong black woman she used to know. She hadn't realized how much she had changed until she and John had a disagreement. Danya knew that she had lost her backbone when they ended up doing it his way. That night she came home and thought about the last few years. Danya was upset with herself for not pulling herself together in the hospital. She'd given up on life, leaving John to take care of all her business. No more; she was definitely back.

It was funny, over the last few months she had accomplished what she should have six years ago. Danya was now handling more of her business. John had thought it best that she only handled a small portion in running the business and concentrate on creating fabulous clothing. Now she was working alongside of him running the business and making new designs. Her company, at one time, was really John's. He had been running everything in the business while she let what had happened ruin her life. Now that she was dealing with those events, the business had become hers. John became a valued top executive, not the other way around. He didn't have to take as many business trips now that she was more involved running it. Danya was thankful for John's advice to see

Dr. Adams. If she hadn't, she wouldn't be back in control of her life.

Dr. Adams made her see that Marcus was running her life. She had cut and dyed her hair because Marcus hadn't wanted her to touch it when they were together. She started calling herself Danya because he hadn't liked her middle name. Danya had changed her life not because she particularly wanted to but because she was attempting to rebel against things that haunted her. Danya was coming to terms with her past. They had a lot to work on, but she was improving. Her life had not become a bed of roses. It had gotten a little rougher because everybody had to get used to her changing.

It seemed odd to Danya that John was having the most trouble accepting the change in her, especially since she was acting in ways she used to before that night. Maybe he'd gotten too used to the way she'd been acting for the last six years. Right about now she couldn't care less.

She was no longer delaying her wedding, waiting to see if Marcus would come after her. There was no way she was letting her guard down, but she could resume living her life. She wanted to throw a little something together and Rick agreed, but his parents wouldn't hear of it. Danya believed that if they could pull off a wonderful wedding in a short span of time then they should go for it. Too bad the churches and reception halls all seemed to be booked up. She was trying to figure out how to be a married woman before the New Year rolled in.

She finally stopped reflecting and looked over the calendar she sat on the kitchen table, then circled the days that said karate classes. It felt wrong to have people thinking she was still taking self-defense but John, Rita, and Rick have been monitoring her behavior like a hawk. Some days she felt like she was on suicide watch how everyone was watching and interpreting her behavior. The last thing she wanted was for them to worry that she was going over the edge, but she wasn't planning to drop her guard. She sipped her coffee as Rita gallivanted into the room with a huge smile on her face.

"How are things going with that Cory character?" Danya shook her head at her dramatic entrance then returned her attention to her calendar.

Rita grabbed her cup and poured herself some coffee. She leans on the counter sipping it. "Going well."

She smiled, not looking up from the calendar. "That's good."

"Does that have to do with your ex?" Rita nodded at the sheet of paper.

Danya folded the calendar and stuck it in her sketchbook. "My ex has already ruined my life once and—"

"He's doing it again," Rita stated matter of factly. "And he hasn't even made an appearance since his release."

Danya absently stirred the little coffee she had left in her cup. "What do you mean? I have to be prepared when he does. I will not let him destroy my life again."

"It seems to me he already is." Rita leaned on the counter with a smug expression. "Instead of enjoying being engaged, you're—"

"Look, I got a lecture the other day because I brought up hiring someone to find him again." Danya put her sketchbook into her briefcase. She grabbed her suit jacket from the arm of the chair and slipped it on.

Shock was etched on Rita's face. "What?" She came around the counter to sit next to Danya.

"I need to be doing more." Danya hit her cell to see the time, ignoring Rita's presences at her side. "I can't sit here and wait for him to make his move."

"There is a thin line between protecting your life and becoming a vigilante." Rita peered over her coffee cup at Danya.

Danya stood, rinsed her coffee cup out, and placed it in the sink. "You sound like John. I only want to monitor his activities so he can't catch me off guard." The desire to fully focus on marrying Rick was strong but she couldn't release the fear that the moment she relaxed Marcus would pounce.

"You've built a good life from the chaos. Don't throw it away for your ex," Rita stated in a stern voice.

Danya frowned as she realized Rita wasn't going to let it go so she switched strategies. "After this lecture, I may have to reconsider asking the question I wanted to." Danya walked into the living room.

Rita followed and took a seat on the couch. "What question?"

"Would you be my maid of honor?" she asked as she slipped her briefcase onto her shoulder.

"Yes, of course! Girl, I thought you had picked someone else." Rita stood and gave Danya a hug. "What took you so long?"

"Let's just put it this way, I've been so busy getting myself together, I forgot to make my wedding a priority."

Rita leaned back and glared at her. "When's the wedding?"

Danya smiled and laughed. "I'll say this, you'll either have to rush or you'll have to wait. I want to get married before it gets cold. If we can't reserve a church and a hall before then, I want to wait till it warms up again. I have a real aversion to freezing my behind off on my wedding day."

"You're sure?" Rita shook her head and laughed.

Danya wrapped her arms around herself and began shivering. "That is not my idea of a good time, what about you?"

"No, but at least you have that frozen beauty working for you." Rita gave Danya a smile that looked frozen in place.

"Ha, ha, ha, very funny." She scanned the room to make sure she hadn't forgotten anything. "I've got to get to work." Danya headed to the door then paused. "Oh, I will be in late. Rick and I are checking out venues tonight."

* * *

Danya made it into work an hour later than she had planned. John was waiting in her office when she got in with new information he dug up about the potential suppliers they were meeting today. They went over the data for the meetings for about an hour before taking a break. Danya made sure John knew she had plans and needed to be out of there on time.

"Well if the meetings stay on schedule we should be finished in plenty of time. How are your sessions with the doctor going anyway? We haven't had much time to talk lately."

"We don't have time now either." Danya flipped her binder closed.

"Yes, we do. It's only 10:45, our meeting is an hour away." John rested his hand over her binder. "We're prepared for the first meeting. And the way our other meetings are spaced, we can prepare in between them."

Danya pulled up the calendar on her computer. "You mean I rushed into work for nothing."

"No, I gave several employees some of our morning work assignments, which they are more than qualified to handle. They worked hard and finished before you got in," John explained.

"Mmmhmm." Danya rolled her eyes.

John leaned back in his chair. "Besides, it didn't take as long as either one of us thought it would when we agreed to come in early."

Danya closed her calendar. "Maybe I wouldn't have been flying through the information if I'd known we had time."

John shrugged. "So tell me, have those sessions with Dr. Adams been helping you?"

Danya debated how much she should tell him. She knew he was already worried about her. The last thing she wanted was to give him more ammunition for his lectures. "I remembered some things that I chose to ignore before."

"Like what?" John pitched forward so close to Danya that the smell of his expensive cologne was in her throat. She coughed then tilted back in her chair.

"You know most of the story so the extended version of it is ..." Danya's phone rang, interrupting her sentence. She held up her finger as she picked up. "Hey, Rick!"

John gave her a grimace as she said, "Yes hold on a sec." She placed the receiver down. "John, we're going to have discuss this later."

"Your future husband upset because you have yet to pick a wedding venue," John teased.

She pressed her lips together giving him the evil eye. "Bye, John."

John waved as he slowly exited the room. Danya was grateful for Rick's well-timed call. There was a feeling in the pit of her gut that told her to keep the information she gave to a minimum. However, old habits are hard to break. He has been her go to person ever since Gena died. Marcus being released from prison had changed things. She was probably being ridiculous but the one thing she had learned from the past was it was better to be safe than sorry.

CHAPTER EIGHT

Marcus was in utter shock at what he had discovered. It took everything in him not to tell Peter what he had found out about their partner or confront his partner about it. He was definitely not going to argue with them about going their separate ways. It would be interesting to see if his partner's wife knew about the money. He was so angry he couldn't see straight. They had to come up with a plan because their business got in a little trouble. Something had been stolen from them that was worth quite a bit of money. Even though they were partners, they weren't exactly working for themselves. The people they owed, some menacing and powerful men, owned the merchandise and wanted them to pay the cash value or retrieve what was stolen. They didn't know how they were going to pay the million dollars for stolen goods that they were supposed to distribute.

Marcus got an excellent job with a firm, laundering enough money to keep them alive. Peter used some of his funds to assist, but he wasn't in full control of them because he hadn't met his father's stipulations for getting his inheritance. It was their female partner's idea to seduce one of the Holmes sister's. Her husband felt it was a greater risk with Gena. Once Marcus started dating Gena, there would be no second chance. However, Gena was the one he was attracted to. Yet he stated Terry would never date a man that dated her sister. In addition to that, there was too much competition for Gena's affection. Peter was more than willing to be the fall guy but no one thought either of the Holmes sisters like cream in their coffee.

They agreed that with Gena's history of spotting a gold digger from a mile away Terry would be their safest bet, which proved to be true. It made him sick to his stomach after her uncle died, finding out that she couldn't touch her money for ten years. Ten freaking years was not what Marcus agreed to. In less than a year it would no longer have been an issue with Terry starting her business, but they hadn't had that month's payment. They had to come up with six hundred thousand dollars and fast. That's when the fact that Gena kept quite a bit of money and at least one or two gold bars in a safe hidden in her house came up. Gena had once told him that with a lot of unexpected trips overseas, she had to keep money on hand. There wasn't always time to get to a bank. Marcus attempted to get the combination and the location of the safe out of Gena once, but Gena passed on it. She would smile and change the subject.

Now that he had more facts, he was rethinking everything that happened after that night. It's not like he didn't know his partner was capable of murder. His partner had killed someone to ensure that their plan would go unchallenged. He remembered sitting in court so confident that he would get off and trying not to show it. He was so focused on that, he'd missed that the events had changed the partnership. He wondered if his partner was actually upset that he had to sacrifice coming home to his wife for the last few years to ensure they all wouldn't end up in prison. No doubt that he blamed him for that. He was so infuriated that they had this backup plan in place in case they needed money but his partner had the cash needed to cover them for a quick getaway. It was unfortunate that saying something would show too much of his hand.

He had to keep his cards close to his vest and switch things up at the last minute to make sure he wasn't being set up for the fall guy.

Marcus checked himself out in the mirror with his tailored black suit, purple tie, and handkerchief to give a pop of color to help catch women's eye in the crowd. He needed one woman, in particular, to help him protect his interest until the partnership was dissolved. It was also time to check up on his ex-wife. He no longer trusted the intel John was feeding him.

* * *

Danya intensely worked at the drawing table in the corner of her office. The angle of the table changed from her norm so no one could see her drawing designs in her personal sketchbook. As John approached her office door, she quickly stashed it under one of her official designs.

"How are therapy sessions with Dr. Adams going?" John inquired.

Danya replied, "They're going fine, but I feel like I need to be doing more to protect my life." She could have kicked herself for saying that. Her old habit of telling him almost everything definitely bit her in the behind on this one.

John's eyes scanned her table then looked back up at her. Danya got up and sauntered away. John attempted to look under the paper, but Danya turned back. He rested his back side on her desk. "What more can you do?"

She leaned on the file cabinet and noticed the file she kept Jax's correspondence in is on top of the cabinet. Discretely as possible, she slid the single file under the pile of files next to it on top of the cabinet. Rick knocked on the door and Danya motioned for him to come in.

John greeted Rick as he approached Danya's desk. "Are the wedding plans coming together?"

"We're going to check out another venue tonight," Rick replied after they exchanged a brotherly hug.

"Hence me leaving early today." Danya walked over to her drawing table and pretended to straighten up as she grabbed her sketchbook.

Rick checked his watch. "Trying to squeeze it in."

"We'll finish talking later," Danya stated, giving John his cue to leave.

John squinted at the piles of files on the cabinet then strolled out. Danya picked the file from under the pile and put it in her briefcase along with her sketchbook. Rick took her briefcase as they exited the office.

Rick apologized again for having to cancel two of their four appointments as he drove to the first potential wedding venue. Danya didn't mind. She thought seeing four wedding venues in one night was a bit much. Not that she would tell Rick but she was actually glad he had to attend his company's after work function. It meant she would get home to follow up on some personal things. She only agreed to see the venues because she felt guilty not putting the same energy into wedding planning as preparing for Marcus. Rick dropped Danya back off at her car after seeing the two venues promising to call her later. Danya headed straight home.

When Danya walked in the door she had the surprise of her life, Rita had a guest. "I didn't know we were having company."

"Danya!" Rita's eyes widen, looking like a deer caught in headlights. "Umm, I'd like you to meet Cory. Cory, this is my roommate, Danya." Cory turned from the window and faced Danya. Her briefcase hit the floor with a thump as he advanced towards her. Danya stood with her mouth wide open as he grabbed and shook her hand and said how nice it was to meet her. Cory didn't give Danya time to speak before he kissed Rita on the cheek promising he'd see her later. Rita walked ahead of him to open the door.

As he walked passed Danya, he whispered in her ear, "We still have some business we need to take care of."

Rita was so happy that Danya had finally met Cory that she rambled on and on about him throughout dinner. She talked about how wonderful he was. Rita was so happy that she did not notice that Danya sat through dinner hardly speaking a word.

The mental debate on how to break the news to Rita continued in Danya's mind. Not saying something wasn't an option. While she didn't want to be the one to ruin this for her, she couldn't put her life at risk by remaining silent.

"I know he's cute but I didn't think he'd render you speechless." Rita put her folk down staring at her.

Danya tried to recover from the shock and process the fact the Rita had been dating Marcus. She fought to remain calm as she got her thoughts together. It would not benefit anyone, especially herself if she got all upset. Her fingers ran lightly over her scalp as they ran through her hair. Danya took a deep breath, hating to have to break Rita's heart. It took the length of dinner to figure out how to handle the situation. When dinner was over, she informed Rita that it was time to have a serious heart to heart.

"Honey, um, you cannot and I stress cannot see Cory Jones again." She grabbed Rita's hands as if somehow that would soften the blow.

"Why? Is he one of your ex-lovers?" Rita instantly went on the defensive snatching her hands back.

"No, he's my ex-husband, Marcus Johnson." Danya fought to remain calm as the reality that not only was the man in her house but he had been dating her roommate for months.

"Your what? Co ... Co ... Cory, he's the one that killed your sister?" She spoke as if his name was stuck in her throat.

Danya couldn't do anything but nod her head. "Cory is, or was, what he wanted his first son's name to be and Jones, well it's just a version of his last name."

"You know, tonight he was trying to get out of here before you got home. I didn't understand why." Rita's body sank into the back on the couch. "He has always been insistent upon coming over here when my roommate was out."

"Now you know." Danya crossed her arms and frowned.

"Man, I truly believed that Mr. Right had come into my life. I was ... He had me fooled. He really made a fool of me. I guess he was stalking me. Damn! I thought I had a winner." Rita leaned forward with her face void of expression.

"I did too, I did too," Danya spoke in a low voice as she comforted Rita. "At least you didn't have to lose the only family you had left to find out. He hurt me in a way no other man could. The bastard ripped not only my heart out but my very soul."

Marcus had played on her weakness and the fact that she thought she wasn't lovable because she was overweight. He gave her what she needed when she needed it. When she was feeling fat and depressed, he'd give her a hug, tell her how beautiful she was, and say how lucky he was to have a woman like her. When her self-esteem was dropping, he'd give her a passionate kiss and tell her how much he loved her. She truly believed that man loved her. She always doubted it in her mind, but it felt nice to be loved, to know that she wouldn't be an old maid with a million cats after all. That she, like her sister, would share her life with someone special.

Danya's face reddened with anger and rage as she reflected on the past. "He shattered all my illusions of him in one night. He lied to me for three and a half years!"

"I don't know what to say." Rita awkwardly shrugged her shoulders.

"Then not only did he murder my sister, he raped her. He raped her! What kind of bullshit is that? Whatever motive he had for going to Gena's house, he did not have to rape her. That man is a sick bastard." Danya's arms cut haphazardly through the air.

Rita rested her elbows on her thighs and clasp her hands together.

"He's an excellent liar. I never once thought he wasn't being honest with me."

"He took all that meant something to me away before the clock even struck twelve. Gena, John, and my uncle told me Marcus was no good, but I loved him and I thought he loved me, and that was all that mattered, dammit! It didn't matter what anybody else thought, he loved me! Wrong, he loved my money! My mistake caused my sister her life. Don't make that same mistake." Danya ended her rant with her fist tightly balled up.

"I hear you." Rita's eyes dropped from Danya to the floor.

"Rita, you were only in the first stages of giving him your heart and soul," Danya stated. "I was three years past that final stage when I discovered the truth. I know that doesn't make it any easier. When you're in love, you're in love, but trust me, you're lucky, very, very lucky."

"Danya," Rita spoke, interrupting Danya's personal thoughts. "Thank you."

"For what?" Her voice filled with strong emotions.

"For stopping me from wallowing in self-pity for a man that's not worth it. Look, I had an early morning and had a rough evening. I need some sleep." Rita stood up with sadness etched on her face and headed for her room.

"I'm sorry. I didn't mean to go on like that." Danya's words made Rita come to a halt.

"That's okay. I needed to hear that," Rita said as she turned and smiled at Danya.

Danya glanced over at her briefcase. "I really would appreciate if you avoid Marcus, Cory, whatever he's calling himself now. I know from experience that he is dangerous. So please stay away from him, okay?"

"No, problema." Rita lifted her hand then dropped it somberly before heading down the hallway.

That night left Danya destitute. It took her too long to discard that feeling of emptiness and it has never completely left her. Now he's back in her life, and she would be damned if she would allow him to leave her feeling that way again. She'd rather die than to give him that pleasure. Danya was too angry to cry. There was no way she was going to let Marcus win.

Danya went to her room shortly after Rita went to hers. "Marcus, Marcus, you've blown it. I now know for sure that you have something up your sleeve. I don't know where or when you'll decide to pull it out." Danya continued to think as she reviewed her file on ideas on how to put him back in prison permanently. "Marcus, darling, you are right. We do have some business to take care of."

CHAPTER NINE

Early the next morning, Danya left the apartment debating whether she would go into the office and pretend everything was normal. The moment she hit the office, John would know something with up. Instead of work, she drove to a restaurant for breakfast and to figure out her plan of attack and decide what was her best use of the day. After her second cup of coffee, her first order of business was to call John to inform him she wouldn't be coming into the office. He could pick the supplier and handle any other business that popped up. It would also prevent him from calling trying to figure out where she was. Next, she called Dr. Adams to see if she had any available appointments and luckily her ten o'clock had canceled.

In Dr. Adams' office, Danya paced the lobby until the assistant retrieved her and lead her into the office. Dr. Adams stood and inquired, "What has prompted this visit?" Dr. Adams stepped back, allowing Danya to enter the room.

"I saw Marcus," Danya said.

Dr. Adams closed the door and led Danya to the couch.

Danya sat down. "Is it odd that I don't remember anything before the struggle in the bedroom?"

"Not necessarily." Dr. Adams took out her notebook. "Not only did you endure emotional trauma, but physical."

Danya exhaled heavily. "I want to try to remember."

"Pressuring yourself to remember may not get you results." She laid the notebook in her lap. "How about you relax on the couch and start from when you remember. Maybe seeing Marcus jogged memories that will trigger those answers you're seeking."

"Okay." She relaxed on the couch with her eyes closed.

"Danya, go back to the night, but look at it as if you're watching a movie and you're not really part of it. Fast forward the movie to where the main character Terry is calling 9-1-1. She turns to see the assailant has hung up on the dispatcher. Now tell me how the movie progresses from there."

Terry cried out in pain then hit the floor, landing on her knees. With the phone muffled against her, her head fell forward onto her lap as she wrapped one arm around her stomach trying to stop the pain.

"Miss! What's wrong? What's happening?" The dispatcher's voice rose slightly to indicate her concern but not enough to sound alarmed.

The pain was so severe, Terry was struggling to speak. She ignored the dispatcher's questions. She held her head to the side so that her voice wouldn't sound stifled. "I also need the police. The assailant is still in the ..."

Terry looked up and saw the assailant standing above her with his finger on the hook, cutting her off. She couldn't move. The pain wouldn't let her. He walked around her laughing.

In a low whispering voice, he said, "She's fallen and it doesn't look like she'll be getting up anytime soon." He walked over to the cabinet where Gena kept her wine.

"The police are on their way."

"You know that it's going to take them at least half an hour or more to get here." He grabbed the most expensive red wine out of the cabinet. "Let's celebrate the passing of a good friend." His voice was still low as if he didn't want to wake anybody. After opening the wine, he grabbed a glass and poured himself some. He took Terry by the arm and dragged her out to where Gena lay. Terry tried her best to make it difficult by grabbing whatever she could and holding on. "This is like moving furniture. You got to put some muscle into it to get it moving."

He let go of her arm and poured the wine down her throat, then he proceeded to pour the rest of the wine over Gena's body. Terry's pain had subsided but only for a few seconds. "Sorry, Ginny, this was not in the plan." This time he wasn't whispering.

Terry was paralyzed when she heard him say that name. Only one person she knew called Gena "Ginny," and that was Marcus. The assailant turned and saw the recognition in her eyes. He pulled off his mask and said, "Mrs. Johnson, I guess my jig is up. Now let me put you out of your misery."

There stood her husband looking her in the face. Terry started crawling towards the door. Marcus picked up the knife that laid next to Gena and went after Terry. She was trying to stand but the pain wouldn't let her. She tried to crawl faster but Marcus didn't even need to trot to catch up with her. He snatched her by her hair, snapped her neck back, then placed the blade to it. She rested on her knees with her back against his stomach. He bent over and kissed her on her forehead then whispered in her ear.

"Good night, sweetheart." The knife pressed into her flesh as he spoke.

In a panic, Terry took both of her hands and pushed the hand that held the knife down and away as he tried to cut her. The knife ripped through her flesh as his hand was forced back. Terry grabbed her side thankful that it was not her neck as she elbowed him then rolled to her back as she held her side. She didn't have time to do anything else before the blade of the knife was coming down at her. His arm stopped moving when he noticed her looking over his shoulder. He quickly moved in time, escaping getting hit with the wine bottle but not in time to avoid the blow completely. Between getting hit and tripping over Terry, he hit the floor.

"Gena," Terry said as if she couldn't believe it.

Gena gave Terry a confused look. Marcus recovered from his shock then lunged at Gena with the knife as the thunder exploded in the air. Terry grabbed Marcus' ankles. Gena jumped against the living room doors as his body crashed against the floor. The knife hit the ground and slid near Gena's feet but within his reach. She quickly kicked it in Terry's direction. Terry retrieved the knife but Marcus pried it out of her hands.

They wrestled fiercely on their backs on the floor fighting for sole possession. Marcus snatched the knife from Terry but she refused to let go of his hands. The lights went out but only momentarily. Gena bent to pry his fingers open as Marcus pulled his hands away from Terry. The light blinked out for less than a second. There was a second of total darkness. Gena was falling forward when the lights blinked back on, directly onto the blade. Gena's eyes bucked. The smell of the expensive red wine on Gena's dress hit Terry's nostril as Gena's blood ran down the handle of the knife onto her hands. Terry's hands dropped away from the knife.

Marcus pushed Gena's body off him then swiftly stood. The lights were constantly blinking. He stumbled towards the door and fumbled with the lock. The strong wind whistled a high pitched shrill as the rain blew in and beat down on Marcus as he turned, looked back, lowered his head, then ran into the storm. Terry watched as she set Gena's limp body on her lap then leaned back on the living room door. The wind whipped her long reddish-brown hair across her face. A shiver raced up her spine as she rested her forehead against the top of her sister's head. Crying, she began whispering in her ear.

"Gena, you can't die. You're going to be a Godmother. That's the good news I wanted to tell you. Your big sister is pregnant with her first child. How about that?" Terry knew that there was no chance that the baby survived but she couldn't stop rambling. "Gena, the ambulance is on the way. Just hold on. Please, you're the only family I got left."

"Terry," Gena said in a barely audible voice.

She applied pressure to the wound. Her eyes frantically searching the area for something that could help stop the bleeding. "Don't talk. You know everybody in the movies that try to talk dies and you can't die."

"Keep your promise," she whispered.

The storm died down but the smell of blood and wine became more potent. Terry didn't know how long she sat there rocking Gena in her arms before the ambulance arrived. The paramedics, police, and John immediately entered through the door Marcus had left open. The paramedic moved Terry out of their way and checked Gena's pulse.

"She has a slight pulse." They had Gena in the ambulance before Terry could blink. Terry tried to get in but John pulled her into his arms and hugged her.

Danya could hear the papers of the doctor's notebook flipping fast. Dr. Adams questioned, "What was John doing there?"

"He worked at an electricity company or something. Anyway, he was checking on a report of a live wire down near Gena's block when the police and ambulance attempted to get through. Once he found out the address and the reason they were trying to get through, he followed them over," Danya replied, trying to sneak a peek at the doctor's notes.

The session went slightly overtime as she finished telling Dr. Adams what happened at the hospital. Dr. Adams seemed surprised at the last piece of the story. She had regained her composure by the time Danya sat up.

The doctor's response to how she should handle all this new information wasn't quite what Danya wanted to hear. The events of the past can't be changed, she had to learn how to deal with it. While that was true, she didn't quite know how. The doctor suggested she find a safe place to take some time to think about everything and figure out how she would proceed.

Danya had to admit the doctor was right, she did have too much going on. Clarity was needed if she wanted to survive this. Danya called John to inform him she was taking the next few days off. John was curious as to where she was going. Her response was vague. Before leaving out, Danya called Rick at home and left a message even though she knew he had already left for work. The message told him where she would be, but he wouldn't be able to reach her for a few days. She was getting away to think. Danya would call him when she got back. Even if Rick tried to call her on the cell phone, the reception in the area was bad. She requested that he only use the main cabin number for one purpose only and that was in case he had an emergency. Rita didn't seem surprised when Danya told her.

Danya made her arrangements online as she made her calls and packed. Doing one final glance around the apartment, she headed out. She threw her bags in the car and headed to her rented cabin in the Dells. When she arrived, she looked towards the lake. After getting the key, she put her bags in the cabin and walked down to the lake.

The lake was not what she expected, but it seemed an appropriate place to think. It kind of reminded her of the way her life was—murky, greenish in color, and moldy but if it was cleaned up it would be beautiful, but not exactly perfect. Danya thought back to the night Gena died. Her life at that point became murky. Yet, her life was full of the green stuff; money was not her problem. Then there were those years that she'd rather forget, those moldy ones. Danya thought of it more like mold on bread—not something she wanted but there was nothing she could do about it once she got it. She inhaled the fresh woodsy scent that floated in the air. The noises from the surrounding forest were a beautiful symphony that went unappreciated by Danya. She walked onto the shabby boardwalk pier and sat on the edge. If she weighed another ounce, she'd swear this thing would break down. Wouldn't it just irritate the hell out of Marcus for her to die before he could carry out his plans? She would love to annoy him but not that way. She prayed that the boardwalk would hold her weight.

Danya had so much on her mind. She felt like a jigsaw puzzle, that even though the pieces were slowly falling into place, they weren't making a pretty picture. There were a few pieces of the puzzle that didn't make sense. Regardless of what angle she turned them, they just would not fit. Why had Marcus spent most of his time after his release dating Rita? What purpose did it serve? How did Rita work into his plan to come after her?

What struck Danya as funny, in a bad way, was that over the last few years she believed that she'd been pulling her life together. But, she found out that she was trapped in a bottle that sat under a dripping faucet. Over the years, water had been slowly filling that bottle. If she stayed in that bottle any longer, she'd drown. The next few days she had to find a way to save her life and to get out of that bottle.

She sat there at the lake for the rest of the day.

Danya had been sitting there alone for a long time when an older man came walking down to the lake. He looked as if he was going to join her on the boardwalk which made her nervous. She truly doubted it could hold both of them.

"It's much stronger than it looks." He sat next to her and introduced himself as Harry.

"Danya," she replied, shaking his hand.

"You must really love the lake." He glanced around. "You've been sitting here quite some time. Personally, I've seen prettier bodies of water than this."

Danya nodded. The man looked as if he was in his late fifties. His salt and pepper hair against his skin gave her the impression that although he looked White he could be mixed with something else, something of Hispanic heritage maybe.

"Colombian," Harry stated.

Danya turned her head towards him. "What?"

Harry explained further by saying, "My father was White and my mother is Colombian."

Danya didn't know what to say. She wasn't used to people reading her thoughts. The sun was going down and here she was talking to a stranger. Now she knew she must be losing her mind, but what the hell. That was not her norm. They talked for a while. He gave her a brief summary of his life. He told her some stories that had her laughing so hard she thought she'd hurt herself. It still seemed to be bright out even after the sun went down. They left the lake and slowly walked the narrow dirt trail as he continued to talk about his family.

When they reached his cabin near the main office, Danya sat in the rocking chair as Harry went in to make tea. This cabin was nicer than the rest; on the porch was a swinging chair, rocking chair, and a beautiful view. The wooded area was really peaceful. The crickets were chirping in the background and a nice breeze was swaying the trees. There was a chill in the air as darkness began to close in on her. Through the trees, she could see the moonlight shimmering on the lake. Danya hadn't given any real thought to the problems she'd left behind since Harry sat down next to her earlier. It kept crossing her mind but Harry kept her distracted. He came back onto the porch and handed her a cup of tea, then took a seat on the top step of the porch. Looking up, he asked her to tell him something about her life.

"Well, I don't have much to say about it." She stopped rocking and shifted her feet nervously. Here it was, the past knocking on her door.

"What about your family?" Harry probed further.

Danya tried to shrug it off but before she knew it, she was speaking.

"Most of my family died before I turned twenty-five."

"Are you married?" Harry studied her face.

Danya held her hand up and looked at her ring. "I'm divorced but I'm giving this marriage thing a second try."

"Was the first one all that bad?"

"No, not until the very end." She thought back to when she and her younger sister first met her ex-husband. If only she saw what Gena saw, she wouldn't experience the sadness and pain Marcus brought into it.

Harry coughed, interrupting Danya's review of the past. "You were saying that it wasn't all that bad until the very end, right?" Danya nodded as she took a sip of the refreshing tea. "What happened then?"

"Well like most naive women, I thought I had a pretty good marriage even with the occasional disagreement over this and that, then one day ..." Danya's voice faded to barely a whisper. She thought about the morning Gena died. It was at the end of August, August 31st to be exact.

"Danya, you were saying?" Harry waited before interrupting, but Danya spaced out a little too long.

In only a few seconds, she displayed a lifetime of sentiments. "Oh, I'm sorry" Danya looked at her companion who was waiting for her to finish talking. She knew the various emotions that probably crossed her face had made him inquisitive. She didn't really even know what the last thing she'd said. "My parents died in a car accident when I was young. My sister and I moved in with our uncle instead of our grandmother. He felt that his mother was too old to be raising two young girls. She died about five years after that and my uncle died just before I married. By the age of twenty-five, all my family was gone and I was in the process of getting a divorce." Her voice lowered in volume as she finished her sentence.

Harry sat his cup down next to him as he asked, "What happened to your sister?"

"She was murdered two weeks before her birthday." Danya set her tea cup down next to her chair feeling the weight of the emotions stuck in her chest. She didn't need to tell this man anything about her life, edited or not. "I'd better be getting back to my cabin. Thanks for the tea and friendly conversation." She walked past Harry on the steps and waved as she headed down the pathway to her cabin. When she heard him yell to her, she stopped.

"What? I can't hear you," she yelled

"How long are you staying?" he bellowed out.

"A few more days," she shouted back. Danya walked back close enough to Harry's cabin to be heard without shouting. She told him she'd stop back by and visit him before she left.

When Danya said she'd be back to visit him, she did not realize how little time she'd have to herself. She spent the next few days enjoying her surroundings and the people in the other cabins. She believed Harry made it his mission to keep her occupied. He gave her the grand tour of the resort which she found out he owned. He also took her on the tour of the town telling her the town's history and everything. Danya hadn't even thought about calling anybody in Chicago, not even her fiancé. Well, that wasn't entirely true. She thought about it several times but she always got interrupted. Besides, the reception in the area was terrible. She was busy playing softball, volleyball, and a few other games with the kids that were staying there. She even indulged in a few hands of cards with the adults. The only time she reflected on everything going on in her life for an extended period of time was her first day. She was too tired to think about it when she'd enter her cabin at night. Most of the time her mind was occupied with the events of that day, or she was knocked out before she could even attempt to ponder upon the craziness in her life. It turned out to be exactly what she needed.

Danya wanted to get an early start in the morning. Her goal was to make it home in time to go to work. She figured if she left early, she'd have an hour to rest before heading into the office. Another thing she wanted to do was get together with John, Rita, and Rick so they could decide how to handle this Marcus situation. It was time to accept that she didn't have to do this alone.

Danya's plans didn't work out like she thought. She ended up staying until after breakfast to say goodbye to everybody. Not wanting to get caught in traffic, she ended up lingering there until after dark. Maybe traffic was the excuse. While she was ready to get back to Rick, she wasn't ready to get back to the madness. It wasn't until she turned her cabin key into the main office that she realized how much she'd miss the place. As she drove back to Chicago, she wondered how she had become attached to that place so fast. Danya didn't know what it was that made her feel so relaxed, but it did and she was glad about it. Maybe because she expected to be wrestling with her demons but the spirit of the place reminded her of love and family. Whatever it was, at least now she had her head on straight again. She had a clear plan in mind. She would stop trying to do it alone and utilize her support system to figure how best to neutralize Marcus.

This was the life she was trying to protect. If she kept going the way she was, she would self-destruct. When she returned, she'd arranged another meeting with Agent Waller. She had gone through and located the shipments that she wasn't aware of. The signature was always either Mary or Trish or the Shipping department's supervisor. She still couldn't believe that someone in her company was working with Marcus. However, after seeing him with Rita, she shouldn't be surprised as to the lengths he would go to undermine her life. Instead of going rogue, she would meet with Agent Waller to see how she could send Marcus back to prison.

CHAPTER TEN

Danya arrived at her apartment late, but Rita hadn't made it home yet. She prayed Rita wasn't still seeing Marcus. It worried her a bit that she wasn't home. She had to remind herself that Rita didn't know when she'd make it in. She called her when she was driving back but all Rita knew was it would be sometime today. She was probably out with some guy trying to get over the fact that Cory was Marcus. If Rita didn't come in before Danya woke in the morning, she'd be truly worried. Danya kept telling herself Rita was a grown woman. If she decided not to come in then it was none of Danya's business. Rita was smart. There's no way Marcus could have charmed her into believing anything that would make her forgive him.

Kicking off her shoes, she picked up the phone and called Rick. Danya knew that he'd been asleep by the way he answered the phone. She apologized for waking him and told him she only called to let him know she made it in safely. They stayed up talking for a couple of hours.

Danya took a shower and made herself some tea before finally checking her home phone's voice mail. She was so sure Marcus would leave a threatening message now that he knew she was aware that he was in town. None of the messages were from him. She went to bed worried about her friend. Checking her phone, Rita hadn't responded to any of her texts or voicemails.

The next morning Danya knocked on Rita's door and received no response. Knocking again, Danya shifted her ear towards the door to listen for movement. She announced herself before opening the door. The bed was made. There weren't any signs that Rita had been there. Danya finished dressing, hoping it was one of those mornings Rita would rush through the door to get ready for work. As Danya left for the office, she wondered if maybe Rita was too scared to stay in the apartment alone since she knew about Marcus. *That was it*, she thought. She decided to call Rita later on at work to put her mind at ease. Danya made it into the office early to play catch up. She wasn't the only person that came in early. In fact, John and Trish beat her there and were in a deep conversation that stopped abruptly when she walked in.

Danya was curious, wondering why they cut their conversation off like that. Immediately Trish started filling her in on current work issue that had gone on while she was away. After Trish gave her a synopsis of what transpired, she took a seat at her desk.

John peeped at Danya in her office. He strolled back and momentarily before entering. "With it being the anniversary of Gena's death, I thought you would still be taking some time."

"I've thought about it," Danya replied. "But it's better to be around people I love than to be alone being haunted by the past."

John updated her on his choice for their new supplier and the reasons he chose that particular company. "Our new suppliers' contract won't kick in until October but our old suppliers are doing a thorough job of blowing it. I'm flying there myself to see if I can pull things together by the end of next week."

"Why the end of next week?" Danya flipped through her notebook to see if she forgot something.

John gave her a concerned stare. "Because we are scheduled to start production on the newer designs the week after that. If those fabrics are not in by then our production will be behind."

Danya read over her notes. They would be swamped with orders. Danya knew they did not want to be in the position of playing catch up, trying to fill all those orders, especially with them coming in so rapidly. If the fabrics were not in by the end of next week, they would have some angry clients to deal with. "Shoot, you're right. When you go, make sure that you see them load those fabrics on to the truck, alright? I don't want you coming back thinking the problem is solved then have to turn right back around." She closed her notebook. "When are you planning to leave anyway?"

John looked down at his watch. "Now."

"I didn't think it was so urgent of a situation that it couldn't wait until tomorrow. I just got back. I thought maybe we'd get a chance to talk." Danya sighed as she took a seat behind her desk. "Couldn't it wait a day?"

"Man, we have a few of the craziest work weeks coming up. I'll be too busy to go. I won't be there long, at least I hope not. My plan is to quickly nip the problem in the bud then be back in time for a late dinner. If I catch the six p.m. plane then I'll be back tonight, hopefully before nine. I'll just stop by your place." John headed out the door. He stopped and turned when he heard Danya speak.

"Call first. I'm going to see if Rick wants to get together tonight."

John gave her a look then left out the office to catch his plane. Danya went over files, reviewed John's choice for a new supplier, and worked on a few new designs.

Trish came in later to see if Danya wanted to handle a few meetings that John was supposed to handle mostly with accountants and supervisors from the factory. She also informed her she had a lunch meeting with a potential client at the usual restaurant. Trish mentioned that the client was specific about the date of the meeting and the executive he wanted to meet with. Trish laughed.

"I like a man that knows when, where, and exactly with whom he wants to see; plus he's a working man. Those are the qualities I'm looking for, a man that knows exactly what it is that he wants." Trish smiled wantonly.

"Yeah, that sounds great. A man who can afford to keep more than one woman and knows which woman he wants and when. Mmm, those are definitely some unique qualities for a woman to desire to have in her man." Danya smiled.

"On second thought, he's not the type of man I like. At least not the way you describe him. I was thinking more along the line of him making up his mind that he wants me and no one else. That his entire world revolves around me." Trish gave her a starry-eyed look.

Danya laughed. "Keep that dream alive because that fantasy is as close as you'll ever get. And, I don't mean that as an insult to you."

Once Trish left, Danya picked up the phone to call Rita at her work number. She wasn't there. Her co-worker said she hadn't come in or called. Danya started to worry big time. She called the apartment. Rita wasn't there either. She stood and began pacing. Well, Cory wasn't the only man Rita was dating. Maybe she was on a date last night or stayed out late with a friend. Then she decided to play hooky from work today because of her late night. If Rita wasn't home later, Danya would call the police.

Trish came in. "Don't forget your lunch meeting."

Damn, she thought. She had better get out of there if she wanted to be on time. "Thanks, Trish."

Danya made it to the restaurant right on time. She quickly handed her keys to the parking attendant and hurried into the restaurant. The day wasn't going as planned at all. Rita was M.I.A., John had to fly out of town to handle supplier issues. Her attempt to call Rick to arrange to have dinner was a fail. He and his assistant were both away from their desks when she called.

Danya approached the host stand and asked if the person she was meeting arrived yet. She was shocked when the host explained that her client called in and made special arrangements.

"What special arrangement?" Danya questioned, confused.

"A change of tables," the host explained as he directed her to a table near the front. Danya had been there ten minutes waiting for the client. If it wasn't for her fifteen-minute policy, she would have been out the door long ago. She couldn't understand why her client requested that their table be changed to one closer to the front. Danya wasn't given time to speculate as the waiter walked to the table with a bottle of red wine. Danya smiled and stuck out her hand to touch the bottle, saying, "I didn't order any wine."

"No, but I did." Her client stepped from behind the waiter. The waiter popped the cork, poured the wine, then left.

Danya's mouth dropped open. "Marcus Anthony, we have nothing to discuss." As she tried to stand, he applied pressure to her shoulder. She knocked his hand away and tried to get passed him. He stood firmly in her way then took her hand in his and gave her a solid handshake.

"No, Cory Jones, ex-boyfriend of Rita. You do remember me? Rita certainly did last night. Won't you have a seat?" Marcus gave her an arrogant stare down.

Danya sat back down. "Rita, where is she?" The waiter walked to the table preventing her from questioning him further. She gave the waiter a phony smile and quickly told him, "We're not ready to place our order yet."

"Okay, I'll come back," the waiter replied as if it was not a problem.

"Thanks." Danya smile at the waiter as he turned away from the table.

Marcus stopped the waiter. "Actually, I think I'm ready to order."

Marcus ordered, but Danya didn't and he took his sweet time doing so, saying he wanted this, no, no, he wanted that. She was ready to shot-put him into the next century. The waiter smiled and stated, "I'll come back."

Marcus held his hand out and replied, "No, I know what I want now."

The waiter finally left after ten minutes of supposed indecisiveness. Danya made it clear to the waiter to take his sweet time getting the order in, that this was a business meeting and they didn't know how long they'd be discussing business.

"Marcus Anthony, cut the B.S. What is this about?"

"What happened to baby, honey, or just plain old Marcus? Don't you know this is our anniversary? Today is August thirty-first."

Danya was dumbfounded momentarily. She and Marcus didn't get married or divorced in August. She figured out what he was talking about as his food arrived. Hadn't she told that waiter to take his time? *Damn that man for ordering something that only took a hot second to prepare*, Danya thought as Marcus plastered a sarcastic grin on his face.

The waiter asked, "Miss, are you ready to order?"

"I'm not ordering anything. Thank you," Danya said politely. All she wanted to do was get back to dealing with the problem at hand.

After the waiter left, Marcus refused to discuss anything until after he ate his lunch. He actually tried to make small talk, asking how she had been and what she had been up to. She couldn't believe him. His calmness let her know that he had been planning this for a while. As soon as Marcus finished his last bite, Danya called the waiter over to the table. The waiter took Marcus plate and left.

"Where is Rita?" Danya was extremely upset that Rita had been brought into this.

"Rita, dear sexy Rita, is waiting for her loving Cory to come home.

She wasn't originally a part of the plan, but since she was your roommate she became an essential part." He gave her a wicked smile.

Danya whispered intensely so that no one but Marcus could hear her. "Marcus Anthony, I don't care about your original plan. Just tell me how much you want. That is what you want, isn't it? Some of my millions. If that's what you wanted to start with, you should have divorced me and took half from the get go. Gena should have never been brought into it."

She understood the reason Marcus changed the tables was to prevent her from causing a scene or walking out. He knew she wouldn't make a scene in the restaurant where she held her business meetings. In the private dining room where her company reserved a table for business meetings, it was another story altogether.

"My dear, naive Terry, didn't you realize that she was always a part of the equation? That Gena didn't like me because she wanted me. That night I was supposed to be gone before you made it there. Did you know your baby sister was into kinky games?" He lifted his eyes and gave her a devilish grin.

"Look, bastard that is one lie you won't be able to convince me of! We are not here to discuss that. It's over and done with." She leaned in towards him speaking through gritted teeth. "You are here to tell me what it is you want, now, in the present. And, I doubt you're here just to tell me lies."

He was still handsome and slightly more muscular. He didn't have the hard look she expected after spending time in prison. It just wasn't in his eyes like some of the other men she'd met then discovered that they'd done time. Regardless, Danya could tell Marcus thought he was "the man" by the way he carried himself. How she would love to slap that damn smug look off his face.

"Terry, darling, don't rush me. Why would I divorce you for only a half when I know I deserve so much more. When I married you instead of your sexy baby sister, I earned every right to a large chunk of your inheritance." He sipped his wine.

Anger coursed through her body like it was her life's blood. "Hmmphm."

"How was I supposed to know that you'd have to wait for your money? I didn't think your sister would get hers before you did. Then it really stung when she'd tripled her money by the age of twenty-two."

His hand reached up and caressed her cheek. He smiled as she knocked it away. "If you only looked like this ten years ago, I wouldn't have minded being with you, not at all. I wouldn't have had to choke down the sickness that rose in my throat while I was touching 223 pounds of disgusting fat instead of 110 pounds of lusciousness."

Danya popped out of her chair.

"Sit down!" Marcus placed an unshakable hold on Danya's lower arm as she stood. "This meeting is far from over."

"It is for me." She brought her face closer to his and whispered slowly, every word laden with anger. "I do not have to put up with this shit from you." Danya tried to yank her arm away from him.

Marcus laughed. "Oh but you do, or will I be seeing you at Rita's funeral?"

"You bastard!"

Marcus grabbed her arm again, this time forcing her back into her chair. Danya was fuming but she had to stay cool for Rita's sake. The patrons near them heads snap towards their table. Marcus smiled at them like nothing was wrong. Danya fingered her knife. She wanted to cut his heart out and place it in his mouth so he could choke on its bitterness.

"I could have been an actor," he continued. "I was pretty good with acting with you but that's beside the fact. Terry, you owe me."

She snarled at him. "I don't owe you jack sh ..."

"What time should we have Rita's funeral?" He calmly drank his wine.

Danya leaned forward wishing that she had an inkling that Marcus would be the one she was meeting with. She would have had the FBI here waiting for him. "Cut the crap and get to the point. How much do you want? This is about money, isn't it?"

"You know I should ask for more but it would take you too long to get it. So, I just want 5.5 million dollars." He gave her a sly grin.

"What? You have got to be kidding me!" His audacity amazed her.

"Lower your freaking voice. I'll call you at your office at three, be there or Rita's dead." Marcus forcefully whispered as he noticed people were staring. His eyes darted around the restaurant.

Danya noticed their waiter was talking to the manager. She motioned for the check. "You're willing to go back to prison for a second time after you just managed to get out."

"I'm not worried about prison. It was like living in a condo." He started laughing. "Besides with 5.5 million in my pocket, I don't plan to get caught. Oh, and when I call, already have the money in hand."

"Look, I can't get that type of money that fast without questions being asked. How am I supposed to liquidate 5.5 million dollars' worth of assets in less than three hours? I don't have that type of money sitting in my personal bank account; it is invested."

"You're resourceful. You'll figure it out. Just make sure that you have your butt back in your office by three." He finished off his wine.

"Are you crazy, silly fool? I need more time than that." Danya figured he wanted her to sell one of Gena's antiques. The dollar figures for what she'd been offered for a collection was too close to his number to be a coincidence. She just didn't know how he knew she hadn't sold them already.

"Three o'clock. Meeting's adjourned." Marcus stood and left the table, leaving Danya to pay the bill. *Damn him.* Danya knew there was no way that Marcus was going to let her and Rita walk out alive after he got the money. She wished like hell that she'd gotten a chance to formulate a plan. Now she didn't have time to do anything but think quickly on her feet. She needed to talk to John. Maybe he had some idea how to handle this.

After paying the bill, Danya left the restaurant then waited for her car to be brought around. Her foot tapped impatiently on the concrete. The valet parking attendant pulled up with her car just as she decided she had a plan that just might work. She prayed it didn't get them both killed. Danya tried to work out the details as she drove to her apartment.

CHAPTER ELEVEN

The door slammed as Danya rushed into the apartment towards her room to changed clothes. She continuously glanced at her watch as she took off her business suit and changed into black sweats and black canvas shoes. Digging in her purse, she pulled out her cell and called the office.

"Hey, Trish, I won't be in the office until a little before three but I won't be staying long." She logged into her personal laptop and retrieved the information she needed.

"Anything else?" Trish asked.

"If a Marcus, Cory, or the client from my eleven o'clock meeting call before I get in, put him on hold and call me immediately." Danya hesitated for a moment. "And track down John and tell him to get on a flight back here, pronto."

Trish repeated the names back then paused, Danya assumed to jot down the instructions. Danya checked the time. She needed to wrap this call up. "If John is being stubborn tell him that a few angry clients making my life difficult is nothing compared to the problems M.A.J. would cause me."

After Danya hung up the phone, she kicked herself in the butt for hoping that Marcus would let it go without seeking revenge. *If he thinks he's still dealing with that naïve, overweight girl he married, he is dead wrong. Dead wrong!* she thought as she took a deep breath to calm herself.

Danya attempted to call Rick next. She stared at her watch as the phone rang. If John didn't make it back in time, she needed someone she trusted to know what was going down. She became frustrated after finding out that Rick was out of the office at an all-day conference and couldn't be reached. *Damn.* If her Plan B fell through before her Plan A, she might as well shoot Rita herself.

"That will work," she said as an idea popped into her head.

It was time she called in a few favors. She had two hours to get everything she needed done and be back in the office. Danya left her apartment and went to work. She reached out to someone who once offered to pay her quite a bit for three painting she had in her possession. It was the quickest way to get cash. She placed the call letting him know the offers expired in two hours. The return call came within ten minutes. He asked for an hour to make the arrangement. She told him she would retrieve the paintings and have them ready. Danya also knew someone else who wanted Gena's antique pieces but she didn't want to part with them unless it was her last resort.

Danya made a detour to the beauty supply store. The cashier seemed insulted by her snippy attitude, but Danya didn't care. She had been putting a few surprises up her sleeve when John called.

"Terry! What's going on?" John yelled through the phone.

"Hold on, John." Danya made her purchase and exited the store. Once she got to the car she began talking. Pulling away from the curve, she told John an edited version of what happened.

"At three o'clock, he's supposed to call and tell me where to meet him."

John asked if she phoned the police.

She simply replied, "You know the routine, no police. Besides, why would I call the same people that let the bastard out?"

"I'll be on the first plane out. I should be there by six-thirty. Do not meet with Marcus until after I get there. Okay?" John commanded.

She huffed. "I won't." She hung up then added, *or at least I will try not to.* Danya kept watching the time as she sped through the streets back to the office.

Danya made it into the office in time to take Marcus's call. He made a snide remark about how it sounded as if she was out of breath. "What were you doing, running a marathon?"

She replied with an apparent attitude, "You know what I was doing."

"Look, Terry, you are in no position to get an attitude with me. Rita's death will be on your hands," he threatened.

Danya silently cursed Marcus out. "Just tell me where you want to meet."

"Where it all started." Marcus's voice was filled with sarcasm.

"If Rita's already in the hospital then there is no need for me to give you this money."

"Very funny. Be at 212 Bell Oak at six."

"Wait, Gena's?" That was the last place she expected him to say. She had John sell Gena's house within a year of her death.

Marcus replied, "Yes, Gena's."

"I can't be there until seven." Danya needed more time.

"Six, a minute late and Rita's ..."

"Alright six!" she hollered into the phone.

"Ring the bell." He hung up leaving Danya cursing a dial tone. Danya's finger held the button down a few seconds before she released it to dial Rick's cell number.

"Baby, I'm praying you get this message before it's too late. Marcus wants me to meet him at 212 Bell Oak at six. I don't have time to call the police and try to explain everything. So, I need you to do it for me and have them meet me there. Tell them Rita is being held hostage. Rick don't ..." Beep. "Dammit!" She was really starting not to like his voicemail. She left her office heading for Trish's desk. Trish stared at her outfit, but she ignored the look.

"Trish, when John calls you back tell him if his plane arrives on time, he's going to be at least thirty minutes late for our 212 Bell Oak meeting." Trish nodded her head.

Danya never stepped into the office in anything other than business attire. Now she looked like she forgot to change out of her gym clothes. On top of that Danya had come in, taken a phone call, barked out some orders, and bolted out of the office. That was something she'd never done before. She knew Trish and everyone in the office was trying to figure out what was really going on.

Tonight, Danya planned to close a chapter of her life. She had a serious score to settle. She drove to her apartment like a bat out of hell. It hit her giving the message to Trish may have been a mistake but there was nothing she could do about it. Once she entered the apartment, she immediately tried to reach Rick again. She was about to call the police when she thought better. They would slow her down asking for details. The police would probably want her to let them handle it, or she'd have to answer too many questions. Whichever one it was, it would slow her down in being prepared for her final confrontation with Marcus. She was wasting time. Damn. She picked up the phone and dialed the number. It wasn't only her life that hung in the balance tonight. There was no way she was going to let Rita die because of her stupidity.

The phone rang. She paced back and forth as far as the phone cord allowed her to. When somebody finally picked up, she asked for Officer Bally. The person told her he wasn't in but could transfer the call to another officer. Danya tried to explain to the officer what was going on but he asked too many repetitive questions. She was totally pissed off by the time he asked the same question for the fourth time. Twice is understandable, the third time was irritating, but the fourth time was inconceivable. The conversation was over.

"Look." Her teeth clenched as she talked. "Just make sure Bally gets this message. His technicality is running amok."

"What?" the officer asked.

"Tell him Marcus Johnson is going for a repeat performance. Just with one new character. This message is from Terry. You got that Terry, T-e-r-r-y. He'll know who it is." She slammed the phone down. "Dammit, that was a waste of my time. I swear if that man doesn't give him that message, I'll be on America's Most Wanted as a cop killer."

Rick was the only person she had to pull her butt out the fire if she got into a crunch. So, she left another message.

"Babes, it's me again. I need you to call Officer Bally for me. He's on the force out in the suburbs. It's about four, four-thirty now. I have some errands to run before I meet Marcus at six. And Rick, don't come trying to play hero, okay? If I don't make it back, remember I love you." She prayed he could understand her. This time she wanted to make sure that voicemail didn't cut her off. Danya had spoken so fast, it almost sounded like she was speaking in a foreign language.

Danya got the money and put half into a suitcase and half in a bag. Marcus had taken away more than $5.5 million could ever replace—her family and ten years of her life. She couldn't get her family back but she was going to reclaim her life. Mr. Johnson was right, she was resourceful and he'd find out just how resourceful she was tonight. Danya laughed. Marcus was going to get more than he bargained for. She was giving him three choices, either leave her alone, go back to prison, or if it came down to him or her, die.

Danya made a few stops before heading out to meet Marcus. She even changed her clothes. It felt as if she was driving back in time. Danya scolded herself for getting emotional. Dr. Adams stated that if the doctor at the hospital said that she hadn't been the cause of Gena's death than Danya needed to believe that. Danya fought to pull herself together. She was falling right into Marcus's hands. He thought that being back at Gena's would cause her to fall apart and not be able to handle things. She refused to let him have his way. She started reviewing her plans and her back up plans. *This has to work*, she thought to herself. *It has to.*

After getting John's voicemail, Danya broke down and called Trish to see if John had been in contact with her. Trish apologized. Danya told her there was nothing that she could do so don't apologize. She reminded Trish that she needed to give John the message as soon as possible. Even if John didn't call back before she went home, Trish was to reach him with whatever number she was at and give him the message.

Marcus was cocky enough to believe she still loved him. Danya knew that. It was in the way he spoke. If she confirmed that, she'd blow him out of the water. If she was wrong, she still had at least one other thing she could use in her favor. If that didn't work, she would have to resort to Plan B. She pulled out her phone. Danya was definitely getting tired of not being able to reach people but she left a message anyway. She needed back up to her back up.

CHAPTER TWELVE

Danya pulled into the circle drive, fighting the urge to replay that night over in her mind. Marcus had even placed what looked like Gena's mustang in the driveway; it even had Gena's personalized plates on it. He was trying his best to play on her emotions. There was no way he was going to get the best of her. *At least he couldn't control the weather,* she thought. If it was storming, she might not have been able to take it. Danya knew Marcus figured with the right combination he would make her lose it. Didn't he know better? He was about to learn. Six years ago, he taught her so many lessons she nearly choked on them, but she learned them well.

At six on the dot, Danya rang the doorbell. Marcus answered the door. "You know you are a fool to have come."

"You can put the gun away. I'm unarmed." She smiled and kissed him on the lips, noticing he had on a similar outfit to the one he had on that night. She twirled around lifting her jacket not only to show that she had no gun but also for him to appreciate her shape.

Marcus didn't put away his gun but he stopped pointing it at her. Shocked was scribbled in his eyes as Danya sashayed passed him with the duffel bag in one hand and a bottle of red wine in the other.

Marcus stood staring at her. She could only imagine what was going through his mind. Danya had on heels and a short form fitting black dress with a small quilted looking jacket over it that was slightly opened. She also wore a wig that looked like her hair had before she'd cut it, except it was darker.

Danya turned, taking a wide stance with her hip stuck out and asked, "Are you planning to stand there all day with your mouth opened or close the door and come on in?"

"Just, just go into the living room." Marcus gestured with one hand, pointing at the double doors, as her laughter echoed in the hallway. The way she strutted made the bottom of her dress swing just enough to see where her behind started to curve. She peered over her shoulder to see him slide his gun back into his waistband. Marcus softly bit his bottom lip examining her shapely legs in the black stockings.

Danya smirked as he muttered, "Mmm. Too bad you didn't look like this when we were married."

Danya paused slightly before opening the door then went to sit the bag and the wine down. It was right before these very doors that she'd held Gena's bleeding body in her arms. She shook off the memories and opened the door to see Rita sitting in front of the bay window gagged and tied to a chair. The way her hair flowed over her face, it reminded her of the wig she had on. Danya walked in and went over to the bay window behind where Rita sat mumbling from behind the bandanna how glad she was to see her. Of course, Danya couldn't make out a word she said. Her eyes scanned every inch of the room. Marcus tried his best to make this room appear to be the same way Gena had it, but he didn't know what antique really meant. Danya sauntered over to the bar and grabbed two wine glasses, ignoring Rita when Marcus entered the room.

"Terry, what are you doing?" He watched her walk over to the coffee table.

"It's our anniversary, remember?" she replied with a sensual raise of her eyebrow.

Danya set the two glasses, a cork screw, and the bottle of wine on the coffee table next to the duffle bag. She unzipped the bag and pulled out a gun. Marcus went for his gun but Danya had already gotten off two shots before he could get to it. Rita's body slumped over in the chair.

"We're celebrating the passing of good friends." She put the gun on top of the bag then opened the wine and poured two glasses. "Again."

"Dammit, Terry, why did you go do some stupid shit like that?" He slowly advanced toward Rita's slumped over body, looking at the red spot form on her stomach, keeping a close eye on Danya.

"Oh, I'm sorry. Did I take the fun out of it? Oh well, life goes on, at least for us." She stepped in front of him and handed him a glass of wine before he could check to see how badly injured Rita was. She attempted to pull him towards the couch.

"You don't even like red wine." He snarled at her then sat the wine glass down on the table and took a couple of steps back.

Danya sat on the couch, crossed her legs, and took a sip of wine. She smiled up at him, thinking, *Maybe because it reminds me of you pouring it all over me and my dying sister*.

Marcus turned and placed his hand over his mouth as if he was coming up with Plan B or couldn't figure out what she had up her sleeve. She gave him an evil sneer until he turned to her.

Danya patted the cushion next to her on the couch. When he didn't come, Danya stood and walked over to him. She pulled him to her and kissed him. At first, he tried to pull away but when her hands started to roam, he stopped resisting and gave into the pleasure. Danya hoped all thoughts of checking on Rita would exit his head. It made her wonder how deep his obsession with Gena goes. Danya stepped back and looked wantonly into his eyes.

"I've been waiting a long time to do that." She smiled, trying to resist the urge to gag.

"Terry, your act is not fooling me. Where's the money?" He snatched off her wig and threw it at her, then walked over towards the bag.

"In the bag, but it's only half." She took a seat on the couch.

Marcus grabbed the duffel bag. He glared at her and said, "What?"

"The other half's here but it's in the car. I want to know the truth before we go our separate ways. Why did you kill Gena?"

Danya waited patiently as he flipped through the stacks of hundred dollar bills. Marcus should have been able to tell by looking at it that it wasn't all there.

"Give me the damn keys to your car," he yelled almost frantically.

Danya refused. Marcus threatened to break the window. She smiled innocently knowing it wouldn't be that simple. The rest of the money was in the trunk that required a key to get into. She laughed as she warned him, "Let me put it this way. There's a little something, something other than money on the inside of my trunk if you catch my drift. I'm not quite sure it will work but I was warned that I'd be looking for a new car if it should happen to explode."

"You are full of it." He started feeling for pockets on her jacket.

Danya held her hands up knowing he wouldn't find any keys on her. "I wasn't too thrilled riding here with it in my trunk, but sometimes you have to do what you have to do. It's amazing what money can buy. I see you don't believe me, so why don't you go find out for yourself."

"You expect me to believe that?" He scowled at her as she sat on the arm of the couch and crossed her legs.

"Marcus, baby. There's only one way to find out," she stated nice and sugary sweet with just a hint of sarcasm.

Marcus may have thought she was bluffing, but he seemed unwilling to find out first hand. He reached to pick up the wine glass she poured for him. He paused as if he thought better of it then walked to the bar.

"Look, honey, all I want to know is when Gena invited you over, did she tell you to lie to me about being out of town? When I called that day, she made all sorts of lame excuses about why I shouldn't come over. I went anyway because I had something important to tell her." Danya lied and picked up the bottle of wine. She stood and walked over to Marcus who was at the bar pouring himself a stronger drink. She took the wine and set it on the bar.

"What?" he asked as Danya placed her finger on the rim of the glass to prevent him from drinking it.

"Stick with the wine. The vodka will just mess with your performance. Don't worry. I didn't put anything in the wine. See." Danya took the wine bottle, turned it up, and drank some. "You want to taste?"

Marcus downed his vodka then poured himself another. "Terry, just stop."

"I knew she wanted you for herself." She lightly caressed his head. "She couldn't come to terms with the fact that you picked me over her. That's why she pretended to dislike you so much."

Marcus moved her hand. "At that time, you couldn't steal a fly away from her."

"You don't have to lie for her anymore. She's gone." Danya pressed her body closer to his.

"I always believed you were naive, Terry, never stupid." He placed his index finger over Danya's lips.

"Why does loving you have to be naive or stupid? If that night hadn't happened, we would have been a family. You, me, and the baby." Danya slightly turned her face away from Marcus, a single tear hanging from her eyelash. Marcus swiftly turned her to face him again.

"Baby?" Marcus glared at her as if wondering what the hell she was talking about.

"That night I had to tell someone. You went out of town and didn't leave a number." She wiped her eyes. "I went to tell Gena. Marcus, what happened to you wanting a family?"

His face softened as he replied, "Nothing."

"So why didn't it affect you knowing you killed your unborn child for a piece of ass and some cash." She willed herself to remain calm when she really wanted to scream, yell, and punch his smug face for what he did.

"I never knew there was a baby. I was never told." Marcus started mumbling words that Danya couldn't make out. He reclaimed his drink. He gulped the vodka down in one swift move, then set the glass down. Danya grabbed his hand and led him over to the couch before he could pour himself another drink. Handling a drunk version of Marcus was not the plan.

"It's okay, sweetheart. I forgave you, long ago. Now I just want a second chance. Once I saw you again, all those feeling I had for you came back. I didn't want to admit it, but then I realized that it was you I loved, not Rick. Rick could never be half the man you are. I wanted to be able to taste you one last time." Danya wrapped her arms around him trying not to choke on those words. "Let's try to get back to who we used to be before that night."

Marcus didn't respond to that last comment she made. She didn't know how much more of this she could take. Marcus caressed her thigh like Rick does. Suddenly he shook his head and unwrapped her arms and leaned back into the couch for a moment. Danya didn't say anything. She watched the plethora of emotions cross his face before he rose to his feet and headed to the bar for another drink. Danya didn't like the fact that Marcus was drinking vodka like it was juice. Handling a crazy man was bad enough. He didn't need to be drunk, too. Danya prayed that Rick got her message. Any more of the lovey-dovey bull and she was going to be sick. Man, that bar situation was more than she planned for.

She had to imagine he was Rick to have a chance at making it seem real.

Danya was trying to buy herself some time. She had to keep Marcus distracted the best way she knew how, and talking wasn't cutting it. Even though she kissed him and allowed him to put his vile hands on her, sleeping with Marcus was absolutely not an option. Danya knew if she did, there was no guarantee even then that she'd walk away alive. She mentally scolded herself. She needed to focus on keeping Marcus occupied, without this fake flirting. He sat next to her again. The one thing she knew was that something had him worried, but she had a feeling it wasn't her.

* * *

Rick didn't go back to the office after his meeting. He didn't even bother to call the office. Whatever needed to be done someone else could handle it. It had been a rough day and all he wanted was a little rest, relaxation, some food, and maybe a little quality time with his woman. He wondered if Danya was up for some company tonight. The conference location had terrible cell service but it was probably his boss's doing to make sure attendees abided by the no cell phone rule. He tried to call Danya from one of the remote offices at the conference but got her voicemail.

He headed straight to his favorite restaurant for a bite to eat. Rick waited for the waitress to finish with the couple in front of him so he could place his order.

"Will you be dining in?" The waitress accidentally dropped the menu then stooped over to pick it up.

Rick couldn't help but notice her nicely shaped backside. He glanced away checking the time. It was still early. Since it was closer to Danya's place he decided to eat there, then call her when he was done to see if she wanted to spend some time together. The waitress led him to a table with a seductive stroll. If he wasn't engaged, he would definitely be willing to see what she was offering for dinner and dessert. Rick's eyes roamed over her voluptuous figure as she took his order. He laughed to himself. When they came up with the term brick house, they must have had her in mind. He mentally checked himself and reminded himself what he loved about what he had. Nothing was wrong with looking as long as he didn't touch. Getting married didn't make him blind. This waitress would not be the last of the beautiful women that crossed his path. The one thing he knew was outside of this Marcus situation, his life was exactly what he wanted it to be. Rick knew Danya made it in late last night but he didn't know if she stayed in to rest or went to work. Maybe they could get a little bedroom exercise in tonight. There was nothing like that type of R&R to make a man feel better.

By the time the waitress brought his food to the table, he was smiling. She flirted a bit then went back to work. Rick enjoyed his meal and his attentive waitress. He asked for the bill but instead of giving him the bill she took a seat.

"What's a handsome man like you doing eating alone?" She placed her arm on the back of the booth. "Where's the wife and kids?"

Rick shifted a bit as her breast came in contact with his arm. "I'm not married, yet."

"I'm willing to bet it won't be long before some lucky woman claims you for her own." She slowly ran her hand from his shoulder to his hand then smiled as she pulled the bill out from her breast pocket.

Rick reached his hand out for his bill. "You are probably right." He gave her a sexy smile. If she only knew.

"Before I give you your bill, are you sure you don't want dessert?" Her eyes flirted.

He told himself nothing was wrong with a little harmless flirting. "What's the special?"

"Me, any way you like. Whipped cream and strawberries preferred. I have nice sized melons on the menu. I'm told that my peaches are very sweet and juicy. You do eat peaches, don't you? It doesn't matter. I'm creative, I can come ... up with something you'll like."

Rick had to lick his lips on that offer. "Dessert sounds real nice, but," he inhaled deeply and sighed, "I think I'll have to pass."

She slid out the booth. "Maybe next time."

Not likely, Rick thought as she leaned over placing the bill in front of him, giving a nice view down her blouse, then she handed him another piece of paper.

"If you change your mind about dessert, call that number. I still may be able to hook you up with one of those specials." She leaned over more to where Rick's mouth was just an inch from her cleavage then smiled and walked away. Rick shook his head and paid the bill. He nicknamed her Delilah. He was sure that woman had gotten many men caught in her web of seduction. If it had been another time in his life, he would have been one of them. He hoped Danya was in the mood for company.

Rick got into the car thinking about his waitress. He reached into his pocket for his cell and realized he didn't have it on him. He leaned down, remembered he'd put it in his briefcase. He got it out and noticed the missed calls from Danya. Checking his messages, he started swearing. He took a glimpse at his watch. "It's after six, dammit! Why hadn't I thought to check my messages earlier?"

Rick pulled out the parking lot trying to estimate the time it would take him to get there. If he sped all the way there, he could make it before seven, seven-thirty at the latest. If he picked up a couple of cops on the way, it was all the better. Rick phoned Officer Bally, but he was told that the officer had left on an urgent matter. Rick didn't want to assume the urgent matter was Danya. He had to make sure. He tried to think of others that he could call for help that could get to Danya quicker, but he couldn't keep his thoughts focused and off his guilt. While he had been eating, enjoying himself, and flirting with a voluptuous waitress, his fiancée went off with no assistance to meet the man that had killed her sister.

* * *

Danya sat, peering out of the bay window. Someone should have arrived by now. The seduction ceased to work. She quickly discovered that he wasn't as easily distracted as she thought he'd be. It made it even harder for her to understand what he did to Gena. She watched as he searched for her keys. Glancing over at Rita, she knew she'd need someone to arrive soon otherwise she'd never become Mrs. Cameron. He pulled out his gun and aimed at her demanding that she hand over the key. She reached for her jacket zipper. She refused to tell him where it was. He shook his head and pointed his gun at her hands. Reluctantly she dropped her hands away from her zipper. Marcus seemed to be in deep thought, formulating a new plan with the gun now aimed at her chest. The shrill of his cell phone ringing startled her a bit. Marcus answered and hadn't said a word to her since he got the call. That was not a good sign at all.

"If you want to kill time till to the Calvary arrives, how about we go up to one of the bedrooms?" Marcus grinned, wickedly.

Danya gave him her best innocent look. "I'm not killing time."

"You came ready to seduce when earlier you couldn't stomach the sight of me." Marcus snickered.

Her eyes were glued to the window. "A woman can have a change of heart," Danya stated, relaxing as she saw a patrol car on the only section of the circle drive that could be seen from where she stood.

He cackled. "The wig was a nice touch. You know I've always had a thing for long hair."

"I never really got over you." She turned to face him thinking she could go back into the charade since he brought it up. Especially knowing her back up plan had arrived.

"Come on." Marcus nodded toward the door.

Danya took a seat back on the couch. "Why don't you come on over here?" She was quite cocky now that her Plan B was in place.

Marcus stared over at Rita's body. "I don't think so."

The doorbell rang. Danya looked. It threw her. She was kind of expecting them to just bust in. She reminded herself that this wasn't a movie. Things may not work that way in the real world. It still struck her as odd. They were probably giving him a chance to open the door first then when he answered it, he'd get arrested. Marcus told her to sit tight and don't try anything; he'd be right back. Danya got an uneasy feeling when Marcus went to answer the door. A shiver went through her body. It felt like it was about to be do or die time. She zipped up her jacket and waited.

* * *

When Marcus opened the door and the four of them walked in, she should have been relieved to see them but something wasn't right. "Good lord, does this nightmare ever end?" she whispered.

"Hello Officer Bally, John, Rick. So nice of you all to join us." Marcus smiled smugly.

"Marcus, what happened to Sharrita?" John noticed the slumped over body in the chair. He turned, grabbing Marcus by the neck.

"John, my man, your million dollar female shot her." Marcus pried John's fingers from around his neck, then strolled over to the bar to get himself another drink.

John's focus snapped towards Danya. "Terry?"

"Have some wine." Marcus tilted his head towards the bottle of wine. "We are celebrating the passing of good friends. And John, after Ms. Terry Danya finds out about your part in this, I have a feeling you'll be included in that." Marcus snarled at John.

"Come on, Marcus!" Bally stated. "Don't make this worse."

"Terry, I'd like to introduce you to the fo ... mmm, the three musketeers, myself, Peter better known to you as Officer Bally, and your lifelong friend, John. Welcome to your worst nightmare." Marcus started cackling like a crazy man.

Danya could tell he was extremely pissed at John's presence.

"I can't believe you were involved in this." Rick scowled at John.

Rick was handcuffed when they came in. At least she was positive he wasn't involved in this. Or she hoped not. There was a sense of relief at getting that confirmation. That relief was quickly replaced with terror as John moved his gun from behind Rick's back and held it to Rick's head.

"So much for damage control." Marcus looked at John, lifting his glass to him.

John glared at Danya with disbelief. "I can't believe you shot your own roommate, your best friend for the last three frigging years."

"Don't sound so heart broken. It hasn't been quite three years yet, has it? Call it the survival of the fittest." Danya gave John an innocent look, resisting the urge to run her fingers through her hair. "You know that theory, only the strong survive. Do you know who said that? I can't seem to remember."

Bally stared at Rita then looked at Marcus and stated, "It doesn't matter—"

"John, how was your trip?" Danya cut Bally's statement short.

John stared at her. "Let's not play games."

"Danya don't ..." Rick stopped speaking as John pushed his head with the gun.

Danya started laughing. "Oh, I'm really scared now."

"Look, it didn't have to be this way." John looked toward Danya with sincerity. Although his eyes seemed to hold genuine feelings of sincerity that emotion was not there—in any shape, form, or fashion—in his voice. "Especially if Marcus had stuck with the plan."

Bally moved Rick into a chair while John kept his gun trained on him even though his focus was on Danya. She recognized that John was extremely upset with Marcus. From the way John's face tightened up, she could tell it wouldn't be long before she found out why. John gave Marcus a deadly glare and began speaking with a murderous edge to his voice.

"Marcus, why did you modify our plan? Look what a mess you made of the situation." He shifted the gun from Rick to Marcus. "Or was it your plan to take the money and leave your partners' ass out?"

"You're one to talk." Marcus looked at Bally. "You know me better than that."

Bally kept his gun on Rick.

"Wasn't the original plan to have it happen on the same date as last time? If I wanted to cut out on you, why would I bring—"

"Alright!" John yelled. "Let's just clean up this mess and move on. I'm damn sure not planning on spending the rest of my life in prison, on the Virgin Islands maybe, but not prison."

There was a deadly silence hanging in the air as John finished his sentence. Danya realized John was actually going to kill her and Rick or have one of the others do it. Her heart ached at the thought of someone she loved and trusted all her life was just seconds from permanently destroying it.

CHAPTER THIRTEEN

Danya scanned the room carefully. Rick was sitting in the chair across from her with a dazed and confused look on his face which probably reflected on her own. She assumed he was having regrets about trying to play hero. Officer Bally was deep in conversation at the bar with Marcus, both drinking her wine no less. She assumed they were trying to decide on the best way to handle the situation or dispose of them. John stood with the gun pointed at Rick but his focus was clearly elsewhere. Danya assumed this by the way he kept looking over at Rita's slumped over body. No one was supposed to be murdered, just a few million richer. She had a feeling that she and Rick weren't getting out of here alive with the knowledge that John was involved in this whole sordid deal. It was time to reevaluate her plan since her back up turned out to be her worst enemy. Danya understood Marcus being in with a dirty cop, but John? It didn't matter. It was time to put her alternate plan into motion and pray that it worked. Taking a deep breath, she stood.

"Okay, John, tell me the real deal." Danya mentally crossed her fingers and prayed she could buy enough time for Plan C to kick in. "You owe me that much?"

"Actually, I don't owe you anything." Whatever sincerity Danya saw in his eyes earlier was no longer there.

"Wow, it amazes me that you feel you don't," Rick stated.

"Since Marcus already put my cards on the table, you know I'm in this mess up to here." He gestured with his hand going over his head while cutting his eyes at Marcus. Bally offered John a glass of dark liquor but he shook his head. Bally sat the glass on the bar. The way Marcus shifted the position of his gun, Danya knew that wasn't a good sign. Bally put his hand over Marcus's gun preventing him from lifting it. Marcus gave him a searing glare.

"You conveniently forgot to inform me that Terry was pregnant with my child." Marcus demanded to know why he hadn't been told that Danya lost their baby. John told Marcus, in a none to pleasant tone, that neither he nor Bally thought it was important. They were all focused on fixing Marcus's mistake. Danya watched, hoping that her other plan would kick in or they were dead. There was no way she could take all three of them.

John continued to speak to Marcus in a callous manner. "Anyway, after killing Gena, why should it have mattered that you killed your unborn child. It's not like you couldn't have anymore."

"Dammit, John! You should have told me." Anger shook Marcus's voice as he spoke.

John looked at Marcus as if he was debating moving the gun off Rick. "It's irrelevant now. We're back in the process of cleaning up another of your messes."

Danya didn't give Marcus a chance to respond. "John, if you are the master mind behind all this, then why did you bother helping me? I can understand why you helped me get my business started. The answer to that is pretty obvious. But what I can't understand is why you sent me to self-defense class and Dr. Adams."

"Let me answer this one. It's simple. We needed you alive, but, Marcus here had always had a way of making fatal mistakes," Bally answered eager to make that information known. "We needed you to be able to protect yourself from any of his unfortunate mistakes—"

John interrupted Bally and shifted his gun towards Marcus. "Gena was never meant to die."

Bally took over telling the story. "All Marcus had to do was to scare Gena into giving him the combination to her home safe, get the money out, maybe lock her in a closet, then leave. As you know, he deviated from the plan."

"Neither of you have told me why." Danya noticed that John's gun was pointed at Marcus. The tension seemed to crackle in the air. Something was going down among the ranks. Danya nervously tugged on her zipper.

"We owed a large sum of money to some dangerous people. And although you weren't broke, you and Gena were destined to be two extremely rich women with your dear Uncle Chris dying." John spoke her uncle's name as if it left a sour taste in his mouth.

"The people we owed money to weren't willing to wait until you met the requirements to receive your money. They wanted their lump sum. We paid them to keep them at bay until we figured out a way to get your money." Bally continued the story.

"If Mr. Brilliant hadn't decided to get some before going through with the plan, Gena would have been out of some money but still alive." John glanced at his watch as he finished his sentence.

Danya knew that John was tired of talking, but she needed to keep them talking anyway. If they turned on each other, it would make it so much easier for her. Even if that happened, it still wasn't going to be easy making it out alive. They may have turned on Marcus, but John and Bally were on the same team. One player out was better than three players in. She stalled for time, waiting for her Plan C to kick in. *Damn, keeping Marcus off balance was effortless compared to this.*

"I'm missing a piece of the puzzle, fellows. Why? You all had good jobs and bright futures." Danya sat back on the couch hoping they would relax.

John answered, "Every dime we made went to keeping us alive another day."

"Terry, you know what Marcus's excuse was for what happened that night. Do you remember that Bally?" John asked.

Bally nodded then responded. "Yeah, he thought he needed a Plan B."

Marcus shifted a bit as if he was strategizing his next move. John followed Marcus' movement with his gun as he walked over near where Rita was slumped in her chair. "Where raping Gena came into the Plan B, we have yet to figure out."

Bally looked at John and Marcus. "We need to handle this situation at hand and stop this stroll down memory lane."

"Would you stop pointing that thing at me?" Marcus yelled at John.

"For a smart man, Marcus, you sure have a tendency to do some stupid things. Was it in your idiotic Plan B to kill Gena?" John's voice had a slight snarl to it.

"If you hadn't fumbled your part, Gena wouldn't be dead. You had the easiest part. Keep Terry away from Gena's house. What was your excuse? Oh, I remember it. 'I missed her at work.' Yeah, that's a real good excuse." Marcus's tone became sarcastic.

John must have caught Rick shifting because he turned his gun back towards him. "How was I supposed to know that Terry left work early and went straight to Gena's?"

"I'm not so sure of that." Marcus tapped his gun against his thigh as if he was debating using it. "It made you a hell of a lot richer. It seems you're a man of many secrets. Maybe things would have been different if you told us that Gena left you …"

"What?" Bally's head snapped towards Marcus then John. "Richer …"

"What, Peter? You didn't know that John—"

"Marcus, I am tired of you," John said with venom seeping out of his voice.

Marcus immediately aimed his gun at John. Before he could pull the trigger, John shot him in the head. Marcus hit the floor with a thump. Rick shifted in his chair. Bally quickly pointed his gun at him. John and Bally started talking to Danya about how Marcus had become a liability that they couldn't afford so they had to rectify the problem. John aimed the gun at Danya's heart and gave her a wicked laugh.

"There were a lot of things he didn't know, now he'll never know." John gave Bally a look that indicated he knew what he was talking about even though Danya didn't have a clue.

"Yeah, one being that we paid the money back long before the police even picked him up. Since you told officers that weren't on our payroll that your husband did it, Marcus had to be the fall guy. We convinced him that they'd never convict him."

"We didn't lie to him about that, he was our partner after all," Bally stated. John closed his eyes and shook his head. When he opened his eyes again he glanced and nodded at Bally.

"Terry, that night you became a very wealthy young woman." Bally shot Rick before John finished his sentence.

"No!" Danya jumped up and yelled.

"Too bad you won't live long enough to be an extremely wealthy old woman," John concluded his sentence then pumped two bullets into Danya. Danya's body went flying back onto the couch then crashing to the floor with a thump. Her eyes fluttered. She didn't realize it would hurt so much. She watched them through the slits of her eyes trying not to breathe every time they looked her way.

"Make sure Danya is dead." He gave Bally his gun. "We need the bullets to be the same. That is not your police issue gun."

"No. I'll take Marcus's gun. Plant yours on Marcus." He wanted it to look like Marcus got one shot off before Rick killed him.

"Rick here is about to committed suicide." John yanked Rick from the chair.

Rick laughed at John glancing down at the gun in John's hand. "No one will believe it."

"It won't really matter if we make sure our boys are on the case," Bally informed. "This is a precaution for if we happen to have a rookie on the case."

The doors closed softly behind John as Bally went to the bar and finished his drink. He had a feeling he'd need a few more before the night was over as he walked over to Danya's body. Bally shook his head and aimed for her heart. Danya lifted both her legs, catching him off guard as he stood over her kicking Bally solidly in the thighs. The impact made a loud thudding noise as Bally's body hit the floor.

"You shouldn't have paused so long," Danya roared as she scrambled to her feet.

Bally scrambled to his feet but Danya knocked him back down. His gun slid under the couch. He tripped her with his feet, sending her stumbling. He punched her with every intention of doing bodily harm. Danya brought her knee up but he blocked his attempt. She tried some self-defense move then remembered he was a cop. Danya put the heel of her shoe into his foot, giving her a fighting chance. She got a few good punches in before he flung her over the couch. Danya rolled on the floor hitting her head on the coffee table. *Damn, I'm not cut out for this*, she thought as her head throbbed. Her chest was burning and her back was killing her.

Bally went over and grabbed her gun she'd sat near the bay window. She stood, grabbing for the halogen lamp, and yanked it out of the socket. He pulled the trigger. Danya laughed as she stepped around Marcus's pooling blood.

"Sweetie, what did you expect to do with an empty tranquilizer gun? I'd think you'd recognize the difference." She watched as Bally looked at the gun." I thought it best to keep Rita out of harm's way." Danya swung the lamp like a bat. The force of the blow broke the lamp when it made contact with Bally's stomach and knocked him against the window. Bally stood only to say hello to Danya's foot. She kicked him extremely hard, her heel sinking into his chest, sending him flying against the glass. Danya flipped off her heel.

"Catch!" Danya yelled.

Bally instinctively went to catch it, then she kicked again with such force it sent him through the glass. "Oh, did I forgot to tell you. I've been taking karate."

It felt as if she was watching him in slow motion. His face filled with terror as he became hysterical and his arms began to flail. The sound of the bay window glass breaking and frantic screams filled the room. Damn, there was a chance he was still alive since the window wasn't that incredibly high off the ground. If he was alive, it would be a shame she'd ruined a beautiful bay window for nothing. Danya looked out of the broken window. She shook her head. "Damn!" She heard rustling noises and low moans behind her; sleeping beauty must be awaking. Rita slowly opened her eyes and quickly closed them. *Oh lord, she was going to be sick. Keep it together. You need to get to Rick*, Danya thought as she hobbled over in one heel to untie her. She undid the bandanna first then the rope. Rita inhaled then exhaled and opened her eyes again.

"Danya, you shot me." Rita's words slurred as she checked for blood. There were red stains on her clothes but no blood on her hands.

"No, just knocked you out." Danya zipped up the bag of money, dropping it in Rita's lap. "Look, I need you to stay out of the way. Take this bag. My car's out front. The keys are taped to the inside of the front bumper."

Danya pulled Rita by the arm guiding her towards the door. Rita turned her head as she stepped over Marcus.

"Listen carefully. Use my cell phone, it's in the compartment between the seats and call the FBI. The number is on the dashboard on the back of a parking permit. Don't call them here. Call while you're driving back to the city. If you see John, either run like hell or run him over. Okay?" Danya didn't wait for a response as she pushed Rita out the door. She took off her other heel and walked over to look out the window to make sure Bally hadn't moved. Danya shook her head. *How in the hell did John and Rick end up underneath the window near Bally's body?*

Why did Rick run after John? From what she saw, John still had the gun. Danya stared out the broken window trying to see if they were still near the pool. Frustrated, she ran her hand through her short curls. When she became engaged, she did not think she was marrying a man who had a death wish. Danya went over to the couch and pushed it until she could reach Bally's gun. Grabbing it, she hurried up the stairs then exited the living room. On her way out, she flipped on the bay window lights. She wanted to see who was outside and where they were.

Danya ran down the hall, out the front door, then slowed to a trot. As she stepped outside she paused briefly to glance down the drive. She was relieved to see her car was gone; at least she didn't have to worry about Rita going off trying to get herself killed like her fiancé was attempting to do. She took off running in the direction she last saw John and Rick go. Danya had to get to Rick before that silly fool got himself killed.

* * *

John was glad Bally only shot Rick in the arm. They needed him to be the fall guy for Marcus and Danya's murders. He'd caught his fiancée in bed with her ex-husband then committed suicide. It would work as long as they didn't leave Rita's body there. John took off Rick's handcuffs and twisted his injured arm behind his back. They exited the room. John closed the door and guided Rick towards the bathroom. He was thinking the car but he didn't want to risk anyone happening by the driveway and seeing something. He wished he could have avoided killing Danya. Now he needed to find a way to get her assets and her company's assets before the police discovered the bodies. John's thoughts were interrupted by a thudding noise in the living room.

"What the hell?" John turned and looked in the direction of the living room.

Rick took advantage of his distraction and hit John square in the jaw with his good hand. The gun slipped from John's hand. As he tried to catch it, Rick knocked him over. The gun clinked as it made contact with the floor, then Rick kicked the gun out of John's reach as he ran for the door. Rick was heading out the door before John could react. There was no way he could get the gun without a fight. Rick must have known he didn't have the advantage.

"This man is about to piss me off." John retrieved the gun then ran, following Rick out the door.

Marcus just couldn't wait, could he? John thought as he pursued Rick. He had to come back to this house on the same date Gena was killed. Marcus could have waited one day; he knew John would have been back from his trip tonight. The plan was supposed to happen the next day when he knew for sure he would be back in town. No, Mr. Johnson couldn't do that. It had to happen on the anniversary of Gena's death. John's only consolation was that he didn't have to worry about Marcus anymore. If Trish hadn't called him, the situation could have been even worse, not that it wasn't bad enough. John wouldn't have rushed over if he thought Marcus could have pulled it off. All Marcus had to do was get the money from Danya and be on the next plane out of Chicago. He hadn't recovered from the shock that Danya shot Rita. Marcus should have stuck to the original plan. He knew what happened the last time he didn't follow the plan. Now John was running around, looking for a man that basically held his future in his hands. John didn't want to think about what would happen if Rick made it to the FBI. He knew if he was caught, he'd be spending the rest of his life in prison. All because Marcus couldn't stick to the plan.

The plan had been so simple. Danya would have a business meeting with a potential client that turns out to be Marcus. He'd inform her that he had Rita and wanted $5.5 million by three o'clock. She'd drop the bag off at a secluded location. Bally would be there to make sure she didn't try anything funny. John knew that Danya was never to be underestimated. Rita would be released. Officer Bally would inform Danya that Marcus had been caught and taken into custody. This was all to happen after John came back from his trip. That way, he could make sure Danya didn't call anyone other than Bally. Marcus and Bally would get on a plane to the Bahamas, then he and ...

A fist interrupted his thoughts as John slowed near the bushes to see which direction Rick went. Rick came out of his hiding place in the bushes, throwing punch after punch, most were from his uninjured arm. John didn't bother trying to fight back. He immediately grabbed Rick where he had been shot. John dug his fingers in and squeezed. Rick's teeth sank into his bottom lip to keep from screaming. He could taste his blood as it oozed out of his lip.

"How does that feel? Does it feel good?" John applied more pressure to the wound. "I hear this helps stop the bleeding." Rick cringed in pain, no longer able to bare it. His injured arm was twisted upward as he was pushed to his knees. John put the gun to Rick's forehead. The sound of shattering glass exploded in the air followed by a blood-curdling scream. John's eye shot up to see Bally as he released the item in his hand then began moving his arms frantically as he went flying out of the window. Bally's body hit the ground. John cringed as he heard the bones in Bally's neck crack.

John pulled the trigger. Damn. Nothing came out. He hit Rick, sending him back in the bushes. Rick's head fell inches away from Bally's empty stare. Bally's neck was turned at an awkward angle and red fluid dripped slowly out the corner of his mouth. Rick couldn't get up fast enough. John took off around the pool as he put more bullets into his gun.

CHAPTER FOURTEEN

On the grounds, Danya didn't see either John or Rick. At least she knew that they had run past the pool which meant that John was probably heading toward the bushes that lead to the next block behind them. The only lights on were the ones from the bay window, but they wouldn't do any good near those bushes. She raced around the pool, taking a quick glance at the light. It was strange. They no longer created an exotic picture in the pool. It was now a mass of colored lights with an occasional design here and there from the pieces of glass that were still intact.

Her thoughts went back to the situation she had at hand. Damn, John knew the grounds about as well as she, maybe better. Danya couldn't believe this was happening. All she wanted now was for her and Rick to get out of this alive. "Okay, think! The bushes are hard to get through because they make a very solid, thick barrier. A person would have to literally cut his way through to hit the back street. That's it. The shed!"

John was going to cut his way onto the next block. Danya remembered there was a space in the bushes that didn't need to be cut and it had a little pathway to the next block. Gena was going to put a fence around the perimeter with a gate door right there. She never got the chance to do it. Danya hoped that space didn't still exist. If it did, she prayed John didn't remember it. Either that or it has grown as thick as the rest of the bushes.

Danya started to wonder if it was such a good idea to turn the lights on as she glared into the darkness. She couldn't see much as she looked towards the shed. Anyone standing near the shed could see her without a problem. It would be easy for John to shoot her before she even saw him. *Too late now,* Danya thought as she slowed and neared the gardener's shed. She jumped as she heard a crash. Her breathing became rapid, her heart seemed to thump in her ear. She hesitated then she yanked the door open, letting it rebound off the shed. Her foot caught the door as the force of it hitting the shed was about to close it. No guns were fired when the door opened. She assumed it was as safe as it was going to get to go in. The gun went in first. Scanning the space, her arms swung the gun from side to side. She lowered it and looked at the back of the little metal shed. Danya couldn't believe her eyes. If she had any thoughts of being mistaken about them being here, there was no need. They'd clearly left their calling card. The back wall of the shed was gone. Danya had a feeling this was going to be one of those nights.

"It is likely to send me to an early grave," she stated as she ran towards the opening.

* * *

Rick followed John across the grounds to a shed made out of the flimsiest metal. The door made a clank on the metal as it closed behind John. Rick knew John had the upper hand and that he should go back to the house and call the FBI or something, but anger clouded his judgment. There was no doubt in his mind. John would shoot when the door opened. If he managed not to get shot and grab a hoe, rake, or something then he could knock the gun away. At least then he and John could go toe to toe, injured arm and all. The shed wasn't all that large, so how would he get in without getting shot? John had to come out sooner or later. Rick stood at the shed door. This was the only way. There was no back door. Maybe he should wait it out, and then what? What if John starting shooting through the shed. Rick slowly backed away. He decided to go back to the car and call for help. He was concerned that if he walked away he'd give John a chance to shot him in the back. He paused then realize John had his car keys. Since he didn't know who killed Bally, he had no interest in going back into the house to search for a phone.

Rick opened the door and entered, crouched down almost to the floor. John fired but his aim was too high. Rick was relieved that John wasn't willing to take any shot. The shed was dark. He attempted to look in the direction the gun was fired but he couldn't see John. His eyes weren't adjusted to the darkness of the shed. He wondered if John moved while he went for cover. Rick backed into a rake. He quickly grabbed it to prevent it from hitting the floor and then decided to use it as a weapon. John made the slightest of movements but it was enough to reveal his position behind the metal shelves. Rick instantly came around the shelf and swung the rake at John.

John was taken aback by the stinging blow. Rick swung again. John grabbed the rake, yanked it forward, then pushed it back into Rick's stomach. Rick grunted as he stumbled back, releasing the rake. John slammed the length of the handle into Rick's ribs. Rick went to his knees, his hand holding his ribs. John swung the rake quickly over his head but Rick jumped up. His shoulder connected with John's midsection sending them smashing into the back wall of the shed.

The wall collapsed from their weight. They crashed onto the grass on top of the flimsy metal. John had the wind knocked out of him and was stunned momentarily. Rick took advantage of John's dazed state, punching him repeatedly. His punches were vicious as he held John with his injured arm and punched him with the other. His hold on John was weak because of his injury. Rick noticed that John had managed to keep the gun during the fall. He wanted to wrestle the gun away from John before he fully recovered from the fall.

John hit Rick in his injured arm, but Rick refused to give John a chance to finish him off.

They wrestled, flipping each other over, each claiming the upper hand. John was on his one knee, attempting to hit him in the face with the gun. Rick blocked the blow. John stood and pulled Rick to his feet. Rick elbowed him forcefully in the nose. John's head jerked back then Rick hit him hard in the chest knocking him off balance. John's reflexes automatically sent his hands down to catch himself, causing him to lose his gun.

Rick swiftly stepped on John's hand with his left foot to make sure he didn't get the gun then kicked it out of his reach with the other foot. He slammed his knee into John's chest and started choking him.

John tried to pry Rick's hand away from his neck. Rick's grip got tighter. John could feel his air supply being cut off. He slammed his fist into Rick's arm, again and again. His hand was covered in blood. Rick banged John's head into the ground wishing it was concrete instead of grass but it was enough to stop John's vicious assault on his arm. Rick's fist connected with John's face.

John frantically looked around for his gun or some type of weapon. Rick was full of malice and rage, as he choked John until he was just moments away from taking his last breath. John forced Rick's neck back by getting his hand under Rick's chin and pushing. Instead of releasing John, Rick squeezed tighter.

John suddenly released Rick's chin then slammed his fist into Rick's face as it fell forward. The blow left Rick grasping for air. John shoved Rick off him. His eyes rapidly scanned the area then brighten as if he remembered something. John kicked Rick a few times then fled hastily to the bushes. Rick ignored the burning sensation as he crawled over to the gun. He extended one foot forward to a kneeling position and rested on the other one. At least this time he was in possession of the weapon. John was now a dead man. Rick aimed at the dark figure retreating towards the bushes. If John got to the bushes, he'd never get a good shot. It was now or never. He pulled the trigger.

* * *

Danya saw the piece of weak metal wall lying on the grass. John and Rick made sure she knew which way they exited. She slowly moved towards the opening, not wanting to take any chance. There was no way she could be certain this wasn't a trap. The last thing she wanted was to step out of the shed's new backdoor and get shot. She paused when she reached the back and peeped out. Danya stepped on the flimsy metal wall then onto the grass. There she saw just two shadowy figures that she knew were John and Rick wrestling a couple of feet away. She aimed her gun.

"Dammit," she mumbled.

She couldn't get a clear shot, besides, from where Danya stood she couldn't tell them apart. Danya was amazed at how similar they were built. She'd never paid attention to it before. Now she wished she had. Maybe she'd just shoot both and take the guessing out of it. Rick would never forgive her for that one. It was an insane idea anyway. Danya quietly moved closer trying not to make her presence known. All she wanted to do was get near enough to tell the two men apart then put a bullet into John. She didn't want to kill him unless absolutely necessary, only to detain him or slow him down.

Before Danya got close enough to the men, one ran towards the bushes while the other retrieved the gun and took aim. She didn't know if it was Rick or John running. If it was John heading towards the bushes, he'd get away. If it was Rick, she'd saved his life. Danya made a millisecond decision, sprinted to attack the guy kneeling with the gun. Before the guy pulled the triggered she lunged at him, the gun went off as Danya's body made contact.

His aim wavered as his body fell forward. He reached to catch himself with his left hand. He grunted in pain as his arm gave out and he hit the ground. Danya, off balance, struggled to not get flipped. She felt her body flipping over his back as she took a moment to take in who it was. Breathing heavily, he straddled her then aimed the gun at her forehead with his right hand with his left arm hanging painfully at his side.

"Danya! Are you trying to kill me?" Rick leaned back on his heels breathing hard but didn't lower the gun. Shock, relief, then happiness displayed on his face.

Danya was near tears. She was so happy to see him alive. "You're the one with the gun aimed at my—"

"Drop the gun!" the voice yelled from behind them.

Rick brought his arm down to his side then let the gun dangle from his finger before he dropped it. Danya looked over her shoulder. Her eyes filled with relief as she saw two men and several further away running in their direction. Rick slowly moved off her as they commanded, turning slowly, his movement jerky. He reached to hold his injured arm.

Danya sat up. Terror replaced the look of relief in her eyes. One of the two men aimed his gun at Rick. She opened her mouth to say something to the men. Her words were drowned out by gunfire. Rick turned as if he was attempting to shield Danya. He was hit before he made it completely around to face her. His body jerked as the bullets penetrated his skin. He looked at her for a split second before his body fell forward.

Tears made a steady trail down her face as she watched Rick's eyes get that same blank look as Gena's six years ago. His body fell onto her with a slight thud. Danya immediately rolled Rick onto his back as the men stepped closer with their guns still trained on Rick. Tension filled the air as the agent realized his mistake. As she applied pressure to his wounds, she could hear the agent say, "I thought he was trying to go for the gun."

This couldn't be happening again, she thought as she fought to keep it together. This was the second time tonight that her back up plan ended up being one of her worst nightmares.

"Get an ambulance, now!" Danya violently pushed the guy away and told him to help. Danya pointed the other agent in the direction John disappeared. "You go after John. He just went through the bushes a few minutes before you arrived. Get your asses moving or I'll be wearing your behinds as leather boots! You hear me. Move it, idiots!"

They stood there for a minute stunned at this woman barking out orders, but Danya gave them a deadly, searing glare. They took off after John. A few other men arrived in time to hear her angry commands. Four other men took off in the direction Danya pointed while the other agent went for the ambulance that was already on its way.

This was John's fault. She'd be damned if she was going to let him get away. She wanted him caught, dead or alive. Right now, she couldn't care less. Two FBI agents stayed behind with more running across the lawn, but Danya ignored them, placing her full attention on Rick. She leaned her ear close to his mouth; to her relief, he was breathing. His eyes opened and closed every so often. She only prayed that the bullets missed all major organs. "Where is that ambulance?" she screamed.

"Don't you die on me! I am not going to let you get out of marrying me that easily!" Rick made a weak attempt at smiling as Danya kissed him on the forehead. She sat on her heels trying not to cry when she noticed Rick's lips moving. She assumed he was trying to say something and leaned closer to his lips to hear.

"I love you." His words were barely audible even with her ear pressed so close to his lips. Danya looked into his eye. Rick's eyes fluttered rapidly as her tears hit his eyelids.

"Dammit Rick, you can't die on me!"

The paramedics drove onto the grass to get to the victim. They got as close as they could. Danya moved away from Rick to give them room to work. She wiped her hand on her dress knowing that wouldn't remove Rick's blood from them.

Agent Waller came down from the house after being informed of what happened. He frowned as he watched the paramedics put the stretcher into the ambulance. Danya was not too far behind. She paused in front of Waller who stood near the doors of the ambulance.

"If Rick dies and John gets away ..." She didn't finish her sentence as she got in the ambulance. The paramedic reached down to give her a hand.

The trip to the hospital was a blur for Danya. She hated that Rick was taken to the nearest hospital. She would feel better if he was at one of Chicago finest, but Rick was in no condition now to be taken there. She knew that. Maybe once he was in stable condition, it could be done. Danya knew it was crazy not to want him in this hospital, but two people she loved had already died there, six if she counted her parents and her baby. She did not want to add one more to the list.

Rick was listed in critical condition, but he had a fighting chance. She stared down at her hands. Rick's blood was no longer on them. She glanced at her black dress. She knew his blood was on it. To anyone else, it just looked like wet spots because the red color couldn't be seen, but she knew that it was there. She didn't know who she'd become if she lost Rick.

* * *

Rita got the key and threw the bag in the trunk. She looked around and got into the car. The key was shaking in her hand as she started the car then pulled off, driving down the curving pavement to the street. This was crazy. She had no idea how to even get to the expressway. At the end of the drive, she just picked a direction and drove. Rita looked at all the mini-mansions to see if she recognized anything. She drove straight for a couple of blocks then made a right turn and another right. Her hands were shaking so badly that she had to pull over and park the car in an attempt to pull herself together. She glanced around trying to see if there was anything familiar from when Marcus brought her here.

"Yes!" She sighed her relief. She spotted Marcus's car a half a block up which meant she was on the street behind the house. Rita remembered Marcus parked there and made her go through the thick bushes to the house. She examined the places where the bushes had snagged her clothes. Rita leaned forward to look in the rearview mirror at the small scratches on her face remembering how Marcus pushed her through a small opening in the bushes. She leaned back into the seat not liking what she saw in the mirror. Her eyes were blood shot, her face looked grimy, and she looked twenty years older than she was. She held her hands in front of her. The tremors had reduced themselves to only small ones even though she felt she was seconds away from losing it. It was the worst feeling in the world, not knowing what was happening.

"If I wait here maybe the police will pass by or maybe I'll hear their sirens when they go to the house. Just keep it together until then. No nervous breakdown, okay? Just keep it together until you know what's happening."

Rita couldn't get the image of Marcus lying in his own blood only a heartbeat away from her feet. Then there was Danya. "I can't take this! I need to know. No!" She put the car in gear. "Don't be stupid. Wait a few minutes after the police arrive and then go back to the house."

Rita put the car in park staring in the mirror again. She was in no condition to drive. She was jumpy, jittery, and frightened. "I can't take this. I need to know."

The street was dark with only the lights from the houses to see by. The car was in park but still running. Maybe it wasn't a good idea for her to be sitting here. Rita knew she was being paranoid but she was nervous and scared. She had no idea what had gone on in that house. Now someone she loved was in danger. Rita cried over the steering wheel.

Not even a full five minutes passed before Rita decided she'd waited long enough. She put the car in drive and pulled off. The car rapidly picked up speed and suddenly a dark figure ran into the street right in front of the car. Rita's heartbeat quickened as she slammed on the brakes. The car didn't want to stop. The tires came to a screeching halt. Rita felt a weird tingle go through her body as she put it in park then rested her head on the steering wheel as her body began to tremor.

This was too much. Rita felt like she could still hear the sound of the brakes shrieking and the tires fighting to grip the ground even though sound had ceased. The car had only stopped centimeters from the person at the rate she was going. She lifted her head. The person's hands were on the car as if he could have actually stopped it. Rita's heart rate was beating rapidly and her breathing became erratic. She didn't even think to call the FBI until she glanced over and saw the parking permit slid forward on the dashboard when she hit the brakes. She leaned her head back onto the seat with trembling hands, feeling the thumping of her heart through her chest.

* * *

The bullet whizzed past John's ear. An inch closer, it would have been his ear, or worse, his head. He couldn't think about that now. He had to find the space in the bushes. John staggered down the slight grass slope right before the bushes. He ran along the fence of thick bushes but couldn't find the pathway. It wasn't that far from the shed. It had to be here. He went back in the direction of the shed.

"Yes," John said as he found it. The bushes had grown out quite a bit but he could still make it through. John knew once he made it onto the next street, he'd need to get out of sight quickly. He decided to run to the house across the street. The chances that someone would be home were fifty-fifty. He had no choice but to take a chance. If someone was home, he'd tell them he needed to use the phone to call the auto club. The bushes scratched and clawed at his clothes as he forced his way through. He came out of the bushes running onto the sidewalk then between the parked cars into the street. He turned and froze as two headlights began bearing down on him. His face filled with horror as the car seemed not to want to stop.

John turned to see the headlights bearing down on him. He was momentarily paralyzed. It was a moment too long as the car narrowed the gap between them. The smell of burning rubber penetrated his senses. The car didn't want to stop. His body wasn't doing what his mind said. Run! He felt the car's bumper against his legs. John's hands went out as his screams stuck in his throat.

John stood there stunned with his hands on the center of the car as he watched the driver lay her head on the back of the seat. Her eyes were closed and her hand was over her heart. *Rita.* John looked again. Things were falling into place after all. He moved closer to the driver's door. At least he didn't have to break the window. Her door was unlocked. When the car door opened, she jumped. "Move over!"

Rita seemed to be in shock. She didn't move or say anything. She just stared at him. He was surprised too but he knew he didn't have much time. John pulled her from behind the driver's wheel and walked her to the passenger side. He rushed back to the driver side and got in. John put the car into drive. He peeked over at her, her whole body shook uncontrollably. John reached over and buckled her in only giving her a sideward glance. She started shaking and crying. John glanced in the rear mirror to make sure no one had rolled up on them.

CHAPTER FIFTEEN

There was no way Agent Waller could get around his bad judgment call. He should have kept Agent Stevenson with him. Waller had known his agent had been jumpy lately but it had never affected his performance on the job before. This was one time Waller wished he had left Agent Stevenson behind. Waller maneuvered through the scurrying hospital employees. The sound of beeping machines and the smell of disinfectants invaded his senses, reminding him of his rookie mistake. Waller lingered a moment before he approached Danya who sat in the hallway leaning forward in her seat with her elbows resting on her lap and her head in her hands. He lowered himself into the chair next to her without uttering a word. She didn't even bother to lift her head.

"I already told you what happened at the house. Several times, I might add. You already gave me your lame excuse for what happened and why John's not in custody. I know Rita is missing and John may have her. So, in fact, I already know that you've messed up big time. What more do we have to discuss?" Danya's words were sharp but delivered with a calm tone.

Waller didn't speak as he observed her. This woman had a rough night and he didn't want to rub her the wrong way. He was awed at this black woman's intelligence, her quick and clear thinking. Most people would have panicked in situations like these. She was a serious danger to him. Danya Holmes had his butt seasoned and ready for the roasting. If Rick died and he didn't get John behind bars, Waller knew she'd throw him into the fire without the frying pan. Danya wanted someone to pay. If it wasn't John, Waller was next in line. The negative press would almost ensure her success. He had people watching both John's and Danya's place hoping for John or Rita to make an appearance.

Danya glanced up. "Still here?"

Waller was glad looks couldn't kill. He hated that Danya's cell phone had been cut off. They knew Rita headed back towards Chicago but then the phone was cut off. Without the cell phone, they couldn't track Rita and John couldn't even attempt to reach out to Danya unless she was at home. "We figured John may try to contact you if he has Rita. We need you to be available for him to reach."

"You must be out of your mind if you think I'm going to leave this hospital!" Her back straightens up as she issued a deadly scowl.

Waller needed Danya home in case John reached out to her. John probably had no clue Rick had been shot again. He wasn't crazy enough to let her know when John was captured his sentence would not be what she imagined if he cooperated. They were after the man they worked for. She stared at him waiting for a response. He began to speak, "Well ..."

"Yes, doctor!" Danya popped up from the chair, preventing Waller from saying anything else. She scurried over to the doctor who told her that Rick was now in serious but stable condition. Both the doctor and Waller tried to convince Danya to go home. They both offered to call her if there was a change in his condition. The doctor informed that Rick lost a lot of blood and even though he had no broken ribs, they were severely bruised. The doctor went on to explain about Rick's gunshot wounds. Waller watched as Danya listened intensely.

Danya's face was full of concern as she asked, "So, he is going to make it?"

"I can't answer that right now." The doctor looked at Waller as if to say you know the routine. Waller nodded, completely understanding.

"Why?" Danya's voice hardened.

The doctor held the tablet to his chest. "I would just rather not say one way or another just yet. But, we'll be keeping a close eye on him and running a few more tests."

"Then I'll stay until you can give me some definite answers." She went back and sat down in her seat.

Danya refused to leave Rick at this hospital despite the doctors continuously telling her that there was nothing she could accomplish by staying. Waller didn't interject much. He thought any commentary from him would make it worse. Danya explained that the only way she'd go home was if Rick was stable enough to be transported to a hospital in Chicago. Other than that, there was no way she was leaving. If Rick's condition changed for the worst, he could be dead before Danya made the drive back. Waller prayed he was in good enough shape to be moved. Unfortunately, the doctor didn't recommend moving Rick to another hospital.

"That's fine. I'll stay here." Danya tilted back in the chair and closed her eyes.

Both the doctor and Waller looked at each other flustered. Waller needed Danya at home so if either Rita or John called, she'd be there to answer. If Rita was too scared to go home and John didn't have her, Waller knew he had a big problem on his hands. John could be anywhere, on any plane, if he didn't have anything tying him here. That situation would make it harder on Waller and that was a predicament that he knew he didn't want to be in. Waller knew he was wrong for praying John had Rita but that scenario increased his chances of tracking John down. He needed to be able to tell Danya that he had John in custody. Danya wouldn't sweep the incident under the rug unless either he or John paid for what happened to Rick. Waller thought back to the conversation he'd had with Danya when they first arrived at the hospital.

"You idiot. Why in the hell did your man shoot Rick? He'd dropped the gun." Waller made an attempt to answer but she cut him off. "Don't give me that bull! I'm not hearing you. You were supposed to be there to help, not shoot my fiancé, all while John escaped through the frigging bushes."

Danya stepped closer to Waller, stood on her tippy toes, and grabbed him by the collar. She yanked the 6'5" massive man down to where his slightly crooked nose just about touched hers. "If Rick dies, you'll have only two choices, either John Davis pays or you do. No ifs, ands, or buts about it. There's no way he's getting away with this. Do you hear me? There's no frigging way that this night is going to slip through the cracks of the justice system."

Waller attempted to step away but she violently pulled him back down. He decided it was best not to aggravate her but if she had twisted his collar any tighter he'd need a doctor or a lawyer.

"Don't make me get physical with you. I'm not playing! Your man messed up and I'm bringing somebody down. You may be meaner than a Pitbull, uglier than a Rockweiler's back side, and bigger than a Mac truck, I don't give a damn! I'll annihilate you as if you were a toy solider. Somebody will be brought down to their knees for this. If I were you, I wouldn't try me because you'll be taking a beat down for more than just yourself."

Danya eyed him up and down, released him, then gave him an evil stare that would send chills down the devil's spine. "Oh yeah, there is going to be hell to pay. For your sake, make sure it's John who's paying." She gave him a feeling that she wasn't making an idle threat as she turned and walked away.

Waller was in total shock to have this female not only threatening him but actually get physical with him. Most men would back down from him because of his sheer size alone, not to mention the deadly scowl that usually graced his face. Yet this woman, no taller than 5'7", bare foot on her tippy-toes with torn stockings and hair all over the place, without enough weight to be pushing any man, let alone one of his size around, was in his face like she was twice his size. Not to mention she looked as if she was about to do some serious bodily harm to him. From the condition of the house, he didn't want to cross this woman or even try her for that matter.

Waller brought himself back to the present conversation. He had no real leads. John was his best chance to make a case against them stick. They were working on getting all the appropriate papers to go to Mystic Fashions to go through John's office hoping to find the link that leads to their actual target. With Rick shot, he wanted to cover his behind. The last thing he needed was Danya claiming that she didn't give permission for them to search John's office. Waller and the doctor left Danya sitting in the hall while they talked. Waller asked the doctor if he could get Rick to a hospital in Chicago and discussed the risks they'd be taking by doing so. Waller strolled out of the doctor's office back to Danya. She leaned back in her chair when she saw him coming.

"Let me guess, you pulled a few strings," she stated, smugly. "When will Rick be moved?"

Danya insisted that Rick's car be brought to the hospital so that she could get home. Waller told her that one of his men would take her. He should have known better. Her response was none too pleasant.

"You must be on some serious stuff. You think I'm about to get in the car with any of your idiotic agents. They need to be finding John instead of playing chauffeur. I already warned you about the cost of not finding him. I have nothing else to say."

It was a good thing we found Rick's car keys on the lawn, Waller thought as she scowled at him. Danya wasn't giving him even an inch, making him fight for every single inch he got. Damn, where could John be? Waller wanted him found and found now. Trying to save this case, his behind, and Rita was going to give him gray hairs. Waller hadn't mentioned to Danya that they planned to question her receptionist Mary and her assistant Trish. She had enough on her plate.

To Waller's relief, Rick made it safely to the new hospital. His condition hadn't gotten any better but at least it had not gotten worse. He even got a promise from Danya that after the new doctors ran and got the results of their tests she'd go home and get some rest. Now his fingers were crossed that John would contact her.

* * *

John kept within the speed limit as he drove to Chicago. All he needed was to be pulled over. He'd be arrested in an instant. After a call from Trish came in, he turned off his and Danya's phones. There was no going back to his apartment. That's the first place they'd look. While his place had a private entrance, he couldn't risk going near there until he had a plan in place. The cops were probably patrolling the area. There were some important items that he required from his apartment, like certain files, flash drives, and other documents he had taken out of his safety deposit box at the bank. He needed some personal things, too.

"Dammit!"

Rita jumped at the sound of him banging his hand against the steering wheel.

He turned into the parking lot of the building. John escorted Rita into the elevator up to Marcus's condo. He was happy he had Marcus's spare key on him. It was a relief knowing Marcus always kept guns handy in a cabinet near the door. John opened the drawer and got what he desired before Rita could even turn to see what he was doing. Rita was in front of John as he lightly pushed her in the direction of the bedroom. John planned to keep an eye on her.

Danya will be expecting Rita home. When Rita doesn't show up, she'll be worried. John smiled. He'd leave Rita occupied in the condo then he'd call Danya once he got a disposable phone. John decided to make her go to his apartment and get everything he needed in trade for Rita's safe return. It sounded like a plan to him. It was late, he was tired, and he needed some sleep. He was not exactly thinking clearly. John decided it would be wise to get some rest. He would handle things in the morning.

John's sleep wasn't peaceful. He got up earlier than expected and got to work after checking on Rita. He had considered asking Trish to go but quickly ruled the option out. He would have to use Terry for the one last time as he hung up the phone. He knew he could get into his apartment unseen but he didn't know the extent to which they were watching his building. Were they watching the entrance, or were they in his place searching for clues? Besides, other things required his attention if he were to get out of here in the next twenty-four hours. Terry picking up the items he needed at his apartment was the solution to his problem. It was a risk but he was willing to take it. With how well some of those items were hidden, he knew it would take her awhile. Even if the FBI had searched his place by now, he doubted they'd found anything. John smiled as he entered the building where he was meeting with an associate. He'd glanced at his watch. *I'll have plenty of time to finish taking care of business before I need to get back,* he thought as he approached his associate.

Time had passed quicker than he thought. John hadn't finished making the necessary arrangements. He asked his associate he'd been meeting with could he have a little privacy while he used the phone.

"Trish, hold on." John turned to make sure his associates had left the room then pressed the button on his phone. "I'll be on my way soon but Danya will probably beat me there." He didn't speak for a moment as he glanced again at the door and pressed the button on his phone again. "Okay?" He went over a few details to make sure she knew what he wanted her to do.

"John, should I release—"

"No, don't do that." He cut her off knowing what she was about to ask then told her exactly what he wanted her to do. John was feeling good as he hung up the phone. He hoped this would go off without a hitch but he was preparing for it not to. He hoped she didn't blow it. This was their last chance—do or die.

* * *

Danya sat in the waiting room as they got Rick settled into his room. She called the apartment to make sure Rita went home. Danya was hoping that by some miracle Rita made it home safely and she'd have one less person to worry about. The phone kept ringing and ringing until voicemail picked up. She checked the voicemail, there were no messages. Danya hung up. The doctor wanted to check her out and she agreed to let him after she made the phone call. She knew that all they were seeing were dollar signs but she wanted to be sure she didn't have any internal injuries. At the other hospital, she had refused care. Since she felt better at this hospital, she might as well get checked out. Besides, they were intent on sending her home to get some rest and that was the best way to stay a little longer.

By the time Danya made it to her apartment building, the sun was coming up. She was a bit incensed that the FBI followed her home. Danya didn't think she needed baby-sitters, especially ones that couldn't do their jobs right.

She headed for the shower upon entering the apartment. It only took a few minutes fiddling around before Danya stepped into the warm running water. The drive home gave her plenty of time to think. There had to be at least one more person working with them. Danya couldn't get that thought out of her head. It was just one of those thoughts that kept nagging at her. It could be Rita. She was supposedly dating Marcus, or maybe it was Trish. She and John have been working a lot of late nights together. Those two had been very secretive lately, ending conversations as soon as she walked into the room.

"Dammit! It could be anybody. Another Officer Bally for all I know." Danya leaned forward letting the water rush over her hair and onto her face. She did not want to think about it. Frustrated, she took her hand and pushed the hair off her forehead, slicking it back. It wasn't over and she knew it.

This was like a nightmare that she couldn't wake up from. She wanted to cry so badly, to let her tears be rinsed away by the flowing water, but she knew she couldn't risk an emotional break down until it was over and done with. If she broke down now, she wouldn't be able to pull herself together in time if anything else went down. Grabbing her shampoo bottle, she squirted some into her hand and began lathering her hair.

At first, she didn't hear the phone ringing because she was rinsing out her hair. It wasn't until she brought her head from under the water did she hear the persistent ringing. She decided not to answer it. By the time she made it to the phone it would probably stop ringing anyway. Danya quickly changed her mind thinking about Rick and jumped out of the shower. She took an oversized towel off the shower rack and wrapped it around herself, tucking it in at the top. Danya then grabbed a smaller one and wrapped it around her head as she did a swift trot to the phone. She held the towel on her head with one hand as she reached for the phone with the other. She picked up the receiver then cursed at it. Whomever it was had just hung up. She dialed the number the doctor gave her. He happened to be in his office but he hadn't been the one calling. Maybe it was Rita calling. The caller came up unknown. She would have to wait until the person called back.

The shrilling of the phone woke Danya up. She must have dozed off on the couch when she was supposed to be blow drying her hair. She answered the phone groggily. Danya wasn't surprised to hear John's voice coming from the other end. Before she knew it, she dressed, grabbed a few things, and headed for John's apartment.

CHAPTER SIXTEEN

John instructed Danya not to let the FBI follow her. No one would recognize her dressed the way she was, especially since she kept the hair in her face. She wore a wavy wig, wicked, black high heel combat boots, black leather gloves, and a black outfit. As she walked the hall to the door her heart raced as she wondered if this was John's attempt to put her six feet under. She hesitated, debating her decision to come alone. Yes, she brought protection, but she didn't know what was beyond the door. Would John really kill Rita? The image of John shooting Marcus formed in her mind and she knocked at the door.

As the door opened, Danya was shocked, at first, then truly pissed off. She strolled into the luxurious condo feeling mixed emotions. She'd hoped that she was wrong about her theory but it proved to be correct. Danya didn't want to believe it. When Rita answered the door with a gun aimed at her, Danya had no choice but to believe. Rita, her roommate that Marcus and John in two separate incidents had supposedly kidnapped, was a key player. Rita snatched the bag out of Danya's hand and told her to sit on the couch.

"John wanted to see you before we left." Rita closed the door and nudged Danya with the gun towards the couch. "I have no idea why John insists upon talking to you. Personally, I think it's best if he lets me kill you then dispose of your body later."

"If you say so."

"Don't even think about screaming for help." Rita smirked. "We are the only people on the entire floor. Marcus purchased this whole floor and remodeled it as one unit."

Danya lowered herself down onto the couch. "After sitting in prison, I guess it's to be expected."

"Marcus never went to prison, sweetie. Bally made sure of that." Rita cackled as she sat on the back of the love seat across from her. Rita's feet sank into the cushion as she rested her elbows on her legs keeping the gun aimed at her.

"You have got to be kidding me." Danya's mind was blown. All this time she thought he was serving time for murdering her sister and he was living in this lavish condo.

It took her a minute to recover and realize Rita was still talking. Danya focused on listening to her as she talked about how she hoped John wouldn't let Danya live because she'd always be a threat to them.

Rita's words sounded calculated to indicate John's plans for her were good. However, Danya saw a glint of doubt in Rita's eyes as she tried to make it perfectly clear to Danya that John would be back to take care of her. By the way Rita sat, she was scared to get too close. Clearly taking out Peter Bally had changed Rita's perception of her abilities. Rita examined Danya closely.

Danya wondered if the way she dressed reminded Rita of anyone. The outfit and wig were definitely inspired by Rita's style.

"What's with the leather gloves?" Rita continued to assess Danya's outfit with her eyes.

Danya's bracelet slid down over the wrist of one glove as she extended her hands towards Rita. "I didn't want my fingerprints on the things John wanted me to bring."

"Really?" Rita rolled her eyes.

"Hey. If he doesn't make it out of the country, I didn't want the FBI knocking on my door because you two lied and said I was involved. You are leaving the country?" Danya raised her eyebrow at Rita knowing she wasn't even about to answer that question. "Since we have a few minutes before John gets here. How do you fit in?"

"Let me reintroduce myself. My full name is Sharrita Tiara Drew," she paused slightly then said, "Davis or simply Mrs. John Davis if you prefer."

Danya was shocked, but she didn't want to let Rita know that. She made sure that her mouth didn't drop open at Rita's married name. The heel of her boot dug into the floor to keep her calm. The best way to handle all this was to remain cool. Danya ran her tongue over the front of her teeth. "Mmm. So how long have you two been married?"

"Eleven years. You know Danya, in college John was always talking about you two." Rita spoke as if she was choosing her words carefully.

Danya wondered if she was scared John would kill her herself if she told her the wrong thing. The uneasy feeling permeated her chest as the reality of the position she had placed herself in hit her. "That is interesting since he never mentioned you."

"John had no doubt that his little sisters would be making money hand over fist with or without their inheritance," Rita said, ignoring her comment. "His million dollar women."

"His million dollar woman, huh? When did I become his million-dollar fool?"

"Never. He had a real soft spot for you and Gena since his mother made sure that he kept a close eye on you two." Rita's eyes shifted towards the door. "He felt like your big brother. He never wanted to hurt you or Gena. John actually loves you, you know?"

Danya wondered what was so important among the things that she collected that John couldn't leave without them. They had $5.5 million in cash; they could have gotten new passports. "If that's love, I can do without it."

"Let's not get into that, okay? John knew if he was in a pinch, even if you were broke, that you would figure out a way to come up with the funds needed, simply because you were like brother and sister. It's just that he also knew that if it wasn't legit, you wouldn't get involved. Anyway, our business got into a little trouble."

"What were you? Their girl decoy?" Danya laughed then smiled wickedly knowing that Rita hated when people thought it was her attractive features that got her ahead in her career. "The woman whose looks distract the males and make them forget their real reason for meeting you. Were you the girl Friday, or were you just their female flunky, hmm?"

"None of the above." Rita frowned. "The four of us were business partners, equal partners."

"Whatever." Danya leaned back into the cushion of the couch. If Rita got too comfortable talking then it might be easier to temporarily put her out of commission before John got there. She wanted to have a private conversation with him. Rita would just complicate things.

"Now I understand why John convinced me to go with you as my roommate after I told him we got along great but I was considering someone else." Danya remembered she'd decided to get a roommate. She'd realized she'd shut herself off from the rest of the world. That was the best way she could think to come out of seclusion without getting shell shocked.

"Lucky for us you were sleeping through life." Rita glanced at the clock. "My brilliant husband felt this was a perfect way for us to keep an eye on you and still see each other. You definitely needed to be watched just in case you remembered your hospital stay."

"What was there to remember about my hospital stay?" Danya sat forward then stated, "I was sick."

Rita cackled, "Something like that."

"You haven't told me. What was there to remember?" It hit her in that moment she was a fool to come there alone. Had she not learned anything from meeting Marcus? Danya shifted in her seating thinking of that fact that John had already put two bullets in her. Rita seemed unaware of her sudden panic.

"See, Marcus decided to visit you in the hospital to converse for a few. John walked in on the tail end of what Marcus was saying and didn't like what he heard."

That statement caught Danya's attention and she had a flash of memory. Danya had been so sick that she could hardly stay awake. It was difficult for her to tell reality from her nightmares. Marcus had been quite talkative that night. He told her that at the appropriate time John would have the nurse stop drugging her. Then John would give her some wonderful speech how she couldn't let Marcus get away with murder. Danya acknowledged that Marcus had divulged some relevant information with a simple shake of her head. Things that she definitely was not supposed to know about. Even though her memories of what went on that night were still hazy, she now knew the extent of her knowledge would have destroyed their plans.

"Did you enjoy your nap yesterday?" Danya asked, thinking she should have used a real gun on Rita.

"Did you know what a wreck I was when I woke up? I had no idea how to get to the expressway. You know my sense of direction stinks. I found two of my partners dead. And the only reason I knew John was alive was because you told me to look out for him. See, we didn't know for sure if the FBI was on to John but we didn't want to take any chances. That's why we had to use our ace in the hole, Marcus, to get the immediate cash we needed from you. John placed the majority of our funds in a bank somewhere else. We knew we couldn't touch our personal funds, they'd be all over us. We couldn't have that but don't worry about it. We've got all the details taken care of now."

"The FBI could easily trace that."

"Not if someone clears the account out and gets the cash. Then that someone gets on a plane and joins us. I wasn't sure about the FBI until you gave me that FBI agent's number. That's when I knew we were in hot water." Rita got off the love seat and moved sideways, keeping the gun trained on Danya. She smirked as she retrieved something out of the cabinet. "You'll probably find this funny. I almost ran John over with the car when he rushed out of the bushes into the street. I was so messed up that I didn't know it was him until he opened the car door. There I was worried about becoming a widow, and I almost ran him over. You see, my husband is my whole world, my heart."

Rita moved back in Danya's direction. "I can't imagine being without him. It was different when both of our lives hung in the balance. I could deal with that. The thought of losing him made me an emotional wreck."

Danya watched her features become distorted with anger. Rita spoke through her teeth. "I shouldn't have had to go through that." Venom filled Rita's voice as she spoke then her features returned to normal. Rita was now standing next to her legs. "John is going to have to forgive me for this. He's just taking entirely too long."

Danya was wondering what the point was in telling her all of this. She was also confused as to what John had to forgive Rita about. Did she miss something? She didn't think she had. It wasn't until Rita dropped the tranquilizer gun into her lap that she understood.

"Stand up!" Rita yelled.

Danya looked down then up at her. "What's this for?"

"We're about to have a dual, me near the front door, you near that end of the coffee table. At the count of three, we shoot," Rita instructed as she chuckled.

"Not bloody likely, not with this!" Danya threw the gun up at Rita. She jumped up catching her off guard and struck her. Then grabbed the back of Rita's head and began repeatedly banging her face into the hardwood table.

"Stop," Rita screamed, trying to grab at Danya's hand.

"All these freaking years, I've considered you a friend. I should have laid your pitiful soul to rest when I had the chance."

Rita reached up at Danya's hands trying to scratch her but she got nothing but glove and bracelet. That didn't work. Danya continued to bang her face into the table. Rita couldn't tell if the sound was just her face hitting the table or the sounds of the bones in her face crushing. Her blood was all over the table.

Rita locked her elbows, preventing Danya from slamming her face again. That worked but it pissed Danya off. She flung Rita onto the floor. Rita slid under the table crashing into the back legs, sending the lamp tumbling onto Rita's arm and then it rolled against the front legs of the table.

"I'm glad Marcus was never much for carpet." She grabbed Rita by the legs pulling her from underneath the table.

Rita fought to reach the lamp that lay only a few inches from her as Danya brutally beat her. Rita's relief was great as she finally had the lamp in hand. She hit Danya over the head bringing her brutal assault to an end. Rita scrambled for the gun but she was forcefully yanked by the hair. Her arms began swinging hysterically at Danya. She grabbed Danya's hair but all she got was a fist full of wig. The wig hit the floor. Danya twisted Rita's arm behind her back and Rita's beautiful long hair was scrunched up in her fist. She pushed Rita towards the wall.

"You want to know how I felt ever since the night Gena died." She threw Rita against the wall. "It felt like I hit a brick wall." She hammered Rita's body into the wall again and again until Rita's blood was splattered on it. The sound of Rita's body being pounded against the wall echoed through the room. "That's how I felt every night after that. Then I find out my friend, my roomie of almost three years, was a major player in my nightmare."

Rita's body went limp in Danya's hands. She let go of Rita and let her slide to the floor. Rita looked at her with her face all bloody and battered, her eyes begging for mercy. Danya reached behind her back into her waistband. "This time it ain't no damn tranquilizer gun." She could almost taste Rita's fear.

Rita's eyes widened, not at the sight of the gun, her focus was on the silencer. She started scampering backward. "I'm sorry. It doesn't have to be this way." She pleaded slowly as if it hurt to speak.

"Earlier at the house I forgot my new motto, come strong or don't come at all." She shook her head. She pulled the trigger, sending a bullet between Rita's eyes. Danya's head snapped towards the door as she heard John twist the key in the lock.

He opened the door to Danya putting a second bullet through Rita's heart. He whipped out his gun and shot at Danya but she was behind the chair before he could even fire.

"Honey, you're late but I'm glad to see you brought your silencer. We wouldn't want to disturb the neighbors." She assumed there was some below them that already heard the fight. "Oh, John as you can see, I already had the pleasure of meeting your lovely wife. I'm so heartbroken that she had to die at such a young age. And her face ... What a waste of beauty." Danya shot at John even though she knew she wouldn't hit him. It was the ability to move that she wanted. She swiftly backed up into the other room.

"You know, I was planning to be sitting in that chair instead of hiding behind it. I wanted to be the first thing you saw when you walked through the door. You would have been staring directly into my weapon of choice. I would have made you strip down to your birthday suit to assure no hidden weapons. I even had a little speech in mind. You wanna hear it?"

John advanced slowly. "You didn't have to kill her."

"I was going to have you turn your back to me and say, you now know how it feels to stand butt naked before a friend, exposing your soul, your heart of hearts, only to be shot in the back. I guess you know how that story ends. You would have been ass out in more ways than one." Danya moved along the wall opening the door to the kitchen. She moved to position herself to get across to the dining room.

John walked along the side of the wall using his gun to lead the way. He moved cautiously as if he was trying to ensure that if he stepped out she couldn't get a clear shot of him. His eyes closed as he walked around his wife's lifeless body. "Terry, why don't you come out so we can talk?"

"I'm sorry to inform you, I'm not in the mood to get shot. I'm no longer your foolish puppet. I've cut those strings that had me dancing to your tune." Danya entered into another room when several bullets whizzed by her. John came around the corner shooting. She returned his gun fire with some of her own, sending John back around the corner. Danya took the clip out her pocket and reloaded.

"It's nice to meet a man that can keep his wedding vows, to death do you part." Danya started firing then shouting loudly. "Dearly beloved we are gathered here today on this sad occasion to say goodbye to a loved one, Sharrita Davis. She was a low down, conniving, lying, back stabbing bi—"

"Shut up!" John shifted to move but her bullets were a steady rain and he moved back.

"Don't interrupt me! How does it feel to know your flesh and blood killed someone you loved? But you're still one up on me because I'm not talking about Gena. I'm talking about my uncle and your father, Chris." Danya opened and closed the bedroom door then stepped across and entered the closet across from the room.

The room went silent as Danya reloaded and waited. He slowly entered the bedroom that she had been heading towards. The bedroom door crashed opened at the impact of his kick. John jumped to the other side of the door as if he was expecting bullets to come flying. He slowly entered the room. Danya came from behind and tapped him on his shoulder. When he turned, she slammed her fist into the side of his face. She swung her leg around and kneed John in the gut, then she pounded her fist into his back sending him to the ground. His gun hit the floor as he extended his hands to catch himself. Danya quickly picked up his gun.

"It's nice to know I have what it takes to bring a grown man to his knees." Danya twisted his arm around his back, holding it firmly in place then put the gun to his temple. If John tried anything, the opportunity would cost him a broken arm.

John cringed as she applied pressure to his arm. "This is not you. Don't do this Terry."

"Stand up." Danya tugged John upright, placing the gun at the base of his skull.

John walked in the direction Danya pushed him, the living room. He tried to make a deal with her. If she let him live she could take his three deceased partners' share of the money. Danya laughed. Money wasn't a temptation for her; she had more than enough. John began rambling on about the past, reminiscing about the things they used to do. He was frantically trying his best to pull at her heart strings. Danya stood in front of Rita's body. She pushed John down to his knees then released his arm and turned him to face her. The swiftness of the movement caused John to catch himself with both hands. She immediately jammed the gun in his mouth as he opened it to speak.

"I'm tired of hearing you talk." Danya squatted in front of him with her back to Rita and her feet solidly placed on John's fingers and knuckles. A single tear streamed down his face as he watched her finger on the trigger.

"How touching." She took the thumb of her free hand and wiped away the tear.

"You made me feel good today John, knowing that not only did I bring a grown man to his knees but I also made him cry. Do you have a dying wish or any last words? I guess not." John's head moved from side to side as she moved the gun. She glanced back at Rita as she debating whether she was going to pull the trigger. "I guess you had to have loved her to be married for eleven years. Maybe it helped that some of those years you didn't live together. You know, keeping that same excitement about your relationship y'all had in the beginning. You know after all you two have done for me, or should I say to me, it will be my pleasure to make sure you die together. It's the least I could do for you."

The reality was she couldn't let him live because she knew without a doubt he wouldn't let her live. If she miscalculated an attempt to knock him out, she was good as dead. She had no idea if there were other guns in the house. If she used her gun to get out the door, there was no guarantee that he wouldn't grab another gun and follow her out. Danya pushed John to where his butt rested on his feet then pulled the trigger. John's body went limp, but Danya would not let his body hit the floor. She grabbed him by his shirt. Her other hand picked up his left arm. Danya shifted her weight back so that she could release his shirt and still keep him up. She took the gun and placed it in his hand then wrapped his finger around the trigger. She held his finger in place with hers then put the gun back in his mouth. He was back on his heels when she let him fall.

Through a steady stream of tears, she walked over and picked up the wig she'd lost in the fight. She went over to Rita, placing her gun in her hand, then pulling the trigger a few times. If the FBI tested Rita's hand for gun powder they'd find it. She was about to clean out Rita's nails with part of her belt buckle until she realized that her DNA couldn't be under her nails. Rita had scratched her gloves. After that Danya took Rita's gun and replaced it with John's on the floor where Rita had lost it. Looking over the bodies, Danya knew that the FBI would be able to tell the wig hairs from Rita's hair but that would just have to be evidence that was inconsistent with the crime scene. The thought of actually going to prison because of them after all they'd put her through seemed wrong.

CHAPTER SEVENTEEN

The bag that Danya came to Marcus's condo with was what she left with. She pulled off the gloves then wiped her tears away as she walked several blocks away from Marcus's building. She hadn't thought her plan through. When John suggested she wear a hat to ensure her face wouldn't be recognized, she decided to bring the wig and a different outfit to wear. Her mind didn't conceive she would need a different outfit to return to John's apartment. The clothes she had on earlier were at John's. There was no way she could wear this outfit back. After walking far enough away from the building, she hailed a cab to the small mall in the nearby suburb. She walked into a store, bought an outfit and shoes with cash. The wig hung over her face the entire time. Although she knew from a conversation when she was there earlier in the week the security system was out and was supposed to be fixed next week, she didn't know if they managed to move up the repair appointment. Danya went into the restroom. Once in the stall, she pulled off her entire outfit and stuffed everything into the shopping bag.

After leaving the mall, she walked a couple of blocks putting the shopping bag in a donation bin. Danya kicked herself in the behind for not staying and calling Waller onto the scene. Now it was too late; it would be difficult to prove that she didn't go there with criminal intentions. What they had done to her gave her motive. The way she beat Rita looked more like blind rage than self-defense. *Damn, Danya, you should have let Waller handle this,* she berated herself as tears welled up in her eyes. She caught a cab to the mall near John's apartment building. The mall and the apartments were actually in the same building but there were two heavy glass doors, which were locked when the mall closed, separating the apartments from the mall. Danya attempted to go in the way she came out but a janitor was blocking John's discrete entrance.

There was a huge crowd of people heading to the apartments in the elevator from the mall and Danya hid among them. She needed to get to the alternate route he'd given her. She was thankful for the rush of people, especially for the two black women with similar hair color and style as hers. Danya made sure to walk in between the two women with her head slightly lowered and moving her lips every so often. The tape from the security camera wouldn't show her face, only three friends that were running their mouths. The camera wouldn't pick up that the women were actually talking around Danya. Her pulse was racing and her mouth went dry as she noticed the FBI agents scanning the halls. She continued to act like she was with the other women, then glanced back, doubting that the agents in the lobby paid any attention to her. They were looking for John. The elevator doors opened with the up arrow lit and the black women entered which meant Danya would have to get on to not draw attention and get off on some floor to go down but it didn't happen that way. The first person to get in the elevator pressed the parking ground button. Everyone else got in pushing buttons for upper floors but they wouldn't stay lit up. People that stood in the back of the elevator loudly called off the floor number they needed. It wasn't until the doors closed that everyone realized they were going down.

"What dumb bunny made the elevator go down?" the elderly woman near the front shouted.

"I did," answered a cocky man in an expensive, gray, three-piece suit. "You have a problem with that?"

The elderly woman waved her cane at him. "You knew when you stepped into the elevator it was going up."

"Yes, I did." He sneered. "That's why I made sure I was the first one to press a floor."

The guy and older lady argued until he stepped into underground parking, ignoring the angry yells from behind. Danya pushed through the crowd and exited the elevator behind him. Danya walked close to the wall until the doors closed then took the maintenance door near the elevator to access the door to John's private elevator. She headed up, quickly peeling off the coat that she had on because it wasn't what she was wearing when she came in. Danya changed back into her original outfit she had on when she entered John's apartment then stuffed the new outfit, along with the wig and the bag she had taken over to John, in the suitcase. She paced John's apartment for a while debating if she should come clean with Waller now or continue to cover up her crime. Danya grabbed the suitcase and exited John's apartment. Her eyes scanned the crowd but no one was paying her any attention. She walked over to Rick's car and unlocked the door. It was back to the apartment for her.

Once she was inside her apartment, Danya opened the suitcase. She took out the shopping bag and zipped it back up leaving only John's things. The contents of the bag were emptied on to the couch. Danya deposited the wig, gloves, outfit, and boots she had worn in a plastic bag then she went to the closet and pulled out the oversized purse she usually carried. She stuffed the bag into her purse. Danya zipped up the oversized purse. After that, she folded the shopping bags and put them in the closet with the other ones that looked like them.

Danya called the hospital. After inquiring about Rick's condition, she asked had the FBI agent left. The doctor said he'd left but he'd come back looking for her. She waited a few minutes while the doctor got him on the phone.

"Agent Waller."

Danya dipped her head as she spoke, "John contacted me."

"Yeah, we had that feeling when we followed you into the underground parking in his building. What took you so long to call us? What were you doing in his apartment that took so long to come back down?" Agent Waller sounded like he suspected she was up to something.

"John claims that he has Rita," Danya replied, not knowing if her guilt was reading more into his tone. "All he wanted me to do was go to his place and pick up some items for her safe return. I left as soon as I hung up. John said that he'd call me there around that time to tell me what he wanted. Once I found where he'd hidden the spare key, the phone was ringing. He gave me the list of things. A lot of time passed before I found some of the things. I'm supposed to be heading over there now." Danya knew everything was true except for that last sentence. She rattled off the address of Marcus's condo then she asked should she go over there.

"Don't go over there," Agent Waller commanded. "We did some checking on Rita. She's John's wife."

She tried to sound as if it really was new information to her without sounding fake. "What?"

"Look, I understand it's a shock. What I need you to do is meet my men in the lobby and give them the items. I'll get a few men to head over to the address." He mumbled as if he was talking to someone else in the background.

Danya dumped the contents of the bag into the suitcase. Then put the bag she'd taken over John's into her purse. "Is it alright for me to go see Rick?"

Waller said that was fine. Danya went to the lobby and handed off the suitcase then headed to the hospital.

* * *

Agent Waller entered the condo knowing he wouldn't like what he found. The local police were on their way. Seeing it felt like when he arrived at Gena's house. His partner walked around trying to assess the situation without disturbing too much evidence. Waller stood, staring at the bodies. He took several pictures of the scene with his cellphone when he noticed something near the couch. He stooped down, took a plastic bag out his pocket, and picked up a bracelet. He studied it and then slid it into his pocket.

"Did you find something?" his partner inquired as he reentered the room.

Waller shook his head. "Nothing. What have you found?"

"Besides the two remaining suspects dead and a whole bunch of theories on what happened?" he questioned as he glanced over at the bodies.

"Yes, besides that." Waller's mind was trying to figure out how in the hell did Danya's bracelet get there. His mind was trying to recall if he'd seen it on her wrist at the hospital.

His partner snapped his finger. "Waller, shouldn't we head to John's. Clearly, if Danya retrieved all those items after we had been through his apartment, it warrants another look."

"Yeah," Waller replied, distracted. He followed him out the door after speaking to the local police who had finally arrived.

There is a lot of things about this case that doesn't make sense, Waller thought. He wondered if Danya was withholding critical information. Besides the bracelet in his pocket, they could not prove that she was in Marcus's house since he couldn't recall whether she had it on. How did they not see her leave John's apartment building? He centered his thought. The first thing he needed to do was focus on catching the guy

John and his crew was working with. He'd check into Danya later to see if she was a woman caught in the crossfire or if she was an active participant.

* * *

Danya approached the main hospital desk and picked up a visitor pass. The walk to get to the elevator seemed extremely long. Every time someone glanced her way it felt like they knew what she had done. Her guilt increased with every beep to indicate they were one floor higher. The doors opened and she gave a fake smile to the nurses at the nurses' station as she entered Rick's hospital room. He was still unconscious. His face had gained some of his normal color, but not much. Even when he got shot and was rushed to the hospital, he never looked as frail and helpless as he did now. She sat the balloon on his table along with the card, then she pulled the chair next to his bed.

"Rick, I called your parents. They should be here before visiting hours are over."

Danya made that call before she got rid of the items in her oversized purse. She crumbled up tissue paper in her purse to give it the same fullness it had before she got rid of its contents. She didn't know who was keeping an eye on her, but it would have been obvious to any person watching that her purse was empty. There was no way that she could be sure that the FBI wasn't following her. To people around her, she looked upset over her fiancé but Danya was jumpy, edgy, and paranoid for other reasons too.

At first Danya couldn't decide where to get rid of the stuff. That's when she decided that the best place was in another mall which is where she stopped before coming to the hospital. Danya went to a store that she knew didn't have electronic monitors in the dressing room. Before doing that she picked up some tissue paper, a card, and a balloon. Once she entered the store, she picked up the items she had in her bag. She went to the dressing room, pulling out the items from her purse. She crumbled up the paper and put it in her bag. She left the items with the tags on it along with her stuff in the dressing room. Getting rid of the shoes proved to be a difficult task. She picked up a few shoes off the rack and sat them near the bag that held her shoes. She had to knock over the bag so she could pull the shoes out as she picked up the other shoes.

The salesgirl gave her a funny look. "Can I help you?"

"No. No. I'm good." Danya fumbled with the shoes, looking at the sizes. "Just looking for shoe options for my bachelorette outing."

"What sizes you need?" she asked as she reached for a pair of the shoes that topple from Danya's pile.

Danya glanced at her watch. "I'm sorry. Could you put them back? I've got to get going."

The salesgirl mumbled curse words at Danya before giving her a fake smile and taking the shoes, never realizing that she had an extra pair. "Sure."

"I'm really sorry. I need to get to the hospital." Danya picked up the bag with the get-well soon balloon attached to it.

The salesgirl gave her a sympathetic look and said, "I hope your friend feels better."

Danya thanked her. She headed to her car hoping that if agents were following her, the balloon would be explanation enough of why she had stopped by the mall.

Danya stopped thinking about what she'd done earlier as she stared at Rick. He was all that she had left in a sense. She may still have her company and her money but he was the only person that she loved who hadn't betrayed her. After they were married, he'd officially be the only family she had left.

"Damn you, Rick. You can't die on me!" She leaned closer to his face. "You hear me? Baby, you're my heart. If my heart stops ..." Tears ran down her face making a home on Rick's cheek. She traced his face with her hand. "I love you."

Visiting hours would be over soon. Danya sat there holding Rick's hands waiting for his parents to arrive. There was a chance his parents wouldn't make it since they had to be called away from their convention that was out of town. She felt bad about not calling sooner but it couldn't be helped. The last few minutes she'd been thinking a great deal about their wedding. Rick always hoped that they'd have a good marriage like his parents.

"I decided that if you really don't want to rush our wedding, that's fine; whatever you want." She hoped in the back of her mind that he'd wake up and answer her.

"Why couldn't you have listened to me when I told you to stay away, huh? The voicemail specifically told you not to come. Would that have been so hard for you to follow instructions? I guess we'd better scratch the word obey out of our marriage vows." She laid her face against his hand she held tightly. "Baby, I need you. I need you to open your eyes, to say hi, and tell me you love me." Danya sighed and closed her eyes. The doctor said physically Rick seemed to be getting better. All his vital signs had improved. It was the fact that he hadn't woke up that wasn't good. He and his colleague went over the test results and there's nothing in them that explained why he had remained unconscious.

"I am so sorry that you're here. It should be me laying there. Yet, I don't even have a broken bone." She lifted her head to look in his face. "If you're pissed off with me, it's understandable. I don't care about that as long as you're alive. You can yell, scream, and shout just don't ... I'm not even going to think it. You are going to be alright."

Mr. Cameron cleared his throat. Danya stood, sitting Rick's hand softly back onto the bed. She moved around the chair and wiped her face with the palm of her hand before she greeted his parents. After telling them what the doctors had said, she left the room to give them some privacy. Danya walked down the hall away from the door and leaned against the wall.

That's the position Agent Waller found her in when he came to talk to her, leaning on the wall with her head back and eyes closed. He didn't give any specifics when he told her what had happened once they got to the address. Waller told her from the crime scene it looked as if John killed Rita then himself. Waller kept looking at her wrist as she spoke.

It was in that moment she realized she left evidence behind. She had to resist the urge to touch her wrist. Danya had been debating turning herself in but she couldn't bare not being by Rick's side during his recovery.

Her attention went towards the commotion in the hall. Mrs. Cameron frantically ran out and got a nurse, bringing her into Rick's room; the doctor wasn't too far behind. Danya took off running down the hall before Waller could say anything else. Danya's blood warmed with fear as she reached the door of Rick's room and her body began to shake, dreading what she might find. From where Danya was, she could see Rick's mother was crying and very distraught. "Oh, God! Don't let Rick be dead." She entered the room then lowered her head and sobbed.

CHAPTER EIGHTEEN

Danya was in shock as she sat on the front pew with the family. The whole service was a blur. Before she knew it, she was standing in the cemetery with her heels digging into the moist dirt. She stood there with a blank expression on her face and listened to the moaning and crying of the grieving. She couldn't be burying him, that wasn't possible. It didn't seem real but it was all too real. She was surrounded by a sea of black. The despondency hung in the air threatening to choke the life out of the living. His family sat in the chair right in front of the casket, crying as it was lowered into the ground. She couldn't even look at them. People walked around dropping flowers onto the descending casket. She felt someone's arms around her, moving her in the direction of the cars. Being here at this cemetery, Danya couldn't help but think about all the events that led up to her standing there. The person repeatedly asked her if she was okay but she didn't answer him.

"He was a good man and a hard worker, I know. We'll all miss him. My heart really goes out to you. If you need anything ... Are you sure you're okay?"

Danya noticed the older gentleman standing next to her but really was looking behind him. Her mind was elsewhere. The preacher's words, 'ashes to ashes, dust to dust,' kept repeating in her head. She finally responded to the person saying, "I can't handle going to the house with the family. It's just too much."

"The family will understand but they'd really like it if you made it." He handed her a few tissues. Danya tried to stop crying but this was a reminder that she didn't have any family left and all the reasons why.

It was raining and the wind had picked up by the time she reached her destination. She stepped out of the car only to be assaulted by cold raindrops. The wind pushed her sideways causing her to lean and walk hard against it. The rain had a little sting as the wind whipped it across her face. Danya didn't mind. It was sort of refreshing and maybe it would wash away those feelings that weighed so heavily on her. She wasn't ready to deal with her feelings right now. Danya went into the building. As she entered the elevator she said to herself she wasn't going to cry. She wasn't. She leaned against the wall of the elevator after it ascended and shook out her black leather trench coat. In frustration, she ran her hand through her hair, a habit that she'd developed over the last few months. The doors opened and she walked slowly down the hall, her heels clicking loudly against the floor. She entered and took a seat.

"I'm back," she announced, looking down at Rick. "How are you feeling?"

Rick opened his eyes and took her hand. "I should be asking you that?"

He looked much better. His skin tone was returning to normal. "I'm not the one that had three slugs pulled out of him, losing a lot of blood in the process. Not to mention being unconscious for—"

"I get the point. Now all I want to know is when am I getting out of here. I've been here what seems like forever." Rick slowly sat up. "Personally, I think they're keeping me here for the money."

"It's probably because you're an odd ball case, at least that's what the doctors said." Danya got up, piddling around, avoiding Rick's eyes.

"Odd ball! I'm insulted," Rick joked.

"Well, those weren't his exact words." She returned to her seat next to him. "Anyway, it doesn't matter. He'll be releasing you soon enough."

Rick grabbed her hand. "How was the funeral?"

"How do you think?" She slid her hand out of his and poured him some water. "I really shouldn't have been there. John's family knew what he'd done to me. Not only had he betrayed me, but he had also tried to kill me."

Rick frowned, took a sip of the water, then put it back on the table. "Some of his family know?"

"It was only out of respect for his family that I went." Danya thought about the ones that were good to her and had no clue to the devastation he caused to her life. "I was really tempted not to go, but I laid a guilt trip on myself that made me go. I can't believe that the bodies were released to the family so quickly. But then again I don't really know how the FBI works."

"Baby, you have no reason to feel guilty." He lifted her head so she was looking at him instead of his chest.

Danya gave him a blank stare. "There's still a lot I have to tell you. I had to be there."

"Danya—"

"Don't ask! Anyway, I couldn't handle going to the house with the family. That was too much." The guilt of killing them was eating away at her. She popped out the seat straightening the magazines on his table.

"Why are you acting like it wasn't a double funeral?" Rick shifted in the bed. "John wasn't the only one buried."

"Compared to John's, Rita's was insignificant. I knew her only for what, three years, whereas I knew, loved, and trusted John all my life. Look, I'm through talking about it, okay?" Danya gave Rick a stern look that said the conversation was over.

Rick agreed.

Danya stood and sat on the edge of the bed then leaned over and whispered into his ear what she was going to do to him when she got him home. He attempted to convince her he was up for it now. She replied that she would rather have him crying out in pleasure, not pain.

"I'm about to head home and change. I wanted to see you before I did." Danya's body straightens up. She smiled like everything was okay but her heart was breaking. It was looking more and more like she wouldn't be nursing him through his recovery. She could not live with the guilt of what she'd done.

Rick held her hand. "Are you all moved into my apartment?"

"Yeah, something like that. Once Rita's family clears out her things then I can sell or rent out the place." Danya took her hand back. "Umm, I need to head out."

"So soon?" Rick gave her his best sad face.

"I just wanted to stop by quickly before I went to my meeting." She shoved her hand into her pocket.

"You okay?" Rick asked.

"Yeah. I'm fine." She leaned down, kissed Rick goodbye, and exited the room.

Danya was trying her best not to lie to him but she was not ready to tell him everything. Besides she still had a few things she needed to figure out herself. Her fingers were crossed that she would have it all figured out by the time he was released.

* * *

Danya peered over at the envelope on the passenger seat as she pulled into the parking lot. It was unbelievable that Marcus was still bringing drama to her. She had asked Agent Waller to meet her at Mystic Fashion. It was a good thing he agreed. She couldn't bring herself to go to his office. Picking up the envelope off the seat, she thought about Marcus's letter to her in the envelope. The one thing she could say Marcus was right about was if she'd known it was from him, she wouldn't have opened it. The package had been messengered to her office with only her address on it. Had John not been dead, the information in the envelope would have sent him to prison. She grabbed the rest of her stuff and got out the car.

"Good afternoon, Ms. Holmes." Agent Waller greeted her.

Danya's shoulders jumped slightly. "Agent Waller, I'm glad you could meet. Here's the envelope I was talking about."

Waller grabbed the envelope, opened it, and perused through the documents. "You told me over the phone that John was planning to use your rejected designs to start his own business. But he's dead so none of this matter."

"You may want to look at those documents closer." Danya grabbed the envelope. She pulled out a piece of paper and several photos of John meeting with a man. Marcus had written big boss on the back of several pictures with different names even though it was the same man in all the pictures. One of those names was associated with John's new company.

"Oh damn." Waller studied the pictures. "Thank you very much. This may be the break we need."

The fact was John and his crew was a means to an end for the FBI. They were looking to hook a bigger fish. Danya felt a tinge of guilt as Waller thanked her before walking away. Who was she to want someone else to pay for their crimes when she was not willing to pay for her own? Danya drove home deep in thought.

CHAPTER NINETEEN

Danya was excited that Rick was finally out of the hospital. It was her pleasure to pick him up and bring him home. As she dropped his bag at the door and stepped back to let him enter, part of her begin to dread what she knew would come next. *Enjoy the moment,* she said to herself as Rick smiled at her as she patiently waited for him to clear the door. She locked up then picked up his bag as he did his old man stroll across the room.

Rick stopped to turn on the stereo before continuing to his room. Danya walked passed him, sitting his belongings on the dresser. She stood there and stared at him as he started putting items from the bag into the drawers.

Rick must have noticed Danya had only brought a few things over the way he glanced back at her. She wondered if he realized that most of the clothes she'd put in the drawers were items that were technically his she'd taken from him. Danya would find a pair of jogging pants of his that she liked then tell him, "Thanks." When he asked, "What for?" she'd say, "For the jogging pants of course." That would be the last time he'd see them unless she was wearing them.

"Don't you think that you should get into bed and stop messing around?" she asked him with a stern, motherly tone.

Rick smirked as he slowly sauntered over to the bed and climbed in. Danya took off his shoes and pulled back the comforter for him. After getting him comfortable, she went and washed her hands and started cooking. Rick complained about the hospital food, so she decided it would be nice to cook for him. The food took longer than she thought to prepare.

"Danya, you have this apartment smelling all good. Will I be able to eat some time in this century?" he yelled from the room.

"It's not ready yet." She gave him the same reply she had when he asked the previous three times.

Rick huffed. "Unbelievable! I think this torture will require you to make it up to me in a special way."

Danya laughed and finished cooking.

They sat down at the table, ate, and talked about insignificant things. Rick tried to get her to talk about what happened but she refused to talk about that on his first night home. Danya was buying time before she had to do what she thought was best for the both of them. She sent Rick back to bed and started clearing the table. By the time she finished putting up the leftovers and washing dishes, Rick was knocked out.

Danya got up early the next morning before Rick. She was having trouble sleeping. She didn't want to think about what the day had in store for her, all she wanted to do was exercise. She worked out for a good hour and a half in front of the television before deciding to stop. She was about to grab breakfast but decided to check on Rick first. His eyes opened as she entered the room.

Rick propped himself up against the pillow then reached for

something. He must have realized that he wasn't on the side of the bed with the night stand next to it.

"How's the patient this morning? Feeling okay?" Danya stared at his bare chest that held the white bandages. He was lucky the bullet that went in his arm didn't exit through the other side, if it had ... Then it would have entered his chest doing some real damage. She could feel the tears come on so she stopped thinking about it.

"Just a little battered, bruised, and sore but fine and dandy. And, I feel up to hearing what you have to tell me." Rick smiled.

She couldn't believe he wanted to have that conversation right now; he'd just woke up. Danya thought she'd at least have a few more hours left before they had this discussion. But the countenance of Rick's face let her know he wasn't going to let it go this time. Danya eased down on the bed then handed Rick his watch from the night stand. She scooted closer to him as Rick slid over and rested his head on her chest. Danya wrapped her arms around him. She began telling the entire story from the point where he got shot to what happened at Marcus's condo, even how she got rid of the evidence in the store and everything that Rita said.

"I don't understand. If you thought Trish was involved, why did you dress like Rita?"

"It was split second decision. I needed an outfit that was different from the one I wore to John's. I figured John had to have had another partner. Yes, at first I thought it was Trish. She and John had been working late in the office together and when I tried to reach her to tell her what happened, she wasn't in. She was nowhere to be found at home or at work." Danya told him about the picture with Trish, Mary, and Marcus. It turned out that Mary and Trish were at a networking event when the picture was taken. Danya could only assume that Marcus was there to pass something off to John or as an attempt to get information from them about her schedule.

"Why didn't you say something before?" Rick grabbed his water and took a sip.

Danya pretended not to hear Rick's question and continued to talk. "Later, I found out that Trish had gone to visit her ex-boyfriend in Indiana. Besides, I could never pass for a white girl."

"Rita became your roommate to make sure you didn't remember what Marcus told you about John killing your uncle." Rick grimaced as he shifted positions.

Danya assumed John told Rita about the ad she'd placed for a roommate. He probably told her the best ways to improve her chances of being selected. John hadn't understood why she wanted a roommate when she could afford to live there alone. Danya was only trying to take small steps towards being social again. When it had come down to Rita and one other person, John pushed for Rita. He used the fact that she traveled for her job as a plus to getting adjusted to living with a stranger. She had no idea she'd let the enemy into her home. The fact that she used a private investigator that John recommended was the key reason that she did not discover that Rita was married to John until it was too late. Sometimes she wondered if things would have played out differently had she decided to live alone.

Danya shook off those thoughts and returned her attention to Rick's comment. "I had no idea that Aunt Kesha had told John the truth prior to my uncle's death though. Marcus never explained how John killed his father. All I know is that she finally told John that he was Uncle Chris's son despite her promise."

She wasn't sure how much of Marcus's story was true. According to him, John tried to convince her uncle by suggesting they have a paternity test done. He believed if Uncle Chris had hard evidence that he was truly his son that he'd be written into the will.

Rick asked, "Do you know how long he knew before he approached your uncle?"

Danya shook her head. "His problems would be solved if he could have gotten his father to write him into the will. He and his partners wouldn't have had to go through with their plans. But my uncle, the stubborn man that he was, wouldn't agree to it. Anyway, when everything was said and done, Uncle Chris ended up dying of what the doctors say was a heart attack." Danya didn't think anything of it because he was terminal.

His face crinkled with his deep contemplation. "Do the FBI have any idea about your involvement in Rita and John's death?"

"Waller is suspicious." She shook her head thinking about her putting her gun in Rita's hand. They had both been shot with the same gun and none of the wounds looked like suicide. Clearly, she had watched one too many movies. "There are few inconsistencies in the crime scene but there's not enough hard evidence pointing to me. Especially since they are my alibi."

Rick leaned towards her. "How did you get out without being seen?"

"John had a private entrance that is hard to find that lead out to either the mall or the parking level. Of course, there are no cameras in those particular areas. I was given specific instructions on how to avoid any cameras on the street," Danya explained.

"For all they know you were in John's apartment when it happened," Rick stated as if he was relieved.

She stuck her hands in her pockets, shrugged, and dipped her head low. "They saw me go in but they didn't see me exit the building." The wig she wore out the building hung over her face to assist in the concealment of her identity if she accidentally stepped into the cameras' line of sight.

"Babe, I ..."

"I even left the supposed ransom money at the condo. I brought everything I took over there back. I can't think of any evidence that would point to me being involved except maybe switching guns with Rita." Danya touched her wrist knowing there was one more thing that could tie her to the scene.

"What?" Rick's voice filled with concern.

"Let's just say I wasn't thinking clearly when I put my gun in Rita's hand and took hers." Danya couldn't write a story in her head that made them both dying by the same gun make sense. If she'd put her gun in John's hand, maybe they would have thought it was a murder suicide. Whatever theories they were forming would not make complete sense unless she had lost her bracelet there. It made her wonder if they were coming for her. "It's complicated, okay? But, both our guns were obtained by illegal means. I doubt they could trace it back to me."

Danya wondered how Marcus, Bally, Rita, and John would feel knowing that the clause in her uncle's will that claimed she couldn't touch her money was a lie. It was true that her uncle was about to put it in but she made a deal with him. She wouldn't let Marcus touch her money for a maximum of ten years but would be allowed to invest her money any way she pleased until then. The lawyer upon reading the will, read it as if the clause was actually in there. Only Gena, the lawyer, and she knew it did not exist. The business part of the imaginary clause was her way out of the lie if she felt that Marcus proved he really and truly loved her before the ten years were over. Marcus failed the test right when she'd began to believe that he wanted her and not her money. Uncle Chris's only clause was that no one but Danya or Gena or the lawyers could handle Danya's money and upon Danya's death, it either went to Gena or charity. At first she didn't think it was necessary, but her uncle told her if Marcus did prove to be after her money he could be desperate enough to kill for it. Danya, at the time, didn't believe Marcus would do something like that, so what harm would it do to have that clause in the will?

Danya kissed Rick on the forehead. She doubted he even knew the extent of her wealth. From the story she told him, he knew she was rich. He didn't know between her parents, her uncle, and sister's money, plus what she had earned on her own, she was extremely wealthy. Running her fingers through his wavy, dark brown hair, she sighed. She wondered how he would feel knowing she had more money than him and his parents combined. Her riches weren't from her inheritance from her uncle and the investment or even her business. It was mostly because she had a little sister that didn't play when it came to making money.

"It's odd after thinking something else to find out that John killed Gena. He knew she'd figured out he was involved." Tears formed in her eyes as she thought about everything. "When Marcus visited me in the hospital, he told me Gena didn't die from her wound. She died by lethal injection administered by John."

Rick sat up slowly as he heard her voice tremble. Danya's face crumbled and tears started flowing like someone forgot to turn off a water faucet. He couldn't do anything but hold her in his arms until her sobbing reduced itself to sniffles. He kissed her forehead, wiping away her tears. "I've been meaning to ask how you survived getting shot."

"I thought I was going to step out of my door and be gunned down so I had someone make me a bullet proof jacket."

"Why hadn't I ever seen you in that jacket before that night?" Rick asked as Danya rubbed her tears off his chest.

"I knew I had gone overboard. That was the type of craziness that got people killed. So, I left the jacket in the package and placed in the back of the closet. The jacket was there until Marcus told me he had Rita."

Rick opened his arms to let Danya move. She got off the bed and walked over to the dresser then turned and leaned on it. Rick looked at her, not understanding why she moved. "As I said I thought I had gone over the edge but I couldn't return the gun. I knew how to use it but I didn't want to have to."

"From here on out remember we are a team."

Danya's head dipped as he spoke.

"I didn't think I was capable of murder. Funny, huh, considering. Anyway, with enough money, you can get just about anything. Which is why I ordered the sleeper gun. I paid handsomely to have the tranquilizer gun look as close to a real gun as possible. I wanted the strongest tranquilizer that would knock a person out immediately and slow the heartbeat without killing them." She looked away from Rick as she failed to mention that depending on the body mass of the person there was a slight chance it would be slow acting. It was the reason she shot Rita instead of Marcus. She couldn't risk it being slow acting on him and giving him a chance to go for his gun. "I kept it at my bedside. I figured no one would be intimidated if they thought it wouldn't kill them."

She replaced her real gun at her bedside with the tranquilizer gun, that way she could shoot first and ask questions later. Danya knew it was dangerous, especially if she got in a situation where the other person had real bullets. It was a risk she had been willing to take at the time for two reasons. First, she didn't want to get nervous and end up shooting an innocent person. Second, she didn't know if she could actually pull the trigger if it was a real person and not some paper target. She'd be more apt to do so with a tranquilizer gun.

"Ironic, isn't it? I can't believe how sadistically I murdered them. I beat Rita's face in so badly they had to have a closed casket ceremony. I showed neither of them any mercy. Once you strip away my excuses and John's reasons for killing, we're the same."

"How?"

"We're both cold blooded murderers!" Danya's eyes dropped down towards her feet to avoid Rick's. She twisted her engagement ring around her finger with her thumb. "I'm no better than John. I did the same damn thing he did to me, all under the pretense of the survival of the fittest, 'only the strong survive.' But, I came on a little too strong."

"Baby, you did what you had to. It was you or them." Rick reached for her but she stepped back.

Pain must have hit him because he didn't move for a second. He took a couple of breaths. Danya checked the time and grabbed his bottle of painkillers, handing it to him. "It's not that simple. I murdered them without mercy, without sympathy, not even a drip drop of compassion. I may have been a murderer due to circumstance but I didn't think I was a

murderer at heart. Yet, when you look at the facts, I killed three people."
She held up three fingers. "Out of three of them, Bally was the one I
showed the most mercy for. I knocked him out a window!"

"Remember if they had not come after you then it would have never
happened. It was one of the extremes." He opened the bottle taking out
a pill.

"I'll be an excellent role model for my children—a murderer, a cold-
blooded killer. Oh, children if they come after you don't even bother
to think of another way out, just blow him away. It's just one of those
extreme situations. Rick, you know that crap won't flush! It's pure bull.
What I did is not that easily excused. Bally's murder on some level I can
accept as an extreme."

Rick popped the pill and washed it down with water then said, "It
was self-defense."

"It's Rita and John's murders that are giving me hell. Dammit, I
should have let the FBI handle things. No, I couldn't do that, could I?
I went over there by myself. What, did I think by some miracle that I'd
knock on the door and find out this was all some kind of sick joke? That
John and Rita had only gone temporarily insane and that they're better
now." Danya stalked over to the bed and hit the mattress with her fist.

"Babe ..."

She pointed her finger at Rick. "You want to know what pissed me
off the most? That after all John had done to me I couldn't bring myself
to hate him. Yet, I let my anger and the violent temper I usually control
so well take over and I killed them. I feel like a hypocrite now. Imagine
what I'd feel if I had kids, telling them to control their temper or don't
get violent. God, Rick, I'm a monster. You shouldn't even have to look
at me." Her eyes filled with the sadness she'd felt knowing she knew
what was right, yet and still, she did wrong.

Danya turned and sat down on the bed with her back to him. Rick
scooted closer to her as she rested her hand on the night stand. "I want
you to know that I love you with all my heart and every ounce of my

soul. My heart, with every beat, is bursting with that love. My essences, my very soul goes into loving you and—"

"Danya, I know this. You don't need—"

"Let me finish. I need to say this. I love you so. And you make me so happy. But that night you were shot, I took a risk with your life that wasn't mine to take. If you'd died because I'd made them transfer you ..." A steady stream of tears ran along her face as Rick laid his hand on her shoulder. Danya stood up and turned around. He moved to get off the bed but his soreness slowed him down.

"Don't!" Danya put her hands on his shoulders. "Stop, stay in bed. I'm fine."

"Look that's all water under the—"

"That's not the point!" she yelled at him. "I was selfish and it could have cost you your life."

Danya placed Rick's feet back on the bed. She made him get under the covers with the pillow sitting him upright. Rick didn't argue. She could tell he was hurting and knew his pain killers hadn't kicked in yet. He tried his best to hide his discomfort. She assumed he was attempting to avoid making her feel worse. She could feel him watching as she went and stood on the other side of the night stand. With her hands hidden from Rick's view, she took off the engagement ring and balled it in her fist. Danya balled up her other fist as she leaned on the night stand.

"I need to learn to live with what I did. My heart won't let me have it any other way. How can I expect you to believe me when I profess this eternal love I have for you? This deep down, solid, firm, unshakable, true love and expect you to believe me when I can't love myself, huh? I've become a cruel, sadistic, and violent person. I never thought I was that type of person, but it must have always been in me. People can't become something they're not."

"That is not who you are."

She opened her fist and stood straight up. "I'm sorry for everything

I've done and will do. I need some time to think. You need some time to decide if I'm the type of woman you want to marry. If the woman you want to spend a lifetime with is me."

"Then I have nothing to think about, I know you are," Rick replied.

"Honey, I've changed. The woman you are looking at now is a murderer. You deserve better than that. I thought I could marry you and go on like nothing was wrong. Maybe, in six months you won't feel the same about—"

Rick swung his legs slowly off the bed, interrupting her. "That's bull and you know it."

"I'm sorry, Rick, but I can't marry you, at least not right now. Not like this." She touched a bag in a nearby chair.

"We don't have to get married right away." His eyes went down towards her empty ring finger.

"Look, if several months from now you still want to marry me, I will, happily." She grabbed the bag off the chair. "But only after we haven't seen each other in a while. I don't want to influence you."

"What are you talking about? You're not making any sense." Rick reached for her, but she stepped away.

"I'm so, so sorry, Rick, but the engagement is off." Danya blew Rick a final goodbye kiss and ran out.

Rick ignored his pain as he flipped the covers back and got out of bed. He called her name as he ran after her. By the time he made it to the door, she was gone. He swung the door open and looked out to see if she was still in the hall. The door slammed closed as he went back into the apartment. Her set of keys to the apartment sat on the coffee table. He stood there staring at the door and then at the keys. Rick couldn't believe that she ran out on him like that. He couldn't understand if she wanted to marry him, what was the point of breaking off the engagement? They could just wait until she was ready; at least she kept the engagement ring. This was probably an extreme response to the last few months. He went back into the room.

"Dammit, Danya!" He picked up the ring; the bed sank from his weight.

In front of his eyes, between his index finger and thumb held the symbol of his love for her, a love that had no bounds, no beginning or end, it just was. He sat the ring back on the night stand then picked up a framed picture of the two of them. Danya knew she was going to do this, that's why she hadn't moved her things in. He should have seen it coming.

Rick couldn't justify what Danya did but he understood the circumstances and the bad decisions placed her in the position. Yes, murder was murder but there were extenuating circumstances. Why couldn't he make her see that? It really didn't matter, Danya had already played judge and jury and found herself guilty as charged. He finally met a woman he wanted far more than good sex or a temporary relationship; a woman that he wanted to build a future with. Rick had found a woman that he actually wanted to marry and what does she do? She walks, no runs, out on him. Didn't she understand that he knew that all she did was play out the bad hand that life had dealt her the only way she knew how? It wasn't the best way, but it didn't matter to him, it didn't change his love for her. It made him love her all the more because of the sincerity he felt in her words. There was no way that she could make him believe she had the heart of a murderer. Rick knew this to be true for one reason, Danya's heart wasn't letting her get away with murder. That's not a heart of a killer, it's a heart of a woman that could love so strongly yet did something so foolish. He wished he could convince her that they could make it through this, together. *Damn you, John! Damn you to hell!*

* * *

Danya's attempt to turn herself in wasn't going as expected. She was sitting at one of the officer's desk while he spoke with someone behind her. She couldn't believe they were contemplating letting her go. The officer seemed to believe she was telling the truth. Whoever he was speaking to didn't feel that they had enough for a conviction. He was told to hold her and go in search for the items to confirm her story. Danya didn't understand how her admitting guilt wasn't enough. After being held for several hours, the fact that she was sent home was baffling to her. They stated she was considered a person of interest and was asked to remain in town. Based on the conversation she overheard and the fact that she should have been considered a flight risk, she should have at least been processed and held in jail until that decision was made. Danya shook her head. Even her plan to pay for her crimes went haywire. It wasn't until she made it home that she realized it wasn't about her. It was about public perception. According to the news, the police dragged the victim in for questioning for the murders of Rita and John. Danya wondered if they thought they would get dragged through the mud if they didn't have enough evidence to make sure this conviction stuck. Even if they couldn't find the evidence she had gotten rid of, they had to have her bracelet in evidence. It would be a matter of time before they'd be coming for her.

CHAPTER TWENTY

It was a beautiful day in June. The sun was shining brightly. A nice cool breeze from the lake blew Danya's long, reddish-brown hair ever so slightly as she watched the water crash against the rocks in a set rhythm. It was two months shy of being exactly a year since the day Danya became a murderer. She sat on the jagged rocks on the lake front looking out into the vastness of what expanded before her. It was difficult for her to think about what happened, even to this day. She came to terms with what she did, but it hadn't exactly eased her mind. That day had changed her life and her perceptions of it so drastically that to her life became a novel, a story most people wouldn't even believe. She even had trouble believing it. It was just too unreal, so off the wall and insane yet the basic themes were so common.

Danya's story had eight basic themes, one of love, trust, deceit, betrayal, money, power, manipulation, and murder. Danya loved and trusted John. He deceived and betrayed her. John hungered for power and money. Danya possessed the money he needed to obtain the power. John and his crew manipulated quite a few years of her life. John murdered Marcus, Chris, and Gena. She killed Bally, Rita, and John. Things had come full circle for John. She expected them to do the same for her.

Not to make Bally's murder insignificant, but her mind could comprehend his death. To her, his death was a classic example of the extenuating circumstances that were understood by judges and juries without being an excuse or a reason for murder. If it had not been for that extreme event, the murder would have never occurred. In some degree, Rita and John's deaths had been that extreme. The only difference was Danya placed herself in that situation and in doing so, she'd crossed the line. Even in the manner in which she killed them, a person could see that she'd gone out of bounds. Danya couldn't say it was temporary insanity. She knew the risks she took going over there.

Looking back at how she handled the situation, maybe she did go there with criminal intent. Her heart said it wasn't true though. Yet the fact she brought the gun with the silencer made her question if she was being honest with herself. Danya wanted to give John an opportunity, a chance to explain. She needed to know when he had stopped loving her. Why did he start hating her? When did he decide to play God with her life? And why? Why did he want to hurt her so deeply? He'd known her better than anyone. All that time she blamed Marcus, despising what he'd done to her, and it was John who was the mastermind behind it all. She'd been John's puppet for ten years and didn't know it. He brought Marcus and Rita into her life, took Chris and Gena out, and kept her drugged in a hospital for almost a year even though he knew they were cousins.

When she went to meet John at the condo, she was willing to let him leave the country. She brought the gun along in case John didn't want to take a chance by letting her live. Danya couldn't bring herself to hate him. Even after everything he'd done, she couldn't. He had been a constant in her life, someone very important to her. She couldn't condemn him without hearing his story. Life brought about changes and she desired to know what brought about the change in him. At least that was the story she was telling herself the last few months. She used herself as the example. If anyone had told her that she was capable of murder two years ago, she would have called them a liar. Yet one call on a morning that started off so normal changed the course of her life. It ultimately led her to the moment where she had to ask herself, *How did I get there? How did I become a murder?* She was sure John had a similar story of making choices, unaware of the impact of them would put him knee deep in something that wasn't so easy to get out of.

At this point in time, she needed to believe that his feeling towards her wasn't a lie. That he cared and wasn't secretly hating them all the time. Now Danya had a better idea of what circumstances could have brought about the change in John. She never knew how poor Aunt Kesha was. She was living beyond her means to give John the chance to get to know his father's side of the family. The house and its bills were putting her in debt. Her family helped her keep John in clothes appropriate for the upscale neighborhood. When John was old enough to understand that they were poor in spite of where they lived, he became obsessed with money and power. His mother baby-sat during the day and worked various jobs at night. Once Danya's parents died, Aunt Kesha moved into a house that she could afford in another neighborhood. That way she could save to send John to school. By the time college came, John was working two jobs. One to help pay bills and one to save for college. He realized it would be years before he'd earn a large amount of money.

John had grants and loans for his tuition but it wasn't putting money in his pocket. It wasn't keeping up the lifestyle he had been accustomed to living before he realized that his mother was broke. To him, it was like moving from Beverly Hills into the ghetto. Danya had no idea until overhearing a conversation at the funeral. It was her assumption he met someone that offered him Beverly Hills again, and he took it. In doing that he teamed up with Bally, Marcus, and Rita. Danya, Gena, and his relationship with them were not a part of that portion of his life, at least not until his life was on the line. That's when his two separate lives became fused.

Danya would always believe in her heart that if his life had not been in danger, John never would have let that fusion happen. That's something she'd believe even on her death bed. Rita was right, John did love her, but his love for himself came first. Danya forgave him for that, not so much that she was such a forgiving person but because at the condo she learned something. A person's reaction to life's drastic conditions sometimes can prove to be self-destructive.

Danya's train of thought switched tracks. It was also almost a year ago that she walked out of Rick's life. She'd moved into a townhouse on the south side of Chicago with an unlisted telephone number. The first few months Rick attempted to contact her at work. He'd call or stop by the office but she refused to see or talk to him. She had to give him time to dig deep. Danya couldn't marry him without knowing that he'd seriously thought about what he was getting into and accepted the fact that she was a murderer then decide if he could really live with it. She didn't want to get married and then one day have him actually think about it and decide she was not what he wanted. It was better for the both of them that they give each other space.

Rick finally stopped calling. It broke her heart to know that she might lose him, but it was necessary. She never regretted her decision. It was when Danya went back to the Dells that she came to terms with the events that occurred during her life. She couldn't believe she'd told Harry the story—without the murdering of John and Rita portion. It was probably the fact that he had no real connection to her past and no emotional ties to the outcome of her future. It was a calculated risk but one she was glad she made. Harry made her search deep. His statement to her was, she was listening but not hearing. She listened to the sound of her own voice but was not hearing the opinion of others. Danya knew she'd been seeing only the things she wanted to, manipulating any detail to fit what she believed to be true. Harry believed that she did a foolish thing in going over there alone but it was her heart speaking not her brain. Her heart went over there to say her last goodbye to her friends before she let them disappear into the sunset. The only problem was

Rita had no intention of letting her live. Danya knew that she would never know if John would have let her walk out of that apartment alive if she hadn't killed Rita. She wanted to believe he would have. It's not because it made her feel better but due to what Rita said before trying to kill Danya: "John would have to forgive me." He wouldn't have had to forgive Rita if he was going to do it himself. It doesn't matter now.

What mattered was how much it hurt not to have Rick. Danya hadn't heard from him since the first few months he tried to contact her. She had prayed that after some soul searching, he'd come to the decision that he wanted to marry her. If only life was so simple. Now she questioned whether walking away was the best way to handle things. It's not like he hadn't made the attempt yet she continued to push him away. Frustrated with herself, how did she expect him to give her what she wanted if she wouldn't let him? There was an ache in her heart and tightening in her chest at the thought of permanently screwing up the opportunity to have Rick in her life.

Danya remembered he'd been on her mind a lot lately. It was coming up to one of the three potential wedding dates they selected. She was on her way to attend a wedding that unfortunately wasn't hers. She was depressed about that but glad to be Trish's maid of honor. Earlier that morning all the bridesmaids, which happened to be mutual friends of hers and Trish's, got the 'Queen for the day' package at a total body beauty salon. They all had their hair and nails done, facials, massages, and makeovers—in other words, the works. The odd thing about the wedding was none of the bridesmaids had seen their dresses. Trish mentioned she didn't want any complaints about the dresses. The bridesmaids would get their measurements taken and the dresses would be made knowing any minor alteration would be done right before the ceremony.

It was the kind of day that Danya wanted to be married on before her entire world went crazy. How did her assistant get such a beautiful wedding day? Once they made it to the area of the church where they were supposed to change clothes, Danya saw the boxes with the mysterious dresses in them. She strolled over to the box with her name on it and opened it. With tears running down her face, she read the note and picked up her engagement ring. Danya couldn't say anything. She reached for the beautiful white satin wedding gown and hugged it to her chest. Danya shook her head thinking about all those bridesmaids dress fittings and all Trish questions on wedding dresses.

Trish asked, "Should I tell the groom there is going to be a wedding?"

Danya's smile spread across her face as she told Trish, "Yes!"

Trish opened the door and stepped out, then returned as Danya and the bridesmaids changed into their dresses. Trish grabbed her dress box. "I hope it's okay if I take the role of maid of honor."

"You have earned the titled." Danya chuckled.

Danya's mind was reeling. She couldn't believe Rick had her planning her own wedding via Trish. Now it made sense why Trish wanted to see her wedding planning organizer, supposedly to get the bridal resource list out of it. All the details of the wedding had worked out before her world imploded except for the wedding dress, the venue, and the date. To think she got upset when Trish seemed to be leaning towards her color scheme.

At the sight of the bridesmaids in the dress that Danya had selected, the tears begin to flow.

Trish pulled out a handkerchief. "Don't go messing up that beautiful makeup!"

"I can't thank you enough for helping him out with this." She took the handkerchief and carefully dabbed her face trying not to mess up the makeup.

Now Danya understood why they had a low-key bachelorette party at her house, why there was no rehearsal, and why Trish's sister couldn't make it to the wedding. Rick wrote in his note that he felt that he had to do something dramatic to get her to understand that he wasn't going anywhere. Well, this definitely puts an end to all the craziness. As she stepped into the hallway heading to the ceremony, the water works started again as Harry was waiting to walk her down the aisle. She had visited him several times at the cabins and he never once let it slip what Rick was planning. Yet nothing compared to seeing Rick waiting at the end of the aisle for her.

She had the most wonderful wedding day, better than she ever imagined. Danya would have never guessed that she'd be the one getting married and not Trish. Rick gave her more happiness in that one day than most had over a lifetime.

CHAPTER TWENTY - ONE

The last two years as Rick's wife had been amazing. After all, Danya felt undeserving of it even though she appreciated it. She raised her wedding ring towards her face before grabbing her shoes and standing. Heading in the direction of her car, she strolled away from the jagged rock onto the beach. It was time for her to go home and show her husband how much she loved him. Her feet sank into the sand and she looked down and only noticed one set of her footprints in the sand. It reminded her that even though she felt she walked this journey alone, she wasn't alone. Good people did and endured bad things but as long as those incidents didn't corrupt their soul they have an opportunity for forgiveness and redemption from the one who matters the most. She said a silent thank you. She paused momentarily to slip on her shoes then did a slight jog to her car.

When Danya reached Gena's midnight blue Mustang, she snickered at how she used to tease Gena about her car. Now here she was doing the same, treating it like it's her best friend. Danya did a quick check for scratches as she went around the front of the car to the driver's side. She stopped and squatted in front of her car. For some unknown reason, she felt the need to feel on the inside of the front bumper. Her fingers moved around but she felt nothing. She chuckled at herself for being ridiculous, but something kept nagging her to continue looking. Finally, her fingers hit something, a little pocket. She stuck her fingernail in it and pulled out the object. Danya got into the car, twirling the small key around in her hand. It looked like a safe deposit box key. Danya glanced at her watch; the bank would be open by the time she drove there.

"Whatever possessed Gena to put the key to her safe deposit box on the inside of her bumper?"

Danya was curious and extremely impatient once she made it to the bank as they went through their usual procedures. The banker used his key and the one Danya had given him to open it. He slowly pulled it out and asked her to follow him. Danya followed him to a small room with a table and two chairs. He sat the box down on the table and told her whenever she was ready just come out then he closed the door.

She was somewhat reluctant to look in it once she had the box and a little privacy. Danya stepped towards the table, took a deep breath, lifted the lid, and pulled out the contents. Her legs felt like they were about to give out on her as she glanced at some of the contents. It felt like the air was being sucked out the room. Danya's heartbeat increased. She remembered.

Oh God, I remember everything! Quickly, she took a seat as she finished rummaging through the contents. She poured the contents of the box into her purse then wasted no time getting out of there. Once she was back in the car, she took out her cell phone and made an appointment to meet with Dr. Adams immediately. Danya felt her world crumbling down around her. This couldn't be happening. She thought it was over but she'd remember. Oh no, why did she have to remember?

Danya's thoughts were in an upheaval. She sat in the chair watching Dr. Adams look over the contents of the box. Her mind was a thousand light years away; she could have driven off a cliff and wouldn't know it until she hit rock bottom. Danya imagined Dr. Adams look of shock was nothing compared to how she herself examined the contents of the safe deposit box. The doctor's body dropped into her seat as she continued to examine all the information on her desk and seemed to be in deep thought.

"How is it possible? Tell me, how could I be Gena?" Danya's words penetrated the silence and the doctor's private thoughts.

Dr. Adams replied, "I can't answer that at least not until I heard the entire story now that you know."

Danya began telling the tale like she never had before. Dr. Adams stopped studying the items on her desk. She listened carefully, leaning forward as if she did not want to miss a single syllable.

Glancing around her antique shop for the last time, Gena Holmes smiled. Her life was turning out better than she'd imagined. Gena planned to tell Terry that she'd be retiring from the antique business to work at her new fashion company. It was supposed to be Terry's 25th birthday surprise. At the time Gena started planning this surprise, she had no idea that she'd have a few more surprises to go along with it.

Gena picked up her portfolio that held her latest designs eager to share them with Terry. Terry had always been the better designer of the two but after studying abroad on and off for the last few years, Gena's designs were just as good. To Gena's surprise, she craved the creativity and freedom of designing more than her antique business. Gena didn't feel right starting her own fashion company since that had always been Terry's dream. Working with Terry would provide her with the perfect opportunity to fulfill that desire to create beautiful designs. Gena loved that idea. It would probably work out better for her. She hoped that Terry wouldn't mind her infringing upon her dream.

Now the other surprise was definitely unexpected and unplanned. Gena was pregnant. Gena knew she'd lied to Terry about not wanting kids; she was thrilled to be pregnant. She laughed, imagining Terry's reaction to hearing those words. Gena locked up the shop, trotted to her car, got in, started up her beloved midnight blue Mustang, then drove off.

It looked too gorgeous of a day to storm but she knew better than to believe that. Gena took one hand off the steering wheel and placed it protectively on her stomach and thought about Pierre, the baby's father.

The last time Gena saw Pierre she hadn't even realized she was pregnant. Being tired and a little nauseous at times wasn't normal for her but she thought it was because she was traveling more than usual. Gena still wasn't feeling good on her flight home so she immediately went to the doctor for a checkup and of course discovered she was pregnant. That night she called Pierre to tell him the news and he asked her to marry him.

"Gena, I'm not asking you to marry me because of the baby. I love you, it's just that ..."

"Pierre, I don't doubt your love for me. And I'm not trying to deny your child but I don't see me moving to another country, adjusting to a different way of life while trying to raise a child."

"I want you and my baby here with me, Gena. We can make this work."

"If you truly believe that, move here."

"I, I ..."

"That's what I thought. Visiting often is still different from living here full time."

"Why don't we both give it some thought and decide later. Just take good care of yourself and my baby. And I do love you."

Gena didn't think it would work out until she received a package in the mail. Pierre sent her an engagement ring and a note that said, "When do I move in?" She glanced at her heart-shaped face in the rear-view mirror. There was a stupid grin plastered on her face but she couldn't stop smiling. At that moment, she felt like she had everything that she needed in life. Everything was coming together so nicely. She was getting married, having a baby, and a new career. Terry knew nothing about Pierre but Gena planned to change that all tonight.

On the way home, Gena stopped to place several items in her time capsule. She returned the time capsule key to the specially made pouch on the inside of her bumper of her car then headed home. Not paying attention to much of anything, Gena pulled into her circle drive and drove passed the front door then put the Mustang into park. The car door swung open, she quickly climbed out feeling pretty energized for a tired person. Peering up at the darkening sky, Gena knew by the time Terry arrived it would be raining cats and dogs.

After entering the house and grabbing the mail, Gena headed to her office not even bothering to take off her coat. Leaning her portfolio against the desk, she let the mail drop on the desk top then took off her coat. She threw it over the chair and went through her mail, still smiling but her smile faded as she noticed the manila folder. Gena didn't bother to look in it, she knew by the look on the detective's face when she asked him what he'd found out that it wasn't good news. It would be Terry's decision whether to look at the contents or not. She passed the window and noticed a light drizzle going on. She locked the folder in the safe then headed to the living room to wait for Terry. Gena jumped slightly as the thunder roared loudly, then laughed at herself for letting a little thunder scare her.

Gena really couldn't wait to see Terry; she missed her big sister. With Gena out of the country more than usual, they hadn't seen much of each other. She was looking more and more like Terry. Gena was no longer 110 pounds of tone muscles but 135 pounds of solid weight.

The cherry wood doors of the living room stood before her. She opened them and entered the room. Gena noticed the bay windows lights were off as she began to walk to the stairs. She stopped; she never turned off those light. The color drained from her face, fear rose in her and stuck in her throat. She should have noticed they weren't on when she drove up. She probably would have if she hadn't been in la la land. If she'd noticed, she could have called the police.

"Gena, Gena, you should have noticed," she whispered to herself, immediately turning to exit the room quickly as possible.

Gena never made it out the door. After being snatched and thrown backward, her body hit the floor and slid to the edge of the stairs. Her screams penetrated the air. The intruder loomed before her in black, from the black ski mask over his face down to the black sneakers. Gena watched the intruder's mouth move, the words were drowned out by the thunder. She knew the chance of her screams for help actually being heard was nearly impossible. As he moved towards her, Gena stood and ran down the stairs throwing anything she could in his path. She pushed the end table at the side of the couch then ran the length of it. Gena picked the center piece off the coffee table and threw it at him.

The ceramic centerpiece hit him in the forehead slowing his advance. She stood directly in front the bay window with at least three ways to get to the door. The intruder blocked the center stair. The stairs to the left and the right of her were her only ways out. She wasn't given time to decide which way was best as he stepped over the end table coming at her. He grabbed her arm as she tried to run pass him to the bar. She wrenched her arm free. Gena stumbled up the stairs and struggled to knock the bar over to block his path.

He advanced towards her as he reached over the banister. He spoke. His words sent a menacing chill up her spine as he demanded the combination to her safe. Gena jumped back against the wall out his reach. She rapidly ran off the numbers but she knew that he'd come for much more than the combination. Watching him through the banister, her back hugged the wall as she moved swiftly towards the door. She had to beat him to the door as his eyes carefully watched her every movement. The intruder's movement on the lower level mirrored hers as she moved closer to the door.

Dammit, she thought. Why hadn't she grabbed a bottle for a weapon when she ran by the bar? If she got out that door, she'd have a better chance of surviving. The intruder stumbled over the centerpiece she'd thrown at him, Gena bolted for the door. Her hand twisted the doorknob as the intruder flew up the center stairs. He grabbed a hand full of her dress and snatched her backward. Her body crashed into his with such force, he had to take a step back. Gena stabbed her elbow into his stomach sharply, sending him stumbling into the table next to the door. She heard her beautiful crystal lamp shatter as she ran into the hall.

Before Gena made it out the front door, he grabbed her by the waist dragging her away from the door. Gena slammed her arm into his neck repeatedly. When they neared the stairs, she grabbed hold of the banister. He pried her hands off it. When that didn't work, he began yanking her body to make her let go. Gena release her hold on the banister just as he forcefully pulled her body, sending them flying back on the stairs. She quickly got up and ran.

Dazed, he lunged forward and grabbed her ankle. Her foot came from under her, then her hands went out as she fell forward. The intruder held fast to her left ankle as she twisted her body and tried to use the heel on her shoe to pry his hand away. While he fought to keep a strong hold on her ankle, he reached for her other foot. She lifted it, leaving him with only her shoe. Gena took her foot and kicked him in the head. Her foot slid through his hand leaving him with her left shoe.

The intruder was up on his feet faster than Gena could get to the door. She turned and opened the door. She could taste the rain, the freedom. It was at her fingertips. The force of his body hitting hers closed the door. He turned her around and slammed his fist against the part of the door right next to her head.

"Don't try that again if you want to live to see twenty-five."

Gena's whole body shuttered as he pulled out a knife and ran it over her cheek then slid the cold, hard metal down to her neck. Fear immobilized Gena. He swiftly pulled her away from the door and into his arm holding her firmly by the waist with her back rested against his chest. The blade of the knife bit into her neck ever so slightly as he gave her instruction where to go. While he was asking for the combination to the safe in her room, she was concerned she'd have another issue by what she felt against her backside. This couldn't be happening. She was trying to keep it together but the closer they got to the room the more she fell apart. The intruder breathing became heavier in Gena's ear as a result of the intentional friction he placed against her backside. He entered the master bedroom and threw her on the bed then quickly straddled her.

"It's simple, fight me and you die." Gena's tormentor held her hands over her head by the wrist. Before he'd even finished his sentence, he'd ripped her dress with his free hand making the bottom half looser. The sound of the material ripping to Gena represented how this man, in one big yank, had torn her world apart.

"I'm bursting to be inside of you." The assailant set down the knife next to her thigh and took her left hand from over her head and rubbed across his zipper then forced her legs open with one knee. He placed her hand back over her head.

Gena's thoughts continued to shut down as her chances of escaping this black night continued to by shutting down. Her panic increased. Her baby. She couldn't do anything that would harm her baby, Pierre's baby, but she wanted to be free of this dungeon of despair.

His lips began to make a trail from her neck to her chest. He grabbed the knife, cut open her bra, and seized her with his mouth. He acted like he savored the flavor of each ripe melon. His mouth made a trail from her breast to her lips. Gena tried to turn her head but the blade bit into her neck. If she wriggled, she'd be cutting her own throat. Then he kissed her softly on the lips as if they were lovers. The assailant's passion laded eyes followed the trail he made with the knife down the center of her body. Gena became hysterical as the point of the knife went between her legs. The last barrier was cut away. She faded out.

The continuous roar of the thunder drowned out Gena's single

terrified scream while her eyes begged and plead with him not to do it.
He settled his weight between her legs as he pressed the blade into her
throat.

"Oh God, how I wanted you yet I couldn't have you." He sat the
knife on the night stand.

Gena eyed the knife but he grabbed her hands and held them above
her head with one hand.

"Don't do this," she pleaded as he entered her.

"Did you know how it felt being close to you and not being able to
have you? Oh, mmm, you feel just like I dreamed you would, mmm, even
better." His head dropped forward momentary as he paused then began
talking in a low raspy voice. "I see you gained a little weight but it's
still better than ... Oh, god." His rhythm became intense. His head fell
forward and his teeth sank into his bottom lip as he penetrated deeper.
It got so good to him that he barely held her wrist.

The tears continued to fall as she tried to block out what was
happening. Terror filled her mind as the thought crossed her mind that
he'd kill her anyway. She concentrated on her future, her baby, her
fiancé, anything to block out what was happening.

Danya leaned her head forward and rested them in her hands. "You
know the rest of the story. I, Gena, Dammit, this is crazy!"

"Gena what?" Dr. Adams asked.

Frustrated, Danya didn't even know how to refer to herself. "She
knew what was going on around her but for a moment she just couldn't
..."

"I understand."

"Since you do, explain it to me." Danya frowned at her not giving her a chance to speak. "From the moment Terry came in, to the fall down the stair, is all a blur. I remember everything but it's all in fast forward. All of a sudden, a scream pierced the air, then I heard Terry yelling at me to get the knife, then we were stumbling down the stairs and ..."

Dr. Adams leaned forward. "And what?"

"I woke up in a daze, I was confused. I kept mixing up our names, every time I meant Terry I'd say Gena." Danya thought back to that night.

She tried to sit up too swiftly and got light-headed and had to lay back down. She sat up again but slowly this time. Her head was throbbing and she was slightly dizzy but she didn't think anything was broken. Once she looked around, she found the assailant was knocked out next to her. Her sister was face down over part of his chest. Gena stood feeling as if she was going to faint but she stumbled over to her sister. She knelt next to her and leaned over. Gena shook her ever so slightly and whispered in her ear.

"Gena! Wake up. We need to get out of here before he wakes up. Oh Lord, Gena get up."

Danya looked at Dr. Adams through a water glaze. "At the time I knew it was Terry laying on the floor but I, I couldn't get Gena to stop coming out of my mouth. I mentally corrected myself but ..."

Gena was too scared to move her, but she had to turn her over and check her pulse. She sat there a second and took a deep breath, then turned her sister over.

"Oh, no! God, no." She began screaming as she touched the blood on her sister's body that had not been there before the fall.

Danya's tears flowed down her face as she sniffled. "That's when I ran to call 911. The pain in my stomach was so intense I couldn't stand. I tried to fight through the pain to tell the dispatcher the assailant was still in the house when ..."

Gena looked up and saw the assailant standing above her with his finger across the hook. She couldn't move because the pain wouldn't let her. He walked around her laughing.

In a low whispering voice, he said, "She's fallen and it doesn't look like she'll be getting up anytime soon." He wandered over to the cabinet where she kept her wine. "You know that it's going to take them at least half an hour or more to get here." He grabbed the most expensive red wine out the cabinet. "Let's celebrate the passing of a good friend."

Dr. Adams prompted Danya to finish. "He pulled you out to Terry and poured wine over her body and down your throat, then you realized that the assailant was Marcus."

She stared at the doctor a while before speaking. "Marcus kept his voice disguised in a low raspy voice. Even in the living room when he spoke loud his voice was distorted where I couldn't recognize it."

The assailant looked at her. "Sorry Ginny, this was not in the plan." This time he spoke without disguising his voice.

Gena was paralyzed. The only person that called her Ginny was Marcus.

Marcus saw the recognition in her eyes and pulled off his mask. "Mrs. Johnson, I guess my jig is up. Now let me put you out of your misery."

Dr. Adam interrupted Danya. "Is that the point you began to think that you were actually Terry?"

"I guess so. I don't know!" She threw her hands up in the air.

Dr. Adams observed Danya closely as she asked, "Why did Marcus call you Mrs. Johnson?"

"He used to call me that anyway. When he and Terry would have an argument, he'd say he married the wrong sister then call me Mrs. Johnson and call Terry, Miss Holmes. Terry would laugh it off but I didn't think it was funny. In time, I became accustomed to him calling me either Ginny or Mrs. Johnson."

"Is there any other points you realized that you were Gena?" The doctor rolled her chair closer to the desk.

Marcus's knife was coming down at her as Gena lay on the floor holding her side. His arm stopped moving when he noticed that she was looking over his shoulder. He moved in but not in time to miss getting hit with the wine bottle. Between getting struck and tripping over Gena, he hit the floor.

"Gena," she stated as if she couldn't believe it.

"Gena?" Terry's face crunched up then mirrored her sister's perplexed look.

"It was when I heard her say my name that I knew I was Gena but with everything happening so fast I, I didn't have time to ponder on it." Danya glared past the doctor's shoulder.

Marcus recovered from his shock and lunged at Terry with the knife. Terry jumped against the living room doors. Gena grabbed Marcus's ankle and yanked him down, the knife hit the ground and Terry kicked it in Gena's direction. Gena got the knife but Marcus was trying to pry it out of her hands. They fought fiercely for control of the knife.

"Then it happened, Terry fell onto the knife. She, my ..." Danya's hand dropped forward into her hands. "My hands were still on the knife. Oh Lord, I can still smell ..."

Terry grabbed Marcus's arm from behind. He shifted his body to gain better positioning. His feet became entangled with Terry. She fell forward. He released the knife and quickly rolled out of the way but he wasn't quick enough. Terry landed on top of them both. Gena's nostrils were overwhelmed by the smell of the expensive red wine on Terry's dress. The thick red liquid ran down the handle of the knife onto Gena's hands. Her hands immediately dropped away from the knife. Marcus planted his foot in Terry's stomach and pushed her body off him onto the floor then he stood and ran to the door. Marcus unlocked it and yanked it open then turned and looked back. He stared momentarily at Gena pulling her sister into her lap. His head drooped forward at the sight of his bleeding wife.

Gena watched as Marcus turned and ran into the storm with the knife he pulled out of his wife still in hand. She sat crying with Terry's limp body in her arms and began whispering in her ear.

"Terry, you can't die. I need you too much." She applied pressure to Terry's wound to help slow the flow of blood. "Who's going to be my maid of honor, huh? That's what I wanted to tell you tonight. While I was doing all that traveling I met and fell in love with a guy named Pierre and now we're getting married. We hadn't planned on getting serious but it happened. Now we're going to have a baby. You hear that? Your baby sister is going to have a baby."

Gena knew that there was no chance that the baby survived but she couldn't stop rambling. "Terry, the ambulance is on the way. Just hold on. Please, you're the only family I've got. I love you, sis. What would I be without my twin? I'm special because of you. What's one Danya without the other Danya, huh? Terry, I ... "

"Terry, well it's nice to know that you know who's who again," she whispered in a barely audible voice with a weak smile. Terry continued to talk.

"You're going to be an aunt."

Terry gave her sister a weak laugh.

"That's the good news I wanted to tell you. Your big sister is pregnant with her first child. How about that?" Her voice got softer with every word as her eyes sent streams of tears down her face.

"Don't talk. Dammit, Terry, you can't die on me!" Gena's tears dripped onto Terry's face.

"Don't let Marcus get away with this. Promise?" Terry closed her eyes briefly as if she feared that if she allowed them to stay closed too long that it would be the last time. Gena listened to her sister's words which were soft but had power behind them. She whispered that she promised.

"Keep your promise." Terry's eyes were closed as she spoke, her voice gradually faded into silence.

Gena sat there rocking Terry in her arms and cried softly.

Every other word Danya sniffled. "I, I guess it was after she stopped talking, and, and, I wanted to check her pulse to see, to see if she still was alive then I saw my hands. Oh God ..." She lifted her head up and stared at her hands as if she could see it, and her body began to shake. "Her blood covered my hands. I, I, oh God, it was ..."

"It was what?"

Danya's tear stained face stared at nothing in particular as she spoke. "As I rocked her in my arms, my mind was on all the conversations we had about Marcus. I began trying to imagine what it felt like for her. It was then I started confusing what I said to her with what Terry spoke to me."

She wiped the tears away. There was no need to finish the story. The doctor knew how it ended. "But I don't understand how I could believe I was Terry. I must be a lunatic!"

"Danya, your mind couldn't deal with everything then, so it edited your memory. Since you and Terry had shared a lot of memories and personal—"

"Oh my God!" Her scream cut Dr. Adams off midsentence as a memory flashed in her mind. "I've known for years."

"What have you known for years?"

The doctor received no answer.

Gena was extremely sick. She could barely keep her eyes open. Other than the narrow slit, her eyes were basically closed. She listened carefully to his words while watching his movement through her eyelashes. Gena fought to open them wider but she couldn't. The room was spinning as Marcus continued to talk. She wondered if this was all a dream or was he actually standing in the room. It was difficult for her to tell reality from her nightmare. Marcus was quite talkative but grew quiet as John walked in. Through the tiny slits in her eyes, she watched John motion for Marcus to follow him into the hall. Shortly after John came in with Officer Bally, they left Marcus standing at the door. Gena watched Marcus as he frowned and stared at the two men who were having a private discussion on the opposite side of the room away from her bed and the door. She strained to hear the low but clear tones.

"He didn't even know." Danya remembered their conversation so clearly now.

John wanted to make sure her confusion was more than temporary. They discussed using Terry's personal diary to supply Gena with any information that by chance she might not know. John insisted that Bally pump Marcus for exact details about his marriage to Terry, especially what happened that morning before he left. Bally seemed uncomfortable reviewing all this with Gena in the room but John reassured him that she was out of it.

"Bally, this is between us, alright? Marcus is never to know that it was Terry that died not Gena." John spoke softly to Bally.

"I agree. Marcus wanted Gena too much. If he knew he'd want to stay married to her instead of following the plan," Bally replied.

"We have to keep him away before Gena starts getting better and he recognizes that it's not Terry in that bed." John glanced back at the hospital bed.

Bally nodded. "I agree totally."

"Yeah. Gena may be confused but she clearly remembers that she wants nothing to do with him. We'll begin feeding Gena, Terry's information tomorrow."

Danya jumped out her seat and stepped over to Dr. Adams' desk, leaning until they were face to face. "Everything always comes back to John. I must admit he was smooth quizzing me like he did. He'd ask me a question and then tell me what I told him while out of it until I was repeating what he told me verbatim."

The doctor tilted back in her chair but Danya leaned in more. "Take a deep breath, relax, and—"

"Doctor, everything comes back to John, everything! That man had a reason for everything he did. I understand this now." Danya hopped up glaring down at the doctor. "So, I have one question. Where do you fit in?"

CHAPTER TWENTY - TWO

The room seemed to spin as Danya tried to process everything. Her eyes trailed Dr. Adams' movement towards her cabinet as she unlocked it and pulled out a box. Nervously, she tapped on her thigh and shifted her feet as the doctor approached with the box. Her mind speculated what was in it. None of the possibilities were good. Danya wanted to sink into the floor to cry. She wanted this nightmare to end. It felt like every time she began to find her new norm her world splintered into a million pieces.

Dr. Adams handed her the box then explained, "I believe he assigned me the tasks of delivering these once you no longer felt the need to come to me. He told me that he was moving out of the country and didn't want you to have them until you were in a good mental place."

"You would be the good judge of that. But why didn't you give them to me before now?" Danya questioned.

Dr. Adams stared at her as if she was searching for the right words.

"There has been something bothering you since the second traumatic incident at Gena's. The fact you have yet to discuss it with me had me concerned that you were not ready for the contents of the box."

Danya's eyes cut to the side knowing that she could never discuss Rita and John's deaths with the doctor. She may qualify as crazy but she was not certifiable even after the media storm that resulted from the incidents. Her eyes went back to the box as she took ownership of it. She sank back into her seat and opened it. There was quite a bit of Gena's stuff and journals in there. The journals grabbed her attention because she knew they weren't Gena's. Her hands tremble as she picked them up.

"I'm going let you have this office to go through the contents and take the remainder of my appointments in another room. My assistant is outside if you need to get a message to me." Dr. Adams exited, closing the door behind her.

Inhaling deeply, Danya opened the journal and exhaled as she began reading.

How do you kill someone you love? You don't, but tonight I took my cousin's life. None of my partners understand what I'm going through not even my wife. Terry would have lived if I hadn't stepped in. Not only have I clipped her life line short but I'm about to bury her under her sister's name then feed her identity to Gena. Yet, I claimed to love them like they're my little sisters. I love them both deeply but I guess not deeply enough. Maybe I don't know the meaning of the word love. Where did I get so screwed up?

Danya flipped to another section, her tears wetting the pages.

The transformation is complete. Gena truly believes she's Terry. I've become accustomed to calling Gena, Terry but when I look into her eyes, my heart breaks over and over again. I've accepted the guilt as my constant friend. One day I may gather the courage to tell her the

*truth. But not right now; my future depends on her believing she's Terry.
Dammit, why can't I sacrifice my safety for her well-being? I finally
came to the conclusion that I can't keep doing this to Gena. I'm making
arrangements to move on. I need to allow Gena to be free from the
prison I've trapped her in. I've written her a letter that will be sent to
her upon my death, accidental or otherwise. Telling her everything, even
the fact that I lied to her fiancé, Pierre, saying she'd married because
I was upset by the fact that I had no idea that she was serious about
someone let alone engaged to be married. I broke the man's heart out
of sheer spite.*

Moving to the couch, she sank into the cushions feeling numb as she
flipped to another page.

*By the end of the summer, I should be gone but I'm starting to worry
about the effect it will have on Gena. She also seems to get bits and
pieces of her memory back but because she thinks of them as Terry's it
doesn't strike her as odd. If she remembers something her mind can't
switch around to make it Terry's then ... I don't even want to think about
it but there could be one insignificant thing that Gena remembers that
Terry didn't know and Gena remembers everything. If that happens I
know I can't be the one that helps her through it. So, I've decided it's
best to find her a good psychiatrist to help her deal with it all.*

Danya sat the journal down and picked up the last one she planned
to read.

*I've got this funny feeling that this may be one of my last entries.
Everything I wanted to leave Gena is in a box that will be left with my
lawyers once I include this diary. In a few hours, I'll be meeting with
Gena for what is probably the last time. I'm hoping she'll allow me to
leave and I pray that she won't try to stop me. I know that if it comes*

down to it, it's an automatic thing for me to protect myself.

Something has changed in me. I can't explain the rage, the fury, the violent feelings that develop within me during certain situations. I can't control those feelings that distort my soul; it fills me. I will do anything, anything, to stay alive, even if it means killing. I'm not meeting her with the intentions of killing her. I need to see her. I need to see her just one last time, to tell her despite everything that has occurred, I care for her deeply. To say a sorry she'll never accept but I need to say. However, I'll never be able to explain to her the reason that my love for her didn't result in me protecting her instead of using her. It has been a twisted entanglement of both. That's something even I don't understand.

Looking at one entry, she knew he had to have dropped this off before they met at Marcus's condo. Danya took a deep breath as she began to read.

Gena Danya Holmes, soon to be Cameron, I've got this premonition that this is my last day on this earth and my final entry in any journal. I don't know why but I just can't shake this feeling and if this feeling is correct, it will be you... It will be you, Gena, and not the FBI that will cause me to take my final breath, to lay my soul to rest. There's no doubt in my mind, Gena, you will be the one that punishes me for my crimes. It's destined. But Gena, please grant me one dying wish. I don't expect you to forgive me, just remember me as I was before I became the monster that stands before you in my last hour. The John that knew what the real meaning of love is. Smile if you're reading this, you're enduring the last of the last, after this there is no more. I can't cause you any more pain.

Once you get through this final betrayal, it's over. There's absolutely nothing left as a result of my crimes against you that can pop up and destroy your peace of mind and haunt you in the future. You are free of me forever. That's the best apology I can give you. This is the master key that will release you from that painful prison I've locked you in. Gena, I am truly sorry I wasn't the man you thought I was. Love, John.

Danya's tears dripped onto the page as her bottom lip quivered on the last sentence. She threw the items back in the box then found herself descending to her knees. The tears came like a dam break. She heard a light knock on the door and tried to pull it together. Swiftly wiping away her tears and standing, she managed to get "come in," out. Dr. Adams had attempted to discuss the contents of the box but she wasn't up to it. Danya grabbed the box promising to make another appointment and rushed out the office feeling numb. She wanted nothing more than to curl up in a ball in a corner of a dark room and never come out again. Maybe this was the universes way of punishing her for what she did. Happiness seemed to be a temporary thing for her. What she couldn't understand was what had she done was so bad prior to murdering Rita and John that caused her to deserve what John and his crew had put her through.

* * *

When she entered the house, Danya could tell Rick knew something was wrong by the way he immediately stopped what he was doing. He cautiously approached her with concern lurking in his eyes. More memories and emotions from the past started flooding back. She forced a smile, trying to pretend everything was okay, but it was far from it. *Damn you, John, for screwing up my life from beyond the grave.* How was she going to tell Rick this one?

* * *

Agent Waller and his partner sat up camp in a room they'd rented in the house across from Danya's house to keep an eye on her. Neither he nor his partner was satisfied with how the case turned out. All the people they were planning to use against their target were dead. Waller wished he could have had the opportunity to convince them that playing ball with them and turning against their boss was the best option. It would have made his life so much simpler. Now they were back to building a case that would stand up in court against their real target. That would take more time. The envelope Danya had given him wasn't enough to put this case to rest but it at least laid the foundation they needed to obtain some hard evidence.

"Why are we doing this again?" his partner asked, picking up an empty coffee cup and tossing it in the bag full of others.

Waller turned away from his spot at the window. "Are you absolutely sure we knew all the key players? Come on. Danya's best friend, ex-husband, and roommate were partners in crime. Who else was involved? And who is this guy in there with them? Is he involved?" Waller nodded towards the window.

"Waller, that portion of the case is closed. Why do you still have Danya's life under a microscope?" He observed at the monitor.

"I want to be sure that we have tied up all the loose ends. I've had an old case come back and bite me in the behind once." Waller swiveled around towards him. "I am not trying to experience that again."

"What is it about this case that you can't let it go?" He shook his head as he poured himself a cup of coffee.

"Some pieces of the puzzle were not fitting," Waller explained as he stood, grabbing his jacket off the back of the chair. "Like why Danya thought her ex-husband had served prison time. Or how was Marcus living lavishly, undetected by us, under the alias Cory Jones."

"Danya clearly was a pawn in an ugly game. Just accept that some things we will never understand," he stated, taking the seat Waller had vacated.

"Clearly I'm not the only one feeling this way since you are using your personal time to relieve me tonight." Waller slid on his jacket.

He sat his coffee in the window seal. "The fact that she attempted to turn herself in for the murders of John and Rita has me wondering if the killings were the result of blinding rage or was there more to it."

Had he left her bracelet at the crime scene and they'd been able to find the items she'd dumped, she'd probably be doing time now. *Probably not,* he thought. With all that money, some fancy lawyer would have stepped in to get her off. Waller did not know what he was thinking when he pocketed evidence. Hindsight, it was a combination of wanting to protect a woman pulled into a crazy situation and part of it was to have something to back her off if Rick had died.

Waller's phone pinged. He reached into his jacket pocket. Unlocking his phone, he scrolled to open the new message. Now he had his confirmation that incidents were due to extenuating circumstance and that she too wasn't living a double life like everyone else around her. "Well, it's not necessary anymore. I got confirmation of the identity of the other man. Pierre is on the up and up. I think it's time to let her live her life."

They gathered their equipment and headed out. If they hadn't found any evidence in over three years, it wasn't likely they would. Waller, once he made it home, poured himself a drink. He grabbed a file out of his desk. He sat, opened it, and pulled out an evidence bag. He studied Danya's bracelet through the plastic then returned it to the file. Waller took a sip of his scotch as he flipped through the crime scene photos one last time before closing the folder. Standing, he walked to the safe and put the file in. This time he would be prepared if the past decided to come back to make his life a living hell.

CHAPTER TWENTY-THREE

Danya's life had gone haywire and became more complicated since her unexpected visit to Dr. Adams. Six months had passed since she discovered she was Gena. *My life is more complex than ever*, she thought as she walked into the back room that she considered her own private get away, with her guests following closely behind. Upon entering the room, Danya took a quick but deep breath. Last night she reorganized the room for this meeting with her guests. She moved the television, chairs, spacious cream leather couch, and other things to the sitting room. There was only her piano on one side of the room facing the small three-person cream sofa with a pale blue standing lamp on both sides of it and a sandalwood coffee table that matched the wall bookshelf in front of it. Danya sat the newcomer on the sofa next to her other guest, leaving them no choice but to sit near each other since she removed the rest of the furniture. They waited for her to introduce them, but she went and leaned on the piano facing the window with her back to them.

Danya gave herself a pep talk as she attempted to find comfort in the rippling shimmering blues beyond the window. She scanned the water, noticing how the dark blue faded into a soft blue then changed to a greenish blue. This beauty, many times, had soothed and calmed her nerves after a hectic day since she and Rick had moved in. Today she didn't know if it would be enough. They studied her intensely, waiting for her to speak but Danya stood before them preparing herself to face a difficult situation. The two men, total strangers, sat uncomfortably with the tension increasing every second she didn't speak. Her silence intensified the feeling of uneasiness, causing restless shifting on the sofa from both of the men. She picked up some pictures off the piano and turned around to speak. Danya stood in her barely blue ankle length flowing dress as she leaned against the cream piano with the various blues of the manmade lake as her backdrop seen through the curtain free French doors that occupied the wall behind the piano. She wondered if this image would be seared in both men's minds after the conversation to come. Now that she had them both in the room, Danya debated her decision to tell them the real reason she had wanted them there. Yet she didn't have any other valid reasoning for bringing them together but the truth.

"I'd like to thank you for coming here. Both of you are probably curious as to why I requested your presence here today."

They acknowledged her statement by nodding their heads.

Danya moved away from the piano closer to them and began pacing the length of the sofa. She paused in front of one of them then placed her palm up in front of one man than the other. "Rick, this is Pierre. He was once engaged to Gena. And Pierre, this is Rick, my husband."

Danya waited until they shook hands and mumbled their polite greetings before going on. "Pierre, I appreciate you flying out here on such short notice."

"It really was no problem. I was due for a trip to the States anyway." His accent made his every word sound intimate.

By the look Rick had given her, he had caught the corners of her mouth bending upwards at the sound of Pierre's voice and didn't take kindly to it.

"Lucky for me that you weren't a hard man to track down. I admit I was shocked that you lived where you did almost nine years ago," Danya commented not missing the look Rick gave her. Her smile drooped as she thought about what it was that brought them together. Danya resumed her pacing as she explained why she asked them to the house she still referred to as Gena's place. Rick had wanted her to sell it but despite what had happened there, she wasn't quite ready to part with it. It was crazy that John had never sold it. She only had herself to blame for that. She let him handle too much of her business.

"The reason you're here is because I need to tell you what happened to Gena. But, I'd like you to tell me what happened after you sent that package to Gena and then couldn't get in touch with her, first."

The pacing ceased as she stopped directly between them and peeked down at the picture in her hand. The tears began rolling down her face. She didn't bother to wipe them away because she knew they would only be replaced by others.

Pierre seemed to be reluctant to discuss that time in his life but he didn't deny her the response. He began to tell her about how he tried to reach Gena for two weeks straight but couldn't catch up with her. At the time, he thought she had an unexpected business trip out of the country and would call when she had some free time. Another two weeks passed and she still hadn't called. That was when he began calling around to mutual friends and business associates, but no one knew where she was or had even heard from her.

"I was extremely worried about her because I had started making arrangements to move to the States permanently. It took some doing to fly out and check on her personally." Pierre's expression changed as if he was reliving the shock. "When I arrived, John informed me that she was on her honeymoon with her husband. I couldn't believe it. I kept waiting to hear from her. Eventually, I had to accept it as truth. I was beyond hurt. My heart was crushed. The woman I was about to leave my homeland for, married someone else. The woman that was having ..." His words faded out as his emotion got the better of him and he went silent, lifting his hand as if to say that was enough.

Danya signaled Rick not to say anything but he seemed slightly confused. He was probably trying to figure out why he was there when he already knew what really happened. The way his shoulder relaxed, Danya figured he thought he was there for moral support. Danya strolled over to the piano then leaned on it at an angle where she was looking more out the window than at them.

"Pierre, that's not what happened," Danya stated bluntly.

Pierre glanced up, waiting for her to explain herself but instead she asked a question. "Do you still love her?"

Pierre frowned at her. "It doesn't really matter now."

"It will. It will." Danya paused, eyes shifting down. "Rick, you know most of this already so be patient until I get to the reason I insisted on you being here."

Danya began narrating a tale she knew all too well right up to the part where she murdered Rita and John. Pierre seemed totally stunned. By the way he kept open and closing his mouth, Danya assumed he didn't know what to say or what to think. She held the pictures in one hand and began running her fingers through her hair.

"Did you remember she had a sister?" Danya moved towards them and turned the pictures face down and waited for them to pick them up and turn them over so she could see Rick's expression.

Pierre nodded. "Yeah, I didn't know until today that you were ..."

"Identical twins!" Rick tilted backward, his legs slid forward as he slouched on the sofa staring at the picture in disbelief. "I can't believe you never mention this to me. You only said you had a younger sister, not a twin sister!"

"We weren't exactly identical as we got older. From about five Terry began to gain a lot of weight while Gena gained enough. After Terry became overweight we looked more like sisters than we did twins, at least to us." She handed them each a set of pictures to flip through.

"I don't understand why you're talking like you're discussing two of your friends instead of you and your sister." Rick sat up straight as Danya turned her back on them. She returned to the piano to get the remaining items. She didn't answer him. She came back, stepped passed Rick's legs, and took a seat directly between them on the coffee table so that she would be facing them.

"I'm talking like this not to confuse either one of you." Danya placed the items from the piano behind her.

Rick's face reflected his confusion. "I'm confused now."

"What do we have to be confused about?" Although Pierre had been listening intensely, he hadn't said a word until Danya's last comment.

"This is the point where I talk and you listen. I don't want to confuse you with who I'm referring to when I say a name. There's a reason for talking as if there are three people instead of two and if you listen carefully you'll understand why, okay? Please do not interrupt me unless I ask you a question. The reason I brought you two here is that I want to tell this story only once. If you don't let me get through it, I may never tell it to anyone." She rested her elbows on her thighs with her hands clasped together.

"Rick, remember the day I came home acting weird and you asked why." She took the pictures from them and sat them on the table.

"Yeah." Rick nodded, and stated, "You were reluctant to talk about it."

"I had a session with Dr. Adams and had a lot to think over." Danya didn't know why she felt a twinge of embarrassment saying it in front of Pierre.

Rick suddenly looked nervous. "Yeah."

"That's the day that it hit me. John did everything for a reason, right? So why did he send me to Dr. Adams?" She paused, knowing neither man had the answer to her question. She could see Pierre was completely lost.

"I'm sorry; I'd better start from the beginning so that you'll completely understand the ramifications of what I'm saying." Danya briefly described the events that led up to her being in the doctor's office but the meat of her story was what took her there and what happened after she got there.

Rick and Pierre looked as if they were blown away. "I accused Dr. Adams of being part of it but she didn't even know the half of it. John dropped off the package to her to give to me before he was supposed to meet me at Marcus's condo."

"I'm surprised she didn't give it to the police once everything came out about John," Rick stated.

Danya shrugged her shoulder as her bottom lip quivered. She took the back of her hand and wiped her cheeks. Pierre's eyes filled with warmth like he wanted to take her into his arms. Rick seemed to be debating what was the best way to respond to the situation.

"I'm alright." She took a deep breath, stood, and stepped over Pierre's legs. Danya sat on the piano bench with her back facing Rick and Pierre, internally freaking out. *What now? Do I say what I came here to say or do I leave it at this?* She heard one of them stand. Looking back, Pierre went to lean on the wall near the piano. Rick strolled over and leaned on the piano where Danya originally started the conversation. Danya didn't turn completely to face them, as she regained her composure to continue her story.

"I'd like to make this one statement. My mom thought it was cute to give me and Terry the same middle name. Now it seems only fitting that I am called by the name Terry and I shared, especially since for nine years I truly believed I was her. Although I'm Gena, I prefer to be called Danya, okay?"

"Okay," answered Pierre, as if he knew that tidbit of information was for him and only him.

"You don't have to keep talking about this." Rick spoke as if he couldn't take seeing her crying like that. She was barely able to say the words.

Danya told Rick that she needed to do this. She turned back to face the French doors and asked Pierre to open them for her. After Pierre opened the doors, she asked them to both come and sit beside her. The two men sat on the very edge of either side of her as she began telling them what she read in John's journals.

Rick and Pierre listened as Danya stood, turned around, stepped over the piano bench, and began to play a smooth melody. This was her way of granting John his death wish by playing his favorite song, their last goodbye. She was also saying goodbye to all the illusions that had governed her life. When the song ended and her fingers rippled across the last few keys, she pulled herself together enough to speak. She stood and turned back around to face the open doors.

"This leaves us three, no, it leaves me with a serious problem," Danya announced.

Danya started thinking maybe she did the wrong thing by bringing Pierre here, but she had to be honest with herself and them. Remembering that she was Gena not only brought back memories but the deep feelings she had for Pierre. Now she sat before two men that she was deeply in love with. Why did her life have to be so difficult? Why couldn't Pierre have been happily married? Maybe if he was, she wouldn't be sitting there about to tell her husband that she was in love with another man. This was the moment she dreaded for the last six months.

"What's the problem?" Pierre asked before Rick could speak.

"It leaves me in love with two men." She stood with the quickness and walked out on the balcony. Danya didn't want to see either of their facial expressions.

Rick joined her on the balcony. "You can't say something like that then walk away."

"Rick, I can't. I can't look into your eyes and see the pain I'm causing you. I just can't." Danya turned her head away from him as he leaned into her line of sight. He reached for her chin and turned her face towards him.

"This is not your fault. I understand." Rick's sympathetic tone only made it worse for Danya.

Danya could tell in his eyes that he understood but didn't like it. "I don't want to hurt anyone but I, I can't ..." Danya's tears ran down her face as she tried to get the words to come out of her mouth. "I can't ignore this. It's been tearing me apart."

Pierre stepped out onto the balcony looking like he longed to hold her. "You know I still love you but all I want is to see you happy. Rick makes you happy. I know that there will always be a special place in your heart for me and that is enough for me."

Rick's hand fell away from Danya's chin.

"Pierre, I have something special to give to you to remember me by." Danya unclipped the necklace she wore every day for the past six months. She slid the ring off the extra-long chain and handed it to him, then fastened the chain back around her neck.

"It's the engagement ring you sent me. I put it in my safe deposit box, my time capsule, along with the pictures of me and Terry when we were younger. Little memorabilia, little stuff that was special to me and could be special to someone that knew and loved me. Anyway, the day you sent it to me I placed it in there. I wanted to wait until you flew here. It wasn't because I didn't want to wear it. It was I wanted you to be the one that slipped it on my finger."

"I wanted to be the one, too." Pierre studied the ring he'd given her years ago.

"Rick, I don't want you to take this the wrong way but I need, Gena needs, Pierre to slip this ring on her finger, any finger, it doesn't matter. It ..." She turned back to face Rick.

"Baby, you don't have to explain. Just do what you need to do." Rick was acting like he was trying not to put any additional pressure on her, but she could see he was hurting.

Pierre slipped the ring on her right hand, the same finger that on the opposite hand held her wedding ring. Danya looked into Pierre's almond colored eyes with the same love and passion that illuminated her eyes years ago. She whispered thank you, giving him a hug. Her body tingled as his hand slid up and down her back.

"No, thank you." His lips brushed against her ear, his breath was light on her face. Pierre ended the embrace. Her body remembered what they used to have. Danya slipped the ring off her finger and slid her hand into his then let go, leaving the engagement ring.

"I think it's time that Pierre and I have a private conversation. Danya, could you wait by the piano for one second?" Rick had turned to face the lake to give the situation some serious thought. He had not been able to watch their display of affection.

Danya's heart was pounding as the two men stood on the balcony in a deep discussion. The two men she loved were so different. On the right, Rick stood towering over Pierre, who was to Danya's left, even though Pierre was taller than Danya by several inches. Pierre's reddish-brown skin wrapped a thick, manly, well-built frame whereas Rick's golden skin encased a sexy slim, but muscular build. Even their style of clothes differed. Rick wore a light gray silk shirt unbuttoned to where she could get a glimpse of his muscular chest and loose, black slacks that clung to his small but firm behind. Whereas, Pierre wore a dark blue T-shirt that hugged his well-cut muscles and blue jeans that cupped his nice, round, muscular backside.

The only thing they had in common was they both had features that brought women out of the woodwork. Rick had that dark, wavy hair, those sexy lips, captivating, dark brown eyes and the overall pretty boy look going for him. And Pierre, Pierre had his clear, almond eyes that were enhanced by his reddish-brown skin that gave him an exotic look. Danya remembered how sometimes at night they seemed to glow but he had a way of making her feel that they only glowed for her. She shook her head at that thought and finished listing the features that drew women to Pierre. Pierre had a body chiseled to perfection and strong facial features that caused the word pretty never to enter women's mind when they met him. His hair was a little unkempt, but he was damn sexy. Danya couldn't believe she was in love with these two sexy men. Two men that were so very different.

She had run out of things to distract her from the fact that they were still out there talking. All sorts of horrendous possibilities filled her mind as she waited. Rick and Pierre stood on the balcony in a deep discussion. It terrified her knowing they were in conference about their situation without her. Not having any idea what was being said made her nervous and apprehensive. It felt like she'd been doomed to an eternity of silent torture before they came inside to talk to her.

"We've made a decision that is best for all involved." Pierre stood on one side of her and Rick on the other.

"For the next six months, we'll wine and dine you. When those six months are over, you'll have to choose between the two of us. If it is Pierre, I'll divorce you." Rick looked away.

"If it's Rick, I'll catch the first plane home." Pierre sat down on the piano bench next to her. "It's not a contest to see who's the better man, but neither one of us wants to spend the rest of our lives wondering. I know I don't want to spend the rest of my life wondering if it could have been me waking up next to you every morning."

"And I don't want to spend the rest of my life wondering if it's really him that you want holding you in his arms." Rick knelt down beside her.

"When the six months are over, Rick and I will meet somewhere then we'll drive over here at the same time. Once Rick and I arrive, we'll be looking for the door of this sitting room to be closed."

"And we'll know your answer to which one of us you want by whose ring hangs on this chain outside on the doorknob." Rick lifted the chain around her neck with his index finger. "You will simply have to hang the ring of the person you didn't choose on the door."

Pierre opened her right hand and placed her first engagement ring in her hand then kissed her cheek. "I'll be seeing you."

Danya watched him exit, leaving only her and Rick.

"How is this supposed to work with us for the next few months?" she asked.

"I'll stay at our place in the city and you stay here or the other way around. It's your call." Rick took her left hand in his then slid her wedding ring off her finger. "If six months from now you still want to be married to me, I'd love it."

Rick's words reminded Danya of what she said to him almost three years ago. She watched Rick leave then she slid off the piano bench onto the floor. The back of her head rested on the bench. She wished she knew how to calm her chaotic life. Lifting her head and opening both of her hands, her wedding ring was in the left and her engagement ring was in the right. Rick and Pierre left her alone to wrestle with her feelings. She didn't know what to do but they made it perfectly clear she had to make a decision, either Rick or Pierre. Danya had six months to choose, but the end result was the same regardless of which person she decided to spend the rest of her life with, she'd still be losing a piece of her heart.

EPILOGUE

Sleep evaded Pierre. The only thoughts that were on his mind were of Gena and their baby and his opportunity to have Gena back in his life. He remembered he'd never been so happy in his life that his mother had sent him on an antique gift hunt for his Grams. Gena was a firecracker and his family loved her, which was a rare occurrence. He regretted not deciding to move to the states sooner. Maybe he wouldn't have lost all this time with her. Maybe she would have delayed her trip back home and that night would have never happened. He would never know if that decision would have changed the way things played out.

Pierre stood in the penthouse of the hotel in his sleeper pants staring out at the city line. Part of him wished he had more time with Danya. She'd asked him if he was able to love her as she was now or would he always be in love with the Gena he used to know. Danya was different but she was still his Gena. The problem was he didn't know if that was working for or against him. They had only recently fallen into a comfort zone similar to what they used to be. He needed more time to explore and build on that. However, he knew the longer they did this the harder it would be for everyone.

He sat down and flipped open his laptop. He opened his travel folder and reviewed the flight he was holding, wondering if he'd be returning home on it or if he would have a true second chance with the love of his life. He never knew he could feel so much anger for people he'd never met but Marcus and his crew took away his family. Today would be a long and tortuous day as he waited to find out whether he'd build a life here or be heading home to learn how to live life fully without Gena.

* * *

Rick nervously adjusted his tie, exiting their house in the city to drive to meet his fate. He thought planning a wedding to a woman who wouldn't accept his calls was nerve wrecking. As he pulled out of the parking lot, he thought about how he was sweating bullets waiting on Trish to give him an answer if Danya would marry him. That had been rough. This drive out to the suburbs to see if his wife loved him more than she loved her past was torture. His chest was tight with worry. The change between them in the last six months had to translate into different, not necessarily good or bad. He gripped the steering wheel tightly as he pondered on the facts. In the six months prior to her telling him that she was Gena, she hadn't been able to come to a clear decision that he was the one she wanted to spend the rest of her life with. Even after all they'd been through, she felt the need to fly Pierre in and that scared him. His heart was hurting while his mind understood to some extent why this was difficult for her. Danya had always been driven by her past and Pierre was a connection to the past that she could potentially share a future with. He hated that when they spent time together now, it always felt like there was an elephant in the room. Rick wondered if she picked him would that feeling go away or would it forever haunt their marriage.

He pulled into the driveway and waited. It was early but this day had been a blur of activities intent on keeping his mind occupied and off the fact that he wasn't confident that his wife would select him. They survived so much; he prayed their marriage could endure this. Rick watched as Pierre pulled up. The expression on Pierre's face undoubtedly reflected a mixture of hope and concern. They stepped out of their cars, greeted each other, before entering Gena's house to see what hand they had been dealt. Rick felt his heart thumping against his chest as they neared the door. Both hesitated, only a foot away from the door. Rick took a breath and glanced at Pierre. Pierre acknowledged that they should end the torture. They stepped forward and observed the ring hanging from the knob. The decision had been made.

* * *

Danya remembered when she told them she was in love with both of them and they told her she had to choose one or the other. It felt like an impossible decision to make. The idea of dating them both seemed insane. What did she really expect when she brought them all together? At the time, she had no idea how she would make the decision. Tonight, she had no doubt who it was. Danya sat at the piano playing a romantic song as she waited for him to enter. The room was dimly lit and the furniture was all removed except for the piano, the stereo, and table. In the center of the room, there was an antique table set for two that she brought especially for this evening as the various colored roses created two paths, one from the door to the table and the other from the door to the piano.

Danya loved them both but her love for one man changed into more of a friendship type love. She was shocked that her feeling for this man could change after all the years they'd spent together, but it had. Danya smiled as she looked down at the ring of the man that she wanted to spend eternity with. The ring sat on top of the piano with a long stemmed red rose through it. She wasn't wearing it because she wanted him to slip it onto her finger. She'd almost lost him once what seemed like decades ago and she would never again forget that.

Her fingers strolled over the keys as he entered the room. He was by her side after a few strides down the flowered path. Danya stopped playing, picked up the remote, then turned on the stereo, which was programmed only to play love songs. She stood and picked up the ring and handed it to him.

"Because I love you with all my heart, every ounce of my soul goes into loving you, I wanted you to be the one who slipped the ring on my finger."

"I wanted it, too. I was scared you would choose him." He slid the ring on her finger and held her tightly, kissing her with a passion that stirred his soul.

"There will be no more wondering. It is definitely you that I want to wake up every morning with." Danya felt the joy and happiness warm her skin as she lost herself in her eternal love, her only true love's beautiful eyes.

"Danya, I'm so glad you chose me. I love you too much to lose you again." His lips claimed hers again as he pulled her tightly into his arms.

She walked him back, away from the piano to where they stood further in the rose path. Her lips never left his. Finally, Danya broke their fiery kiss. Her hand reached up to caress his cheek. She stared into her love's face. Her eyes illuminated with love.

"Rick. Our love is something that's just meant to be."

Danya smiled as she hugged him tightly. She wished it didn't take risking losing him to realize who she once was isn't who she is now. The woman Pierre had once loved had changed and they had not been together through that transition. The Gena he was in love with was a distance memory. Rick, on the other hand, was in love with who she was and had been there with her through the mountains and the valley. As she clasped her hands at his lower back, she touched her bare wrist and prayed that her past was done tormenting her.

KAREN D. BRADLEY

was born and raised in Chicago and while she had a creative mind, English and Grammar were never her strongest subjects. As life would have it, her weakest link would become her saving grace. During college, she wrote her first book to help her cope with the death of her father and ever-changing family dynamics. Writing fiction soon became one of her favorite forms of therapy. Encouragement from readers and focusing on positive possibilities motivated her to continue writing. She has penned several contemporary fiction novels—*Love Runs Deep, Tainted Love,* and *Life on Fire.* Recently, she ventured into film making by writing and producing a short film based on one of her novels.

www.ambrosiasands.com

Brooklyn Saunders' life is set ablaze when her ex, Dante Nines, and a newly single friend, Hunter Torres, vie for the number one spot in her heart. Unknowingly, Dante brings trouble to her door causing their personal and professional lives to collide in the worst way. The entanglement unleashes a danger that will have both of the men she loves fighting to keep her safe. Will Brooklyn survive the chaos threatening to destroy her very existence? And if she does, who will she choose?

After Tyler Bradford has a run in with the Chameleon, she finds herself gunned down and bleeding in the snow next to her best friend, Lorrain. Her entire world changes when Lorrain dies. She becomes determined to make the Chameleon pay for his crimes. However, she isn't the only one on a mission. The Chameleon is hunting her down to finish what he started. Their paths will cross, yet only one of them will accomplish their goal. Tyler's love for Lorrain runs deep, but will it be the very thing that gets her killed?

Asya Brown took a bite from an apple that she wished she hadn't! When Asya and Vic Webber's paths crossed, her instincts told her to keep him at a distance. She didn't. Vic slowly inserted himself into her life and into her heart. Their relationship became entangled in lies, accusations and manipulations. Even after breaking up, she couldn't seem to escape his madness. Asya's focus was now all about surviving Vic. The question is, can she?